CHRISTMAS AT MANNUS RIDGE

JOANNE TRACEY

For Grant and Sarah ... always

ONE

The day my life fell apart began as most days begin.

My alarm blared at five as it always did, and as I always do, I dressed quickly in black Lulemon tights and crop top, and Stella McCartney trainers and headed to the gym in the basement of my Flinders Lane apartment complex. It was Thursday, so that meant a torturing forty-five-minute spin class. Afterwards, back in my apartment, I popped a capsule in the machine for my first coffee for the day – black, no sugar – which I used to down a couple of paracetamol tablets. As I sipped, the caffeine pushing away the residual brain fog the exercise hadn't reached, I sent a good morning text to my boyfriend, Otis, scanned my phone for the news of the day and did a quick check on my emails, the usual anxiety growling to attention in my stomach as I flicked through my inbox. While the world at large was in a mess, at least nothing had fallen off the rails in my job over night and the morning numbers were as expected. Nevertheless, I fired off a quick question to a colleague – mainly to let them know I was already on the job – and set a reminder to follow up on their response when I got into the office.

Showered and dressed, I retrieved my Louis Vuitton tote from the wardrobe shelf I'd placed it on last night, glanced at the time on my phone – seven thirty on the dot – and left my apartment.

While the forecast was for a hot day, the sun still hadn't reached this part of the city streets, and I was glad of the warmth my Max Mara trench coat provided and knew I'd be grateful again later this evening as I walked home sometime after the sun had gone back to bed.

At the coffee shop a few doors away, the queue was still short. Second coffee in hand, I nodded my thanks to the barista and began the brief walk to work, pausing at the Swanston Street traffic lights to read the response from Otis (*hi babe, see you tonight x*). A tram clacked by, its bell echoed by another behind it.

At Elizabeth Street, I turned right, then left into Collins. Taking a second to look up – as I did every morning – the sun bounced off the eastern side of the glass-fronted building, the reflection of the sky clear and blue. Not that it mattered, it was unlikely I'd see it again today; I rarely did.

From the coffee shop downstairs, I bought my third – and final – coffee for the morning before riding the lift to the nineteenth floor, smiling tightly at the other occupant when they alighted at the eighteenth. 'Have a nice day,' he said breezily as the doors shut, leaving a cloud of woody aftershave behind.

As it always was at this time of the day, the office was quiet, with just a few employees scattered around – most tapping away on keyboards, some walking back from the lunchroom, coffee in hand discussing the previous night's reality TV. Each looked up as I strode past their desk and chorused, 'Morning, Ainsley.' I returned each greeting, making a mental note of the names of those who were in early, hung my trench on the coat stand in my office, placed my tote under the desk and opened my laptop at precisely eight am. As I always did.

The morning, too, passed as mornings usually do. There was the eight-thirty daily buzz meeting where we went through today's priorities, another at nine with the branch closure team in Sydney, followed by the regular weekly credit briefing and an update on the new deposit product we were due to be rolling out early in the new year. All as it should be.

By twelve thirty, I'd had my midday coffee, and had opened the PowerPoint briefing document for the first of the afternoon's meetings, my pen tapping on the desk in time with my jittery heartbeat, when Drew, one of my employees, ducked in.

'You're needed upstairs.' There was a look on his face I couldn't decipher, but it was one I didn't like. Drew had changed in the last two months: a relatively new father, he had previously been eager to please but was now arriving in the office later, insisting on leaving on time each day, and only last week had had the temerity to push back against one of my requests.

I smiled tightly and nodded. 'Do you know what for?'

'No, JC's EA called down and said you're to get up there.' A sly smirk crossed his face. 'You've been up there a lot lately, haven't you?'

JC, John Collins, was the general manager of our division and the sort of man who would hand a memo back to you with a single red line through it and a throwaway comment like, 'A few suggested changes.' As Drew so helpfully pointed out, I had been up there too often of late – and the conversations had not been pleasant. My department, which had previously run smoothly, had recently begun to falter; I was losing control and didn't know how to get things back on track. A summons via his executive assistant rarely boded well so the churning ball that had taken up permanent residence in my stomach sat up and had a good look around.

Drew was waiting for a response, his arms crossed, his eyebrows raised defiantly so I plastered a 'whatever' look on my face. 'Have I? I hadn't noticed. Don't you have a report due by two?'

Once he left my office with a slight shake of his head, I checked my appearance in the mirror behind the door, reapplying my red lipstick. All was as it should be: my navy Ted Baker shift dress was immaculate, as were my nude Louboutin shoes, and the tight bun I wore my hair in every day was still as tight as it had been when I'd left my apartment that morning, every single blonde hair smoothly constrained. When my phone pinged with a message, I glanced at it – my sister, Jacinta – and ignored it. She could wait.

Upstairs, I sailed past where his executive assistant sat and tapped once on JC's door. 'Come,' came the gruff tones from within.

JC's office on the thirtieth floor was double the size of mine. Even though a large mahogany desk dominated the space, JC was seated at the round table in the far corner, his bulk making the already small table seem crowded, but he wasn't alone. Carmel from human resources was also there, and neither were smiling. My stomach twisted again, and my mouth was dry.

'Take a seat, Ainsley.' Carmel's face was set in stone, jaw firm.

I did as requested, forcing my expression to remain neutral, trying not to look at the prefilled forms on the table in front of Carmel.

'We've had a complaint about you from one of your employees.' No preamble from Carmel. 'It's an allegation of bullying.'

I straightened my shoulders, hating the bitter taste I couldn't swallow away. 'Who?'

'It doesn't matter who,' said Carmel. 'We've completed some preliminary investigations and, in doing so, more members of your team have also complained about your behaviour towards them. Then there was the matter of Tiffany Samuels—'

'But she left,' I broke in, leaning forward and placing my hands on the table. 'And without notice.'

Tiffany had been after my job but had resigned a couple of months back. While her leaving was the result I'd been hoping for, the way she'd done it – in front of several other people at the airport lounge where we were waiting for a flight to the firm's annual high achiever's conference – had prompted a 'please explain' from JC. At the time, I'd haughtily told a story about how she realised she shouldn't have been there in the first place and that it had been an overly dramatic end to my campaign to have her 'self-select', but I hadn't convinced him.

'Yes,' said JC, 'and from what I'm seeing, the wheels have fallen off your department ever since.' His lips – which I'd always thought were too full for a man – had twisted into a grotesque half smile of satisfaction.

'Our informants have advised us she did most of the work and held together the morale in the team – what there was left of it.' With her hands placed lightly on her lap, Carmel appeared relaxed and confident – and the hair on the back of my neck prickled, a combination of caffeine and foreboding causing my heart to race.

'Plus, Matt Delaney over at ZCB has recently poached the high-value Hong Kong clients Tiffany had been responsible for.' JC didn't mince his words.

'How can that be my fault? If Tiffany had looked after them more closely—'

'How could she when you pulled her travel budget? Even with that, she still provided the service they expected, but with her gone ...' JC didn't finish his sentence, his glare and reddening face warning me not to pursue that subject.

I tapped my red-tipped nails on the table, buying time while I composed a response. 'What's the nature of the allegation?'

Carmel didn't need to consult her notes. 'Unrealistic timeframes, rudeness, repeated requests for reports beyond those required. One employee said it now takes them most of a day to put together the report you've requested weekly – and said you rarely comment on it other than to ask for additional figures the following week.'

I lifted a shoulder, my jaw aching from the pressure of maintaining a straight face. 'I simply ask for the data I require to complete a deep dive into our customer's demographics.' I looked to JC and added benignly, 'Wasn't that what you requested at our last meeting?'

As JC would've blustered, Carmel held up a finger of warning. 'As you're aware, Ainsley, that's not an excuse for placing unreasonable demands on employees. Chartered Pacific has a zero tolerance for bullying and takes these allegations very seriously. Because of the seriousness of this issue, we have no option but to take equally serious action.' The remnants of my midday coffee whirled around in my otherwise empty stomach, and I pressed my hand against it to quell the churn. 'However, in light of the service you've provided over the past seven years and the fact that in our current restructure we'd intended to make your role redundant, we're prepared to move that forward rather than place this incident on your file as a first and final warning.' She pushed a document across the table.

The heat rushed from my body and left me icy cold. 'What's this?' I already knew the answer. I'd given the same spiel Carmel had just given to me to others over the years.

'It's a deed of release.' Her tone was even and straight to the point. 'While we certainly don't believe you have grounds for complaint regarding your treatment at Chartered Pacific, or,' she added almost as an afterthought, 'the behaviour of anybody at CP, this document ensures that upon receipt of the payment we'll be making to you, you'll acknowledge that you're unable to make any future claims against the company or any of its employees. As well as a zero policy against bullying and harassment, CP has—'

'A zero media tolerance,' I finished ruefully.

I reached for the document and began to read, my mind in as much a whirl as my stomach. Who had made the complaint? Had there even been a complaint, or was that just an excuse to get rid of me? I snuck a glance at JC sitting back in his chair, legs astride, arms folded across his chest, his shirt straining against its buttons. I wouldn't have put it past him to have instructed Carmel to find a way of getting rid of me. After all, Otis had asked the same of me in the past, and I'd been just as creative with my reasons – I'd even used the no-fraternisation policy against one ex-employee, Alice Delaney. At the time, I'd recognised that for the hypocrisy that it was, but Otis had told me our situation was different. He'd also reminded me that my reward would be further promotion – to this role, in fact. A chill ran through me – had someone found out about Otis and me? Who else knew? We'd been so careful to keep it quiet. Were they worried that if we broke up I'd become vindictive? Carmel had seemed to put an extra emphasis on the words 'or any of its employees' ...

The payout outlined in the document was generous – six months' salary plus my accrued entitlements and annual leave. It had been years since I'd taken any more than the occasional week off, so the amount was sizeable and equated to almost a year's pay. It meant I'd be fine, financially, for a while, but what would I do? My job was my life. I might've expected long hours and weekend work from my employees, but it was no less than what I was prepared to put in myself. I was, after all, on track to crack through the glass ceiling to be the first female divisional general manager. That's what it had all been about – the hours, the sacrifice of my personal life, all of it – and now they were going to take it away from me? That churning ball that had been bubbling in my stomach with the coffees rose into my chest. It tightened, and I struggled to take a deep breath.

Carmel pushed across a pen. 'When you're ready,' she said calmly.

The faintest hint of a smile curved around JC's mouth. 'Excuse me.' He stood. 'I'll just visit the bathroom.'

As he left, I picked up the pen. 'Do you think he needs to go, or he just wants to reiterate that he's so important his office has its own bathroom?' I mused aloud. 'Or maybe it's to remind me what I'll never have if I sign this document?' I twisted the body of the pen to push the nib down and then back again, vaguely registering the clicking sound it made in the silence. 'What happens if I don't sign this?'

Carmel shrugged unapologetically. 'We proceed with our investigations. My understanding is others in your team will come forward. I don't know the details of what went on between you and Tiffany, but there's nothing to stop her from retrospectively making an accusation along the same vein. I have no doubt we'll have sufficient grounds to terminate your employment – and there won't be a payout at the end.'

The bile tasted bitter in my mouth, and every part of me wished JC wasn't in that bathroom so I could run to it. I forced myself to concentrate on breathing, willing the muscles in my face to remain still. I needed to talk to Otis; he'd put a stop to this.

'Can I think about it overnight?'

Carmel shook her head. 'No. This offer is on the table now; JC would prefer it wasn't offered at all. As you're aware, you were never his choice for this position. If you choose to walk out of this room without accepting it, there won't be another opportunity.'

'I see.' Otis mightn't be able to help me on this occasion. As he and JC were both vying for the opportunity to be the next CEO of CP, they had what could best be described as a combative relationship. If JC knew about our relationship, it was an opportunity for him to score points against Otis, and Otis, for his part, wouldn't be able to intervene without losing ground against JC. I was on my own.

'Has she signed yet?' JC was back, but rather than sitting, he stood over me. If he intended to intimidate me, it was working. 'Just sign the damned paper,' he said impatiently.

I flicked to the page requiring my signature. 'If I do, how much notice do I get?'

'None.' Carmel clasped her hands on the table. 'Sign this document and we'll announce your retrenchment effective immediately.'

'Don't sign and you'll move to sack me?' I guessed.

She inclined her head.

'And if you think you'll have help from elsewhere in the organisation and are prepared to risk that outcome, more fool you.' JC thrust his chest out and held my gaze. 'It's not just about the bullying and harassment, Ainsley; there's also the matter of your performance of late. To be completely frank, it's slipped – you've dropped the ball. Even if these complaints hadn't come in, we'd be looking at putting you on a performance management plan.'

Unable to believe what I was hearing, my breath came out in a choked cough. 'So all these years of loyal service, of doing every despicable thing I've been asked to do, means nothing?' The question didn't need an answer; I already knew it.

I placed the pen back on the table and examined the faces before me. Surely this was some sort of elaborate test? If I held firm, they'd back down.

'Tiffany Samuels was one of the best operators I've ever worked with.' JC was on a roll now. 'She could've made it to the top. She was my choice for your role.'

'Alice Delaney was a friend of mine,' said Carmel quietly.

'She shouldn't have slept with a colleague then, should she?' I retorted. 'If she hadn't, she'd still have her job.'

'Perhaps.' Carmel raised an eyebrow. 'It's ironic, though, don't you think?'

Yes, they knew about Otis and me.

Taking a deep breath, I lifted the pen one last time and signed my name, Ainsley St James, and effectively ended my brilliant career.

TWO

In hindsight, you could say I'd been too busy looking down the ladder for threats and not seeing the danger coming from above. That was, in fact, what my best friend (in truth, my only friend these days) Benji said later that afternoon. A magazine stylist, he'd ducked out of work so we could meet at his favourite café in Hardware Lane. He loved it for the boho charm and lumpy vintage couches – I hated it for the same reason.

'Ainsley sweetie, you missed what was coming at you because you thought you'd knocked everyone behind you off the ladder – and in the process, you forgot to do your job. You made it easy for them.'

'That makes no sense.' It made perfect sense when he broke it down. 'I've always been good at my job,'

'I know you have been, but you're not now.'

'Tell it like it is, why don't you?' One thing I loved most about Benji was his habit of telling it like it was, even when the truth was difficult to hear. He wasn't mean but he was a straight talker. 'I mean, don't worry about sparing my feelings, seeing as though I've just been sacked.' The official version might've been that I lost my job in a restructure, but I knew what had really happened. I took a sip of my coffee – my fifth for the day. 'What's happened to me, Benji?' I wailed. 'Where did it all go wrong?'

'Do you really want me to answer that?' His half grin was rueful.

'Yes, I do.'

'Well,' he started, 'the simple answer is, I think you were out of your depth with this role from the start, and that's why you were so paranoid someone was going to take it away from you.'

'Like Tiffany Samuels.'

'Yes. You spent more time working out how to make her fail that you forgot her failure would also be yours.'

'But she didn't fail,' I argued.

'No, which made you look better than you were, and when she left, it exposed you in all the wrong ways.' Benji drained his coffee, sat back in the magenta velvet-covered couch and stretched his long denim-clad legs out under the low table. 'As well as forgetting to do your job, you forgot about the sisterhood.'

'What sisterhood? It's every woman for herself out there, and I wanted to be the first female general manager. After everything I had to do to get there, I deserved that.'

'Maybe she did too.' When I stared at him, mouth agape, for making such an outlandish comment, he continued, 'Can you imagine how she felt having you parachuted in above her? A fair fight would've been both of you doing your jobs to the best of your ability – not the way it was, which was you knee-capping the opposition and doing your best to keep everyone else under control. That must have been exhausting.'

I sighed heavily. 'How do you even know all this?'

'Because I've been listening to you over the past year,' he said simply.

When I'd been promoted into this role and had moved to Melbourne to do it, Benji, who I'd met at uni in Sydney, had been the only person I knew here. With the hours I'd worked, he and his husband, Brendan, were still the only people I knew outside of CP.

'Why didn't you warn me?' I accused.

'Because you wouldn't have listened.' He raised his eyebrows as if daring me to contradict him. I couldn't.

I slumped back into the couch, immediately realising my mistake. 'I'm never going to be able to get out of this chair again,' I grumbled, struggling to sit upright, my heels scrabbling for traction on the smooth concrete floor.

'Well, darling, those heels and that dress are fabulous, but they're made for perching, not lolling. How was it when you left the office?'

I lifted one shoulder. I wasn't going to tell him how everyone had watched in silence as I walked quietly from my office with the small box of personal items, accompanied by a security guard, in case I was tempted to lose my cool. I wasn't going to say how I'd forced myself to return the gaze of the few who had dared to meet my eyes, but how no one had said a word. There were no goodbyes, no expressions of surprise or regret.

'Was that meant to be a frown or something else? Be careful, Ainsley, the injectables are wearing off.'

I looked up at him, ready to throw whatever was to hand in his direction. His caring smile, though, almost brought me to tears instead. 'I'm in my hour of need.' I managed a weak, unconvincing smile in return.

'What are you going to do?' he asked quietly.

'I don't know.' My phone pinged. I cast a quick glance at it and turned it over.

'Do you need to get that?'

I shook my head. 'No, it's Jacinta. She's messaged a few times today.'

'What does she want?'

I grabbed the arm of the chair and wriggled my bum closer to the edge of the cushion. 'Probably just to remind me that Dad's sixtieth birthday is two weeks away, and I haven't responded to her party invitation yet.'

'Are you going?' When I shrugged a shoulder, he added, 'How long has it been?'

'Since I've been back to Mannus Ridge?' I wrinkled my nose. 'No idea. Years.' Fourteen years, nine months, three weeks and a couple of days, to be more precise. 'Don't look at me like that,' I warned. Benji, an only child, was close to his parents and could never understand my reluctance to visit mine. 'I phone home once a week and see my family whenever they come to the city – that's often enough.' Since I'd moved to Melbourne, though, my parents had only visited once and my sister not at all.

'Don't you have school friends you'd like to catch up with from time to time?' He looked perplexed. 'After all, you spent the first twenty years of your life there.'

'No one back there misses me.' I squirmed in my seat, keen to close this subject.

'That wasn't what I asked.'

'I know, but I don't want to talk about it. Anyway, don't you have something fabulous to create or somewhere fabulous to be?' I forced a smile. 'Not that I'm not grateful for you dropping everything to listen to me cry on your shoulder, of course.'

'There wasn't much crying being done, darling – in fact, there wasn't any – but given that the last time I saw you during the week in daylight was many, many moons ago, how could I not come when you called?' He was attempting to make light of the situation, and I loved him for it. He checked his watch. 'But having said that, I'm going to have to love you and leave you.' He stood and offered his hand to pull me out of the lounge. 'Seriously though, are you okay?'

'I don't think it's sunk in yet.' I smoothed down my skirt. 'Everything will be fine once Otis finds out what's happened. He might still be able to fix it.'

Benji cast me a look that had pity dripping from it. 'I think you'll find Otis already knows what's happened.' He double air-kissed me. 'I'll be off. Brendan and I are going to the opening of a new restaurant tonight if you want to pop your glad rags on and come along. Something new from one of the old *MasterChef* contestants – Brendan's doing their publicity, and I know the designer.'

'I'm sure you do.' I patted his cheek. 'Thanks for the offer, and give my love to Brendan, but Otis is in town and I need to see him.'

'Right you are,' he said, then added, 'You know it's not too late to come away with us.' I'd forgotten that Benji and Brendan would be leaving on the weekend for their long-awaited holiday in Bali. 'I'm sure there'd be a villa free in our resort. Just think, nothing to do but lie by a pool looking gorgeous. It would do you the world of good.'

For the briefest of moments, the offer tempted me until I remembered that this was essentially the honeymoon they'd missed out on during lockdown. Reaching across to place my hand lightly on his cheek, I said, 'Thank you, but no, I'll be fine. I'm hoping Otis might manage some time away with me.'

He nodded, but I didn't think he believed me. 'Take care, Ainsley.'

'I will.'

'And ring your sister back!'

When he left, I sat back down, but in an upright chair this time – I wasn't risking the lounge again. I couldn't remember the last time I'd been at a loose end during the week. What did people do on a Thursday afternoon if they weren't at work? Unless Otis was in Melbourne, I even spent most weekends in the office –

there was, after all, nothing else to do and I needed to put those hours in to stay on top of everything – and everybody.

All that stress, all that anxiety – none of it had meant a thing. I'd made so many compromises over the years that I'd forgotten there was a time when I'd battled with my integrity. These days I told myself it was just business, reminded myself I wasn't there to be liked and got on with it. I'd been prepared to do what was necessary to get to the top, because if I didn't get there, what would any of the sacrifices have been for? What would the last fifteen years have been for? It would've all been for nothing.

Benji was right, though; I had been out of my depth with this job. My talent was with numbers; I could look at a balance sheet or a cashflow and tell you the story about that company – where it had been, where it was going, what had gone wrong and what strategy needed to be implemented for goals to be achieved. I was good with details and focused enough to put together a business plan and strategy that worked, yet my last two roles at CP had sent me right out of my comfort zone. I wasn't good at juggling so many different moving pieces, managing upwards as well as down, and for much of the time since moving here, I'd felt completely out of control. I couldn't remember the last time I'd woken without the twisty, churning feeling of foreboding or picked up a call or opened my emails without that same quickening in the gut. The feeling would be there all day, going away only when I had that first glass of wine each evening, becoming sleepier with each that followed. Perhaps I'd been waiting for someone to do what JC had done today – call me out as the imposter I was.

An image of Drew's expression when I left the office for the last time floated across my mind; it hadn't been pity or glee on his face, but relief. I rode those with families and mortgages harder than those who didn't – they had more to lose. It was a strategy Otis had instructed me on, something that had worked well for him in the past.

'It's constructive anxiety, darling,' he'd said. 'The more kids they have and the higher the mortgage – rising house prices and now increasing interest rates have done us a favour – the hungrier they are, and the more prepared they are to work longer and harder for no additional reward. Your dream employee,' he'd added, 'will also have private school fees. They'll do whatever it takes to keep their job.' Take it too far, though, he'd warned, and performance begins to decline.

Once upon a time, I would've argued that it wasn't

fair; people deserved to be treated with respect and enjoy some work-life balance, but as he always said, 'It's just business, Ainsley.'

Under his instruction, I'd embraced the concept and where had it gotten me? My team had detested me so much that none of them said a word as I left. Not. A. Word.

The server approached and began clearing the table. 'Another coffee?'

'No, thank you.' I gathered my bag and coat and paid the bill.

I was halfway out the door when the server called me back. 'Madam – your box.'

Aaah, yes, my box. While security had helpfully provided a box for me – and had supervised the packing of it – I was almost embarrassed to admit that all that was in it was a coffee mug, a fake plant and some leadership books. Not much to show for an entire career.

My phone pinged again with another message – Jacinta. Again.

I know you're very busy and important, but please try and make time to call me back. It's important.

After putting the phone back in my bag, I slung my trench coat over my arm, hoisted my bag over the same shoulder, balanced the box on the opposite hip and began the short walk down to Flinders Lane and up to my apartment.

This morning's blue sky had delivered on its promise, and here in the city, the air was hot, engulfing me and leaving a trail of sweat to pool at the base of my spine. It was weird to be out of doors in the middle of the day, but it wasn't just that that was so strange about this afternoon – it was that my phone hadn't rung once. Normally by this time, my phone was screaming to be recharged, but since I left the office, no one, other than my sister, had called or messaged. No one. The good news must have travelled fast.

I pulled over to one side of the footpath, placed my box on the pavement and messaged Otis:

I suppose you heard what happened? Are we still catching up tonight? A x

Three little dots appeared on the message pane, and when they disappeared, I waited for another few minutes, impatiently refreshing the screen, telling myself he must have been interrupted, but he didn't respond.

The shop I was leaning against was decked out for Christmas with a wreath on the door and tinsel swathed across the window. Wasn't it still too early for that? I glanced at the date on my phone – the middle of November, so no, it wasn't. It seemed these days the city waited only for Melbourne Cup Day to be over before Christmas festivities could officially commence. At least there was one upside to this situation – I wouldn't need to suffer through the office party again this year. My shoulders slumped as I realised it also meant that most businesses would be closing their books on the year in the next couple of weeks. Everyone knew that recruiting was put on hold until after the summer holidays were over and school was back, and it would be February before it started again. What on earth would I do between now and then? Thank goodness the payout would mean I could continue to pay my rent and bills until I got another job, but what would I do in the meantime? Maybe Otis could manage a few days away and we could finally take that getaway we'd been promising ourselves for years; I'd ask him tonight.

Picking up my box again, I covered the remaining distance to my apartment, keyed the entrance code into the door and rode the lift to the fourth floor. Once inside, I placed the box on the base of the closet near the entrance and hung my trench coat. I toed my shoes off, carried them through to my wardrobe and placed them in their box before setting the tote bag on the shelf left bare for it.

What to do now?

I wandered back into the kitchen and living area and switched the coffee machine on – and just as quickly switched it back off again. I'd had too much caffeine today and all of it on an empty stomach. There was nothing to eat in the fridge besides olives and plastic-wrapped parmesan.

My phone pinged, and I picked it up immediately and sighed in relief. It was Otis.

I heard. See you tonight at 7. We'll go to that Japanese place downstairs.

I briefly held the phone to my chest. Otis would know what to do; he could fix this.

Look forward to it xxx

Before I could put the phone down, it rang, and I answered it without thinking. 'Ainsley St James.'

'It's me,' said Jacinta. 'It's about time you picked up. Didn't you get my messages?'

Inwardly I groaned. 'Yes, it's just—'

'I know you're very busy and important, but this is important too. You haven't responded to my emails about Dad's party.'

'Did you send them to my work or my personal account?' I pulled a high-backed stool from under the kitchen counter and sat on it.

'Your personal one of course – you flew into me last time I sent something to work – now you're probably going to tell me you've been too busy to look at your personal account.'

'I have had rather a lot on. I'll get to it when I finish work tonight.' As the lie slipped out, I grimaced. 'If it's about a present, just let me know how much and I'll transfer the funds to you.'

'No, it's not about the present – although I assume you'll do your usual thing and send him a gift hamper from somewhere expensive. It's about his party. He really wants you there, Ainsley. We all do.'

I exhaled and rubbed my forehead. 'It's not possible – I have a branch closure happening that weekend, and I need to be on call.'

'If you haven't read your emails, how do you know which weekend the party's on?' she asked slyly.

Thinking quickly, I said, 'Because his birthday is the same date every year, and this year it falls on a Saturday so it makes sense you'd have it then.'

'Yes, okay,' she admitted grudgingly. 'Even if you have to be on call, you can still come,' she continued. 'It's not like you'll be taking calls in the evening.'

'That's when things can fall over.' I stood and opened the fridge door again, shutting it when I reminded myself it was still too early for wine. Wandering into the sitting room, I sank onto my taupe leather lounge and clutched a cream cushion.

'Surely your family has to come first for a change,' said Jacinta. 'It's been years since you've been home, and Dad hasn't been too well ...'

My breath hitched in my throat, and I sat up straighter. 'What's wrong with Dad? Neither he nor Mum have said anything to me about it.'

'Well, they wouldn't, would they? It's not the sort of thing you can cover in a quick phone call between meetings. How long has it been since you saw them?'

'If they had things to tell me, they could,' I shot back.

'When? When you cleared room in your schedule for them? I'm here on the ground with them, and I'm telling you now, I'm worried about Dad. His blood pressure is up, and Mum said he's had what she calls "episodes" but tells me not to worry. She said he saw a specialist the last time he was in the city. Did you know that?'

My stomach lurched as I remembered back to September – the last time they were in town. They'd asked if we could meet for lunch, but I hadn't long been back from the Top Team conference and was dealing with the fallout from Tiffany Samuels's sudden departure so had brushed them off. We'd had dinner, but Otis had phoned and ... They must've wanted to tell me then, and I hadn't given them the opportunity.

'If she's not worried ...' I started.

'That's the thing – she is. She's fussing over him, and you know Mum doesn't do that.' After a short pause, she added, 'You need to swallow your pride and come home – you'll never forgive yourself if Dad dies and you haven't made the effort.'

I cringed at the baldness of her statement. 'Do I need to remind you I didn't exactly leave Mannus Ridge on the best of terms? It's probably better for Mum and Dad that I haven't been home.' I knew I was making this all about me, but it sort of was.

'That was ages ago.' Jacinta sighed. 'Isn't it time to let it go? Everyone else has forgotten about it – it's been years since I even heard it mentioned.'

'I bet there are people in town who haven't forgotten,' I said, my jaw tightening. 'You were too occupied with your own life to know what it was like. I know it made things awkward for you and Mark.'

'It was a long time ago,' she said. 'Besides, I'd like you to meet the kids – and before you tell me you've met them, the last time was when you were living in Sydney and we were in town for the show.'

I had no argument with that. Everything she'd said was right – I only saw my sister's family when they came to Sydney for the annual agricultural show – and I hadn't seen them at all since moving to Melbourne. I barely knew the man Jacinta's partner, Mark, had grown into, and the kids probably wouldn't recognise me if they saw me. Her eldest must be, what, twelve or thirteen now.

'If Mum and Dad wanted me to come, they would've invited me,' I finally said.

'They no longer ask because they know what your answer will always be,' said Jacinta bluntly. 'That doesn't mean they gave up wanting you to come home; it means they gave up asking you to. There's a difference. They miss you – I miss you.'

I let out a little puff of air, not quite a snort, not quite a short laugh, anything to cover the guilt I didn't know how to deal with.

'Don't you miss any of it?' she asked quietly. 'Home, that is?'

Did I miss where I'd grown up? If I closed my eyes, I could still see the poplars that followed the road into town and the oaks that lined the river – their leaves bright green and providing much-needed shade from the hot summer days and fiery red and orange in autumn. In my mind, I could still walk down the main street with the bakery that made the best sausage rolls in the world on one corner and the hardware store on the other. There was the café where we used to hang out as teenagers and the swimming pool filled each spring from water that had run off from the snow melt high in the mountains out of town and was subsequently so cold it would take at least ten laps to warm up. Idyllic, hazy summer days and long, cold, dark winters where the chill would eat into your bones and you could never feel warm. I'd spent most of the time since I'd left trying not to miss it; there was, after all, nothing left there for me. Deciding that it wasn't too early for wine – I had, after all, lost my job – I got up and walked back across to the fridge.

'I don't miss it at all,' I said dismissively, pouring a large glass of Yarra Valley pinot gris.

She sighed then, the sigh of a woman who knows she's done her best but her best hasn't been enough. 'Please, Lee, it's important – I wouldn't ask you if it wasn't. You can arrive on Saturday, stay for the party and leave on Sunday.' When I didn't reply, she added, 'At least promise me you'll think about it?'

It was the use of my childhood name that almost brought me undone. I wasn't Lee anymore – I hadn't been for years – I'd left Lee back in Mannus Ridge.

'Okay.' Relenting, I sat back on the stool. 'I'll think about it.'

Jacinta seemed to believe the promise I had no intention of keeping and hung up soon after. I, however, stayed where I was, memories I'd tried so hard to suppress crowding my brain – and not all of them were bad. Maybe I should make an appearance for Dad's birthday. I could breeze in and out so quickly *he'd* never need to know I was there – until I wasn't. I slumped forward, my elbows on the counter, my chin propped up by my fists. Could I do it? Should I do it?

Another memory flashed through, one that only ever showed its face at night and, even then, only in my wildest dreams. No, I couldn't go back. Not yet. It was still too soon; maybe it always would be. I drained my glass and poured another.

THREE

'She knows.'

Otis might have waited until after the server had taken our orders before saying the two words that had the potential to shake my world even more than it had already been shaken today, but I'd known something was up from the minute he'd arrived at my apartment.

Rather than letting himself in and walking straight through as he usually did, he leant against the open door, elegant as always in his Hugo Boss navy suit, black Italian leather derby shoes, a crisp white shirt and a loosened lilac patterned tie that somehow made his blue eyes lighter and brighter. He sighed heavily, his mouth curved into a lopsided rueful smile, and ran his fingers through his thick wavy hair. Even in my misery, my breath caught at the sight of him. Although several years older than me and on the other side of forty-five, Otis Wilde was still an attractive man – and he knew it. While his dark hair was liberally peppered with grey, he kept his body lean with a combination of disciplined exercise and diet. It was his charisma, though, that was his true superpower. Otis could make anyone feel as though they were the only person in his orbit who mattered; he could also talk people into doing his dirty work for him, ensuring his hands were always clean. That, and his quick brain, had ensured his meteoric rise through the CP ranks – to the extent that he was now one of the frontrunners for the CEO role when Bud Redman's contract was up next year. If he was successful – and in his mind, he already was – it would make Otis CP's youngest-ever CEO.

'What have you been up to, Ainsley?' he drawled from his position in the doorway, making no move to greet me properly and shaking his head slowly in exasperation. 'You know there's nothing I can do about it, don't you?'

Unwilling to admit that I had nursed a faint hope he'd be able to fix the situation, I turned away from him and walked back into the kitchen, automatically reaching for the wine bottle.

'How many of those have you had?' he asked, having followed me.

I shrugged miserably, holding up the now almost empty bottle.

Shaking his head again, he finally reached for me and pulled me into his embrace. 'I'm so sorry, darling,' he murmured into my hair as I gave way to the sobs I'd managed to hold in during the rest of this terrible day.

'Hey.' His tone was soothing even as his hands pushed me away slightly. 'Careful of the tie, darling. It's Italian silk, you know, and I don't want to stain it.'

He gave a little half laugh as if he was joking, but I took the hint and moved away, picked up my wineglass and took a large mouthful, ignoring his frown of disapproval. My eyebrows raised, daring him to say something, but he dropped his gaze first and took his jacket off, hanging it neatly over the back of the stool.

'Do you want a drink?' I asked.

'Please.'

His eyes followed me as I pulled out a bottle of the beer I kept in the fridge especially for him. 'What did you hear?' I uncapped the lid and handed it to him.

At first, he appeared confused but recovered quickly. 'That there'd been some complaints made against you so rather than pushing it through the disciplinary process and risking media exposure, they've paid you out.' He took a mouthful of beer, the look on his face the one he had when I knew he was trying to choose his words. 'It's probably the best possible outcome, all things considered.'

'What do you mean by that?'

He shrugged slightly, his eyes darting away from mine. 'Simply that any investigation would likely touch all aspects of your life.'

'And they'd find out about us?' I guessed.

'Exactly. You might feel upset about it now, but the payout was generous and it's better this way.'

'For who?' I demanded. The wine had bypassed my empty stomach and was heading straight to my head. 'You? Besides, they already know about us.' I examined his face for some hint of surprise and found none. 'That's why they made me sign a release and a non-disclosure agreement – in case we broke up and it got nasty.'

If I'd expected him to laugh and pull me back into his embrace and say something like, 'you and I both know that's never going to happen', I was disappointed. Instead, he nodded. 'Standard practice in these circum-stances.' He took another mouthful of his beer. 'I can't believe you allowed yourself to get into that position, though. Surely Tiffany Samuels leaving was a warning to you. The trick, you know, is to manage up as well as down.'

My breath caught in my throat again, but this time

it was for an entirely different reason. 'You knew!' When he said nothing, I added, 'And you didn't warn me!'

He exhaled loudly. 'Come on, Ainsley. What was I supposed to do? You know I couldn't get involved – that's exactly what JC was waiting for me to do.'

'So instead you let me be blindsided?' I stalked around to the lounge, the wine slopping over the side of my glass as I sat heavily. 'After everything I've done – and everything I've done for you – you just let that happen.'

He sat in the chair opposite mine, carefully placing his beer on a coffee table coaster. In a stern voice, he said, 'You did nothing you weren't prepared to do, Ainsley. Your ambitions were clear – I simply helped you get there.' His jaw was set in a straight line, his eyes icy. 'You didn't care who you trod on to make it happen – you know that as well as I do.' He forced a smile that didn't reach his eyes. 'Now, how about you tidy yourself up and we get something to eat, hmmm?' Almost as an afterthought, he asked, 'Have you even eaten today?' I shook my head. 'No wonder you're not seeing things clearly. Wine on an empty stomach is never going to end well.'

Nodding numbly, I swallowed the rest of my wine and levered myself out of the seat, stumbling a little as I got to my feet. With my head held high, I walked overly carefully into the bathroom, groaning when I caught sight of myself in the mirror. At some point, my hair had come loose from its bun, but not in the sexy way Otis liked that to happen – when he could unpin my hair and have it fall past my shoulders in a silvery blonde wave – but instead rather messily as if I'd had a terrible day.

Gripping the bathroom sink, I peered closer, cringing as I acknowledged the damage the day had wrought. No wonder Otis had frowned. My face was red and blotchy from either crying or trying not to cry, and my eyes had mascara smudges below them. I tapped at the underside of my jaw. Was the skin slacker than it had been? Did my face look bloated? I knew I'd been drinking too much of late, but what really was too much? Besides, it wasn't showing on my body – I was diligent with my yoga and gym. Most days in the office, I existed on black coffee. A dull thud beat against my temple, and I pushed against it with my fingers before swallowing a couple of paracetamol. Yes, I needed to cut down – just not today.

Inhaling deeply, I reached for my cleanser and began to repair my face.

Twenty minutes later, we were in the Japanese restaurant downstairs from the apartment, more wine had been poured and orders placed when Otis hit me with his two-word sledgehammer. 'She knows.'

For what seemed like the umpteenth time today, my tummy flip-flopped and the pain in my head grew stronger. 'How?'

He shrugged. 'Does it matter? She plays tennis with JC's wife on Saturday mornings, so ...'

I nodded wearily. Of course Melanie played tennis with JC's wife – and probably with every other wife on the executive team. The wives on CPs top team were like WAGs – wives and girlfriends – in the footballing world, and they stuck together.

'What happens now?' Fearing I already knew the answer my heart rate picked up speed again.

His eyes flicked around the room in an uncharacteristic show of uncertainty, and a new dread slithered through my body. While we'd spoken about being together – some day – I'd always understood that day wouldn't come until after he'd reached the top job. 'You need to understand, darling,' he'd once said, 'it looks good to have my family behind me. Any adverse publicity would rattle the conservatives on the board.'

Now he said, 'She wants a divorce.' Before the barest flicker of hope could spark within me, he added, 'Of course, it's out of the question. I haven't come this far to throw it all away now.'

Was he waiting for me to agree with him – or to plead with him to choose me instead? I wasn't able to get any words out.

He paused as the server laid plates of appetisers on the table, each tiny morsel almost too exquisite to eat. As beautiful as the food looked, I'd lost my appetite. I reached instead for my glass and drained it, setting it back on the table with a loud wobble.

'Don't you think you've had enough?' he asked disparagingly.

Defiantly, I poured another glass. 'I don't know, Otis, after the day I've had, I think I deserve it.'

'Why don't you eat something first,' he urged, using his chopsticks to lift a piece of sashimi I knew from experience would almost dissolve on the tongue.

I shook my head, the wine mixing with bile to leave a bitter taste in my mouth. 'What does this mean for me?'

He exhaled and grimaced; that's when I knew there was more to come. I'd seen that look before when he'd had to communicate bad news. He'd do it in such a way that the person who would be left devastated would also be left thinking that it wasn't really Otis's fault, that he was relaying a decision he'd had no part in.

'Just tell me, Otis.'

'I need you out of the apartment,' he said flatly. At first, I thought I'd misheard him, but when he wouldn't meet my eyes, I knew I hadn't. He gave a little half shrug as if none of this was his doing. 'Melanie knows you've been staying there.'

'That makes it sound like you've been paying for me.' A flicker of anger sparked at his inference. 'Instead of which, I've been paying you fair market rent.' How could this be happening? First my job, now my apartment? What else could go wrong today? 'Next thing you'll be telling me we can't see each other anymore.' The words tumbled out shakily, the panic evident in my voice.

I poked at a piece of raw fish with a single chopstick so I wouldn't need to look at his face when he answered me.

'We can't,' he said.

In my rush to get up, my heel caught on my handbag, and to stop myself from falling, I grabbed at the tablecloth, causing the wine glass to topple. As Otis attempted to wipe it off himself, all the while checking to see who had seen, I yanked my handbag free and stumbled into the street and to the ground-floor entrance of the apartment.

Rubbing at the pain in my head, I stabbed my access code into the reader only to have it beep at me. I tried again for the same result, sobs mingling with wine and vomit in my throat. Unable to hold it in any longer, I whirled away from the door towards the gutter and heaved into it, the effort causing one of the pins in my hair to dislodge. Uncaring who saw me, I stayed there like that, doubled over, my hand around my waist holding my stomach, tears streaming down my cheeks, my sobs and my vomiting racking my body violently.

'Let's get you upstairs,' Otis said, stroking my back.

Looking up blearily at him for a sign that it was all a big mistake, all I saw in his eyes was disgust and a need to get this messiness over and done with so he could move on.

Nodding blindly, I allowed him to guide me to the access door and stood back as he deftly entered the code. Once inside, he led me to the lift, silently waiting for the doors to open. At my door, he used his key to let us in.

'Okay,' he said, collecting his suit jacket from where it still hung. 'Will you be right to get yourself to bed?'

'You're not staying?' I'd propped myself against the kitchen counter, half leaning, half sprawled. While my tummy was still churning and my head spinning, there was nothing left inside of me to come back up. I sounded desperate, but I'd lost what was left of my dignity in the gutter downstairs. I'd never be able to go back to that restaurant. A half laugh and a half sob escaped me in a snort when I realised I wouldn't be living here soon anyway.

'No,' he said impatiently. 'I've booked into a hotel; I thought that best.' He shrugged his jacket on. 'Get to bed – we'll talk tomorrow.' At the door, he paused and turned back. 'Take care, Ainsley.' And then he left.

I wanted to scream at him; I wanted to shout and I wanted to pick up the empty wine bottle and hurl it at the door, but I did none of those things. Instead, I sank to the floor, a puddle of tears and misery in a designer dress and heels.

FOUR

I'd forgotten to turn my alarm off last night, so it went off at five as usual. I was about to crawl out of bed and into my gym gear before remembering I didn't need to get up this morning. There was no need to go to the gym, check my work emails, make-up my face, straighten and restrain my hair in its usual tight bun, no need to dress and no need to go into the office. There was, therefore, no need for the familiar twist of anxiety, but still, it was there.

With a groan, I rolled over, pummelled my pillow and squeezed my eyes tightly shut; but it was too late – the beast in my belly was awake and bombarding my brain with their usual message of catastrophes waiting to happen. The endless refrain of what-ifs and you're not good enoughs – I knew it well. It's why I took something to help me sleep most nights – the wine I'd had would send me to sleep, but the resultant blood sugar spikes would have me lying awake in the early hours while my monkey brain went over and over the events of the day, second-guessing what I'd done and hadn't done, turning insignificant molehills into Everest-sized mountains, anticipating what could possibly go wrong the following day and working through potential solutions to pre-empt damage limitation, wondering if tomorrow would be the day they discovered me as the imposter I was.

This morning, though, there was nothing that could go wrong – the two outcomes I'd feared the most had come to pass: I'd lost my job and Otis had broken up with me. I had nothing else to lose – except my apartment; that's right, I'd lost that too. I thumped my pillow again, the tiredness behind my eyes mixing with my hangover.

Falling in love with anyone – let alone a married man – hadn't been in my plans, yet I fell for Otis the first moment I saw him.

It was at a Christmas party soon after I'd started work at CP, so almost seven years ago. I was ambitious and ready to take on the world; Otis was already a senior manager and on the fast track – he knew it and so did everyone else.

It had been one of those summer days in Sydney when the thermometer had nudged well into the thirties, and despite being close to eleven at night, it hadn't cooled down at all. I'd been standing off to one side of the waterside bar watching the action milling around me, unsure how to join in, wondering whether I should duck out and leave them all to it, but worrying that if I did, the powers to be would notice. Using the back of my hand, I wiped the sweat from my forehead and glanced around the crowded bar; then, our eyes had met. I'd been in love before, but this was nothing like that. Lust hit me with a crash that almost took the breath from my body.

With his dark, wavy hair, square jaw and above-average height, it wasn't just that he looked as though he'd stepped from the pages of a magazine – or at the very least a Ted Baker catalogue – I felt his presence from where I was standing as if it radiated out from him in a golden arc. He smiled sardonically and strode purposefully towards me, weaving his way through the throng, his gaze holding mine, his path clearing almost biblically.

My heart stopped for a beat as he paused at the bar to pick up two drinks, but the smile he flashed in my direction told me not to worry. And then he was there beside me, handing me a glass of white wine and introducing himself.

'Ainsley St James,' I said in response. 'I've only been with the company for a week or so.'

'I was wondering why I hadn't seen you before.' Even though his words had a practiced come-here-often sound, it didn't feel like a line; it felt sincere, as if he was *really* interested in me, had *really* been wondering who I was and where I'd been until that precise minute.

We spoke for a few minutes, inane conversation – how it had been so hot, how it was still so hot, how crowded the bar was, where I'd been before CP, what I'd studied, whether I was settling in to work life at CP. And he listened – *really* listened – to my answers. For that half hour, we were the only people in that crowded room, and I was the only one who mattered to him.

Of course it had had to end – someone had dragged him away – and I missed him almost the second he was gone. After that, I thought about trying to get involved, to talk to others, but the party was breaking up. Without saying goodbye to anyone, I edged my way to the exit; after the bar's heat and noise, it was a relief to emerge out onto King Street Wharf. For a second or two, I stood in that almost darkness that exists in a city where the lights are never really out. Music was drifting through on the still air from the bars, the background whoosh of the cars on the Western Distributor, but I allowed it all to enfold me and relived those minutes I shared with Otis, wondering whether he was doing the same.

'You left without saying goodbye.' He appeared out of the darkness, stealing the air from me. Before I could answer, he added, 'How are you getting home? Can I walk with you anywhere?'

'I live on King Street,' I said, trying in vain to control my breathing. 'It's not far.' I dropped my eyes so he couldn't see the wanting in them, because I did want him – so much it was all I could do not to cover the distance between us and kiss him.

He stepped forward and lifted my chin with one finger, that same finger straying to rest against my lower lip. 'I'll walk you home then,' he said, a promise in every word.

Otis stayed that night and when I woke the next morning, he was sitting on the side of my bed, fully dressed. He grinned and said, 'Good morning, sweetheart,' and reached out a hand to trace the side of my cheek. 'You looked so beautiful that I didn't want to wake you.'

I stretched languorously, my body feeling sore in the nicest possible way. 'Do you have to go?'

He tilted his head to the side, his smile regretful. 'I wish I didn't, but I do.'

A wave of heat rushed through my face as I realised what he meant – this had been a one-night-only thing. I turned onto my side, away from him so he wouldn't see the hurt in my eyes.

'Hey,' he said softly, lying and spooning me. 'This isn't a drive-by, okay?' He reached under the sheet, stroking my breast, his little finger catching on my nipple and flicking it lightly. Moving slowly, his hand followed the curve of my hip and back up to my breast, his lips nuzzling in behind my ear, trails of goosebumps following his fingers and his lips.

I tried to turn and face him. 'No,' he whispered, his fingers finding my core, 'this is for you.'

His hands and lips played me to perfection, and afterwards, he held me until my breathing was back to normal, eventually turning me, so we were face to face. 'Now I really do need to go.' He pressed his lips to mine as a chuckle rumbled through his chest. 'But I'll call you later.'

When I nodded mutely, he said, 'Last night was special, Ainsley, and I'd like to see you again. Is that alright with you?'

'I'd like that too,' I murmured and kissed him again.

He'd left soon after but, true to his word, called me that afternoon. He must've been in a park because the background sounds were of a Sydney summer: the squawk of lorikeets, the barking of dogs and the occasional thwack of a cricket ball against a bat. He said he didn't have long to talk, but we arranged to meet again during the week. I told him I couldn't wait, and he'd laughed knowingly. 'There are still parts of you I haven't kissed,' he said, his voice low and smooth. 'And I intend to rectify that situation as soon as possible.'

Even though he couldn't see me, I blushed, desire rushing through me. 'You're thinking about it too, aren't you, sweetheart?' he asked throatily, the deep chocolatey warmth of his voice turning me on even more.

Afterwards, I googled him, and for the second time in twenty-four hours, my heart plummeted. There he was at a CP sponsored charity event and beside him, beaming up at him – with every right to beam up at him – was his wife, Melanie Wilde. With growing dismay, I read Melanie was a partner in one of the most prestigious law firms in Sydney, specialising in family law for the rich and famous and was even more of a high-flyer than Otis. A power couple, the newspaper referred to them as. Unable to stop myself, I went further down the Google rabbit hole, my heart hurting more and more with every photo and article.

That night I caught up with some friends – Bree and Ruby – at another bar in Darling Harbour.

'How was last night?' asked Bree, wincing as the crowd jostled, her margarita slopping stickily over her fingers.

My cheeks must have glowed in the dark as Ruby almost screamed, 'Oh my God! You met someone!'

'It was nothing,' I dismissed, failing to control my smile at the memory of last night – and this morning.

'It's obviously not nothing by the way you're blushing.' Bree wriggled back in her chair and examined my face, her grin widening as I was unable to meet her eyes. 'You spent the night with him!'

Another wave of heat filled my face as I ducked my head and looked back up at them with a bashful expression, biting my lower lip.

'Well?' Ruby made the single syllable stretch into three.

'I won't be seeing him again,' I said, doing my best to ignore the pain in my heart as I said the words. After all, it had been just one night; it wasn't as if I was in love. How could I be after just one night? It was simply a lethal combination of hormones, heat, alcohol and the festive season, and I'd always been a sucker for the festive season.

'Why not?' Bree sounded puzzled. 'If he was special enough to have you come over all coy and embarrassed ... We've never seen you affected by a man like this before, have we, Rubes?'

Ruby shook her head.

I took a sip of my rapidly warming, suddenly too-sweet margarita. 'He's married,' I said bluntly. Ruby frowned in disapproval. 'I didn't know until this afternoon.'

'He didn't say?' Ruby asked.

'Well, he wouldn't, would he?' Bree rolled her eyes good-naturedly. 'I presume there was no ring?'

I shook my head. 'And he stayed the night.' My face burned again at the memory of his farewell.

'That good, huh?' guessed Bree.

I nodded. 'Mind-blowingly, bone-meltingly good.' I sighed deeply for emphasis.

'So how do you know he's married?' Ruby asked.

'I googled him,' I said with a shrug. 'And the first thing that came up was a picture of him with his beautiful and super-smart wife.' I held my phone out to show them.

'He's hot!' said Bree.

'And she's gorgeous,' said Ruby. 'Why would a man

married to someone like her need to play away?' She wrinkled her nose, her brow furrowed.

'Maybe they have an open marriage,' suggested Bree. 'If such a thing exists ...' We were all silent as we contemplated the concept. 'No, it wouldn't be that. Maybe it's a game to him. It says here that she helps Sydney's rich and famous screw their exes for everything, so maybe it turns him on knowing what would happen to him if she ever found out.'

'Maybe,' I conceded, not wanting to think about his wife.

'Did he say he wanted to see you again?' Ruby asked, sipping her martini.

I nodded. 'Next week.'

'So it's not a one-nighter then,' Bree mused. 'What did you say?' She took one look at my expression and chuckled. 'Or weren't you capable of saying anything?'

'Something like that,' I admitted. 'But that was before I knew he was married. I won't see him now.'

The others nodded solemnly, and I truly believed what I told them – at that moment, anyway.

When he texted on Monday, *I can't stop thinking about you,* I wavered but held firm and didn't respond.

When he phoned on Tuesday afternoon and said, 'I'm burning for you, Ainsley,' I closed my eyes as his voice curled around me, touching the parts of me he'd licked and kissed and stroked, but still managed to say, 'I can't see you again.'

'Why not?'

I stood and walked away from my desk, leaning into the window overlooking George Street. 'Because you're married.' The words were barely a whisper.

'Aaaah, I see,' he said. 'That does create a bit of a problem.'

'Only a bit?' Below in the street, commuters were rushing for trains and buses, jostling with Christmas shoppers for space on the footpath.

'I can't get you out of my head,' he said, his voice deepening. 'I'm sitting in my office just a few floors above you, and all I can think about is you and how much I want to touch you again ... taste you again.' I had to stop myself from groaning out loud. 'And I think you've been thinking about it too, haven't you?'

Oh Christ, his voice was rich and dark and sweet, and every single goosebump in my body jumped to attention. 'Yes,' I squeaked.

'So what are we going to do about it?' he asked smoothly.

I took a deep, fortifying breath. 'Nothing. We can't do anything about it.' And I hung up.

When I arrived home that night, he was outside leaning against a black Mercedes. 'Just one more night,

Ainsley?' he urged, reaching for my hands and pulling me unprotestingly towards him. 'One more night.'

I moaned into his mouth as he kissed me, not caring if anyone saw us, knowing that nothing and no one mattered more than being in his arms. 'One more night,' I agreed, melting into him.

Of course it wasn't just one more night, and before too long, I was cancelling arrangements I'd made with friends and making excuses not to catch up. Bree and Ruby persevered with me longer than anyone else but made no secret of their disapproval. I haven't seen or heard from either of them in years. They were both probably happily married now with kids.

Right from the start, he'd made it clear that we needed to be low-key, that no one could know; and right from the start, he looked after me from a career viewpoint – moving me through the ranks as quickly as he could. Of course there'd been a price to pay for that, but I was willing to pay it to stay in his life.

When he pushed me into this job, I'd hesitated. 'If I move to Melbourne, we won't see each other,' I'd said. We were in bed and had just finished making love.

He'd held me close, his fingers tracing the line of my spine. 'I can't see it will be very different, darling. I'm in Melbourne so often. Plus'—his finger drew circles on my bum, the touch so light and feathery I almost moaned in frustration— 'it means we get to have sleepovers whenever I'm in town. In fact, I have a little apartment in the city that I've been meaning to lease out ...' He pushed me onto my back so I was open to his gaze. 'So I was thinking'—his hand drifted below my belly— 'that it would be perfect for you – and perfect for us.' As my breath quickened, his smile grew knowing, his eyes holding mine, forcing them to remain open when I would have closed them. 'What do you think?'

'Yes,' I said, and then when he entered me again, 'oh yes!'

Later he murmured, 'There's just one little thing you'll need to take care of down there.' When I raised my eyebrows, he continued, 'Her name is Tiffany Samuels, and she was expecting to be appointed to the role. JC thinks she walks on water, so unless you manage to get rid of her or make her look bad, she'll be after your job.'

I knew without him saying the words exactly what he needed me to do – remove JC's person, someone who made him look good. Now, though, I wondered whether I'd been played. Had this always been his intention? Had he always known I wasn't up to the job? I'd gotten rid of Tiffany for him, but in doing so, had he also been setting up his way of getting rid of me?

I groaned and reached for the glass of water beside my bed. My throat was sore and raspy – hardly surprising after the wine and vomiting. Tossing back the covers, I struggled to my feet and staggered to the bathroom, managing to avoid looking in the mirror, and swallowed two paracetamol tablets before going back to bed and giving in to the wave of tiredness that crashed over me.

WHEN I WOKE AGAIN after midday, my throat was worse, and I was so hot even a sheet felt too heavy on my limbs. On legs that almost refused to hold me upright, I made my way back into the bathroom. This time, after swallowing more paracetamol, I took a covid test, the double red lines taking mere seconds to make an appearance.

Slumping back onto the toilet seat, I buried my face in my hands. This was all I needed. There was no food in the apartment, and I had no means of getting any. My only friend in the world was about to jump on a plane and fly away for two weeks. Holding onto the sink for support, I levered myself up and went back to bed.

Otis. If he was still in Melbourne, maybe he'd bring

me some groceries – even if he just dropped them at the door. I grabbed my phone and dialled his number. When it went through to voicemail, I hung up and texted him instead.

Hi, Thought you might like to know I've just tested positive for covid. Can you ring me, please?

Nothing.

I was drifting back to sleep when my phone finally rang.

'Otis?'

'Sorry, darling,' came the chirpy tone of Benji. 'Just checking in before we fly out tomorrow. How did you go last night? With Otis?'

'Oh Benji,' I sobbed – which was a mistake as it meant that I couldn't breathe and talk and sob all at the same time.

'Ainsley? Sweetie? What's wrong?'

'Everything,' I sputtered. 'Otis has broken up with me – he said his wife knows.'

'I'll come straight over,' he said.

'No! Don't. On top of everything else, now I'm sick too.'

'Covid?'

I sneezed, reached for the box of tissues and blew my nose loudly. 'Yes. Have you already tested for Bali?'

'We have and we're fine.' He hesitated for half a

beat and said, 'Knowing you, there'd be nothing edible in your fridge. I'll pick a few essentials up and drop them over.'

'You can't come in ...'

'I know that, but I can drop some things off. Give me an hour.'

True to his word, Benji rang my door buzzer barely ninety minutes after hanging up.

'You look dreadful, my sweet,' he said, taking in my bed hair, red nose and swollen eyes.

I propped myself against the doorjamb for support. 'Don't come any closer,' I warned.

'I won't,' he assured me. 'There's enough food in here to last you a week – or at least until you have the strength to get a grocery delivery. Is it very bad?'

'The heartbreak or the virus?' I shrugged miserably.

'Look on the bright side,' he said, attempting to lighten my mood. 'At least you don't have to worry about the emails piling up while you're off sick – and it's not such a bad place to be isolating.'

I closed my eyes briefly as I went back to the thoughts that had been lurking around the edges of my virus-addled brain all morning. 'Except that, I won't be here for much longer – Otis is evicting me and I can't think straight enough to know what to do about it.'

'He's what?' Benji was clearly outraged on my behalf.

I shrugged again, unable to do or say anything else.

'How long have you got?'

'No idea. He said we'd talk today, but he's not answering my calls or texts. Surely, though, he'll understand that I can't exactly get out and look for something now.' My voice was raspy and thick with worry.

'Maybe it's time to buy,' said Benji. 'You've been on a good salary since moving here.'

Suddenly embarrassed, I couldn't look at him.

'Ainsley?'

'I've been paying Otis rent and there's the lease on the car ...' I tried to justify my lack of buying power but didn't fool him.

'And the designer clothes and shoes and weekly manicures and regular injectables and other maintenance appointments,' finished Benji. 'Do you have any savings?'

'A little,' I lied. He didn't need to know the entire truth. 'Let's just say I'm glad I got a payout. Enough to pay the bond on a new rental and see me through until I get a new job. Anyway, you had better go before I sneeze germs all over you.'

'There's a delightful prospect. Stay strong, darling, and I'll see you when I'm back.' More gently, he added,

'Call me if you need me. I mightn't be here, but I can be on the other end of the phone. And you have a spare key, so feel free to stay at mine or even leave some things there if you like.'

I smiled weakly. 'I'll be living vicariously through your social media photos, but thank you. I don't know what I'd do without you.'

My eyes were streaming as I shut the door. I was completely alone, and for the first time in nearly fifteen years, the prospect of it terrified me.

FIVE

While Otis had ignored my texts and calls, his EA, Maria, had phoned me late on Friday afternoon, waking me from my feverish sleep.

'Otis needs to know when you'll be vacating the apartment,' she'd said as her opening line.

My head beating and my nose streaming, I'd groaned and said, 'I have no idea, Maria. It's not as if I've had much time to think about it.' I sneezed and that just made my head ache even more.

'Are you sick or something?' There was no sympathy in the question.

'Yes. Covid – which means I'm not going to be able to look for anywhere else until I'm no longer infectious. I did message Otis and tell him.' As if to make my point, I sneezed again and reached for a tissue to blow my nose loudly before tossing the tissue in a pile on the floor with all the other used tissues.

There was mumbling at the other end of the phone as if Maria had covered it with her hand. 'You have two weeks,' she said.

'Is Otis there?' I sounded weak and pitiful but couldn't help myself. 'Can I speak to him?'

'Two weeks,' she repeated before hanging up.

It had been another few days before I'd felt up to getting out of bed for more than ten minutes at a time and another two after that before my brain was clear enough to examine my options.

The first thing I did was check my emails. I'd had to leave the laptop in the office so squinted at my phone through still-watery eyes. Other than spam and offers I'd be unable to refuse, three needed action. The first was from Maria reiterating Otis's notice to vacate and advising me there would be (undisclosed) consequences if I failed to do so. The second was from Jacinta reminding me of Dad's party and my promise to consider attending, and the third was from the finance company advising me I'd missed the most recent payment on my car and that if I didn't make arrangements for the arrears within the next seven days, they would commence recovery action.

Exhaling loudly, I let my head slump into my

hands, regretting the movement when it resulted in a coughing fit.

Once the coughing was under control, I collected a notepad and a pen from my tote bag and sat at the kitchen bench to begin a list. Today was Thursday, so exactly a week since the bottom had fallen out of my world. Before I could get too caught up in my pity party again, I shook my head, gritted my teeth and wrote.

1. Ring the finance company and pay off the car
2. Find somewhere to live
3. Pack up the apartment
4. Find a new job
5. Buy a new laptop
6. Reply to Jacinta

It all looked simple enough on paper, and in just over an hour I'd ordered a new laptop and sorted out the car (and made a sizeable dent in my bank balance), but with city rentals the way they were, not only would it take me some time to find a new apartment, but unless I got a job quickly, what was left of my payout wouldn't last long.

At the thought of packing up the apartment, a

fresh wave of anxiety began bubbling in my stomach. Forcing myself to breathe (and cough) through it, I ran my eyes around the space. All the furniture had either already been here when I moved in, or Otis and I had purchased it together. A memory of that weekend when I'd pretended we were a real couple with a real future out shopping for our first home together flashed across my eyes. I'd been so happy that day. Pushing the thought – and the memory – aside, for the first time, I wondered whether someone else had stayed in this apartment before me and who would sleep here after I'd gone. Maria maybe? Surely that was too much of a cliché.

Swallowing back a fresh wave of tears, I decided that if we purchased it for the apartment, it could stay in the apartment; I didn't need the reminder, and it would make packing up easier if all I had to take were my few books, clothes, shoes and other personal belongings.

That didn't, however, solve the problem of where to live.

As I was scrolling through my phone at the list of rentals – none of which I could now afford – my phone rang. My attention still on real estate, I answered automatically, without looking at the caller ID.

'Ainsley St James.'

'Is that really you or your machine again?' It was Jacinta.

Squeezing my eyes shut, I closed the rental app. 'It's me,' I croaked.

'Oh my god, you sound dreadful!'

'Thanks,' I muttered, the effort causing me to cough again.

'Is it Covid?'

'Yep.'

Silence. 'I suppose this means you won't be down next weekend.' Disappointment tinged every word.

Rubbing my forehead, I grabbed hold of the get-out clause. 'I'm not sure, Jacinta. It depends on whether I'm testing negative by then – I don't want to bring this home if Dad hasn't been well.'

'No,' she agreed. 'What day are you at?'

'Day seven.' I grimaced, watching my get-out clause escape. 'But I'm still testing positive.'

'Well,' she said more cheerfully. 'You've still got a week, so I'm not giving up.'

'Don't ...' Another coughing fit overtook me.

'What?'

'Don't ... count on it ...' I managed to say in between coughs. 'Better go.'

Within seconds of me hanging up, a message pinged from her.

I'm still hopeful. Take care and hopefully see you next weekend.

Groaning, I typed back:

No promises and please don't say anything to Mum and Dad – I don't want them to worry.

A weekend in Mannus Ridge. On top of everything else, that would be the last straw. No, I couldn't go back – especially not now that I was at absolute rock bottom.

On Saturday, I forced myself to get dressed and, with a mask firmly in place and a list of rentals open for inspection, left the house for the first time in over a week.

Rock bottom, it seemed, was a moving target, and by Wednesday evening, I had to acknowledge that, barring a miracle, I would be homeless within days. The applications I'd made for a couple of properties over the weekend had all been rejected – not surprising, given my employment status. Benji had said I could stay with him, but without an end date, that wasn't fair – particularly as they had family descending on them for Christmas.

As I wearily jammed shoes and handbags into packing boxes, I couldn't help mentally calculating how much I'd spent on luxury brands (many of which I'd never worn) over the past few years and was ashamed to admit the total represented a good proportion of a deposit on an apartment of my own. Not that it mattered now; the money had been spent, and these boxes were all I had to show.

After another night where I went to bed exhausted, yet still managed to toss and turn for all but a few hours, I woke no nearer an answer and briefly contemplated staying where I was. After all, what could Otis do about it if I refused to move? If he wanted to evict me forcibly, he'd need to commence legal action – legal action I couldn't afford to defend. No, if I went down that track, Otis would see that I'd never get another job in finance again.

My phone pinged. I reached across to the bedside table to grab it.

How are you feeling?

For the briefest of seconds, I'd hoped the message was from Otis, even though I knew it wouldn't be. It was, instead, my sister who, true to her word, hadn't given up on me.

I hesitated before replying:

On the mend. Still tired, but it is what it is.

She came back with a single word: *Well?*

Suddenly, I was tired of saying no, tired of making excuses, tired of running. While I'd done my best to convince myself I didn't miss any of it, that I was better off away from there, all I wanted right now was to see my family – even if it meant going back to Mannus Ridge. I could take most of my things to Benji's today, leave tomorrow and be there in time for the party on Saturday night. I could even stay for a couple of weeks after, just while I figured out what I would do next. No one needed to know what a mess I'd made of my life; everyone would assume I'd finally taken some time off work.

Going back to Mannus Ridge would be one of the hardest things I'd ever had to do, but it was also my only real option.

Before I could change my mind, I typed *ok*.

OMG!!!! REALLY????

For the first time in two weeks, I genuinely smiled, picturing Jacinta's surprise, probably mixed with a healthy dose of disbelief.

I won't tell Mum and Dad though, she wrote. *It can be a surprise.*

She might as well have said she didn't believe I'd turn up; I didn't blame her.

The decision had given me the impetus I needed to get out of bed and crack on with the packing.

I messaged Benji and checked he was still okay with storing a few boxes, adding I was going to Mannus Ridge for my father's party and might stay on for a couple of weeks afterwards. He quickly replied in the affirmative and added how pleased he was that I was going home before adding a photo of his feet dangling in a Balinese pool.

I packed two suitcases with the clothes I'd need for Mannus Ridge, including a couple of outfits on the off-chance I needed to come back to the city in a hurry for a job interview, stowed them safely in the car, and by just after nine the following morning was ready to leave.

After checking all wardrobes and closets were empty, I stood in the kitchen and gazed around the room. I'd expected to have been overcome by emotion, to remember all the times that Otis and I were here together, were happy together, but all that came to mind were the nights I sat here on my own, waiting for calls that didn't come, or worse, the last-minute cancellations that had been so much a feature of our relationship in the past twelve months.

I remembered the birthdays and Christmases and anniversaries and weekends spent alone, the early morning alarms, the nights where I staggered in so mentally exhausted I could do little more than reach for a bottle of wine to make it all go away – even for a few hours.

While I'd been confronted with loneliness over the

past two weeks, I realised I'd been lonely for much longer. This apartment that I'd thought was so stylish was, in fact, bland and soulless, much like our relationship had been, much like I felt I was.

I sat my keys on the kitchen bench and left, shutting the door and that chapter of my life behind me.

SIX

It was bad enough that my normally reliable red convertible BMW had decided that now was the perfect time to get a flat tyre, but to do it here, in the middle of nowhere – okay, ten kilometres out of Mannus Ridge, which might as well be the middle of nowhere – in the pouring rain, well, that added insult to injury.

At least I'd gotten the car off the road far enough to ensure I wouldn't be a hazard to any traffic (traffic – a laugh in itself), but where was the closest roadside assist? My alternative otherwise was to change the tyre myself – if, indeed, I had a spare. I'd been seventeen and (officially) learning to drive when Dad tried to teach me how to change a tyre and doubted that I'd remember how to now – even if I had the right tools, which I also doubted. I could always get out of the car and check on the spare, but that would involve getting wet. No, staying here in the dry was the best option. Someone would be along sometime, surely.

I rummaged in my tote for my phone. Great, no signal; this really was the middle of nowhere. I rubbed at the condensation on the window to peer out, the rain pattering against the roof. Wasn't this part of the country supposed to be in a drought? Or was that last year? Either way, I hadn't been expecting rain on the first Friday in December or – I glimpsed the outside temperature on the dashboard – a cold snap.

Against the steel-grey sky, the landscape looked substantially greener than it had on that February day when I'd last seen it. Then the sun had been blasting down, the ground parched, the grass, or what there was of it, yellowed and brittle. Like my heart had felt. I groaned aloud at my uncharacteristic slump into drama – although, after what had happened, surely I was entitled to a little drama?

I held my phone up to the windscreen. Was that a single bar of reception? No. Sighing inwardly, I knew I'd need to brave the elements and step outside – if not to look for a spare tyre, then to try for reception.

After checking for traffic (as if), I opened the door and swung my legs out, stepping straight into a puddle, my white heels sinking into the mud. Christ. Those sandals had cost a fortune. Gingerly, with my arms wrapped around myself for warmth, I made my way around to the boot and clicked it open. If I had a spare, it would be sitting in the compartment under my luggage and there was no way I was taking that out to sit in the rain. Sighing again, I held my phone in the air ... two bars. That would do. I tapped in the number of my road assist. Someone picked up after three rings, and this time my sigh was one of relief.

'Can I please have your policy number?' the operator asked.

'I'm sorry,' I said. 'I don't have it on me.'

'That's okay,' the friendly voice assured me. 'We can look you up in the system. Can I please have your name, date of birth, address and the registration of the vehicle?'

'Sure.' I provided the information requested.

After a little break, where the only noise was the keyboard tapping, the operator said, 'I'm sorry Ms St James, but that membership has lapsed.'

'What?' If I hadn't known that it would splash muddy water onto my tight white capri pants and finish the job of ruining my shoes, I would've stamped my foot. 'How can it have lapsed?'

'We attempted to debit the amount from your

credit card but were unsuccessful,' the operator said, not sounding apologetic. 'We sent you an email.'

'I'm sure you did,' I ground out. 'Can I pay now?'

'Of course you can, Ms St James.'

'Okay, hang on.' I tucked the phone between my neck and shoulder as I tried to step across the puddle to reach into the car's front seat for my bag. As I did, the phone slipped and fell into the water with an ominous splash. I quickly fished it out and dried it against my (previously) white capris, holding onto the car door for balance. 'Are you still there?' My hair was coming out of its tight top knot, and I tucked the damp locks behind my ears.

'I am. Do you have your credit card?'

'Hang on, I'm trying to get it,' I rummaged through my bag for my wallet.

A vehicle whizzed by, and a wave of muddy water crashed over me. I cursed and dropped the phone again – this time on the car seat.

'Are you alright, madam?' came the voice from the call centre.

'Yes, some idiot just sprayed me with water. Oh god, it's muddy too! Okay, here's the card.' I straightened and read out the number.

There was silence as the operator attempted to process the payment.

'I'm sorry, Ms St James, but that payment has been declined.' Rather than apologetic, her voice was laced with pity.

'What? Are you sure you typed the right number in?' I sounded accusing but couldn't seem to help myself.

'Yes, madam. Do you have another card you might like to use?' Was that a judgemental tone in her voice?

'I do, but I don't like the attitude you're taking with me. I've been a customer of this service for more years than I care to remember,' I said, balancing on my toes as my heels would have sunk further into the mud, trying vainly to remember whether I'd paid my last credit card bill.

Before I could say more, a mud-splattered white twin-cab ute drove past, spraying me with more mud. You've got to be joking. I wiped the sodden grit from my cheek. Rather than continuing into town, it slowed before reversing to pull up in front of me.

'Don't worry,' I said to the operator. 'Someone has just pulled up to help me.'

As I hung up, I belatedly realised I should've kept the operator on the line until I could determine that the man at the other end of the muddy riding boots that were now emerging from the open door wasn't going to murder me. But then again, this was Mannus

Ridge. Nothing interesting had happened here since the day my great-great-great-(I think there's another great in there)-grandfather had set down his knapsack and decided it would be a nice place to build a house and a hotel – or that he was too tired to walk any further. The difference hardly mattered – the town had grown up around him regardless. Just in case, though, I snapped a photo of the registration plate of the ute before realising I had no one to send it to and no one who would care if I was murdered.

Over the last two weeks, I'd lost my job, my lover and my apartment, yet somehow it was only here on a lay-by in the middle of nowhere with a flat tyre and about to be approached by a strange man who might or might not have help on his mind that it hit me how no one knew where I was (other than Jacinta who didn't really believe that I was coming) and, more to the point, hardly anyone cared.

Up until a fortnight ago, I hadn't cried since that day I drove away from here, but now I couldn't seem to stop. As if in sympathy, the rain beat down harder, the drops like icy pellets against my bare arms, the water running down my face, mingling with my tears and washing them away. I had no idea whether I was crying for what I'd originally left behind in Mannus Ridge, or the circumstances that had meant I had no choice but to come back now, or frustration at the flat tyre and the woman with the judgemental voice on the phone, or even gratitude that someone had stopped to help me, but my tears were warmer than the rain, and just as persistent.

The man's steps had halted by the front of the car. I swiped the rain and tears from my eyes as they travelled from the muddy, leather battered and worn riding boots up equally well-worn denim to the hem of an oilskin jacket, the colour of the best dark chocolate, buttoned to the neck against the horrid weather. When they reached the man's face, my heart faltered and the world stopped turning.

His mouth, which had been curved into a smile of greeting – the sort of smile you'd give to a stranger with an offer of help – tightened, and his eyes darkened almost to the colour of the sky, his gaze narrowing as it ran up my body from my ridiculous white sandals and expensive, body-hugging white capris to the mushroom-pink sleeveless knit that was now clinging to me as if it were a second skin. His lips curled into a sneer and he stuffed his hands into his pockets, turned his back and walked purposefully back to his ute.

'Wait!' I yelled, pulling my heels out of the mud and staggering onto the road. My tears had stopped, but goosebumps peaked on my arms and my teeth chattered from a combination of cold and reaction. 'Angus!' He stalled but didn't turn. 'I know it's you, Angus; please come back.'

After what seemed like forever, he turned slowly to face me but made no move to bridge the gap between us. 'Lee St James,' he finally drawled, the rain streaming over the rim of his well-worn Akubra hat and down his jacket. 'What are you doing here?'

I forced a tight smile and waved my hand towards my car. 'I've got a flat tyre.'

'I can see that. But what are you doing here?'

I shrugged, the movement enough to dislodge the rest of my ponytail from its topknot. It fell heavily down my back in soaking clusters. 'I thought I'd come and see Mum and Dad,' I said as if it was an everyday occurrence.

'After all this time?' He sounded disbelieving – and disapproving.

'It's been hard to get away.'

'From your important big career in the city? Yeah, I heard.' His hand cupped his darkly stubbled chin, the forefinger and thumb pulling at it in a way I remembered too well.

My chin firmed. 'I'm here now,' I said, my hands moving to my hips. I would've tossed my head, but everything was too wet. 'For Dad's party.'

'So I see.' He looked at me derisively again. 'Do they know you're coming?'

'Jacinta does but I thought I'd surprise them.'

He nodded slowly. 'Yeah, you'll do that for sure. How long's it been since you spoke to them?'

'I stay in touch.'

'That's alright then.' With a little shake of his head, he turned away, facing his ute. 'I'm glad you've been bothered to speak to someone.' Through the rain, I could barely hear his words.

'Please, Angus. I know you probably think you have reasons not to like me very much, but'—I swallowed hard—'I really need your help.'

For a minute, I thought he wouldn't acknowledge me, that he'd keep walking and climb back into his ute, but after a few seconds, he turned and asked resignedly, 'Do you have a spare tyre?'

I nodded. 'I think so.'

Eyeing the car disparagingly, he said, 'Is it one of those space-saver tyres?'

'I don't know,' I admitted.

'Of course you don't. Well, get your bag out of the car and I'll drive you into town.' He thrust his hands back into the pocket of his coat, his shoulders hunching against the rain, his scowl making his displeasure clear.

'Can't you just change the tyre? I can't leave the car here.'

He shrugged. 'Your call. I either drive you into town, or you stay here and wait for someone else to come along.' His derisive half smile told me how unlikely that was on a Friday afternoon in this weather.

I turned and looked back at the car hoping it was far enough off the road to be out of danger, but even so, it was the only thing – other than my clothes and shoes – that I still owned ...

'What's it to be, Lee? It's not getting any drier out here.'

Other than on phone calls with my family, no one had used the derivative of my name in years – and his use of it brought unwanted memories.

'Well?' He looked me up and down unsympathetically. 'Are you coming or not?'

I nodded jerkily, my now loose ponytail flicking water into the air.

'I'll wait for you in the ute.' This time when he turned away, he kept walking.

'But my bags ...' I yelled after him.

'You've got arms and legs, don't you?' he called back without a break in his stride.

I watched as he opened the door and climbed back into the cab, took off his jacket and hat, and tossed them into the back seat. Seriously? He really wasn't going to help me? He beeped the horn, and I trudged to the back of the car and yanked my suitcases out, almost overbalancing when my heel stuck into the mud as I struggled to take the weight of the second one.

After dragging them to the side of the road, I reached back into the front seat for my tote bag, slinging it over my shoulder. Locking the door, I pulled the suitcases behind me over the wet gravel, stopping every couple of steps to haul one or the other out of the potholes the wheels stuck in. I was breathing heavily when I finally reached Angus's ute – although, on the upside, I was no longer shivering.

'Where should I put them?' I asked, raising my voice so he could hear it through the half-open window.

'In the back will be fine,' he yelled back, avoiding my eyes.

I eyed the tray suspiciously – how was I going to lift my bags over the top? 'It's not under cover.'

'So?'

'These bags are designer.'

'What do you expect? Cushions?' He sounded frustrated, as if he wished he'd never stopped and now wanted to get this good deed over and done with as quickly as possible.

He opened the door and got out, walking around to where I stood, lifting my feet one after the other to take the pressure off where the wet straps on my sandals had rubbed my skin into blisters.

With the rain plastering his dark hair to his head he eyed my bags on the side of the road. 'How long are you staying for? That's a lot of luggage for a weekend.'

When I didn't reply, he lifted the cases and heaved them into the back as if they didn't weigh a thing. I glared at him when the second landed with a hard thud against the first.

'Now, are you ready?'

I nodded mutely and hobbled around to the passenger side and opened the door. In the passenger seat sat a black and white dog, a border collie. Its ears were back and its mouth was open in a doggy grin, its tail wagging. 'Is it friendly?'

'Yep.' He climbed into the driver's seat, and ruffled the dog's head. 'Into the back, Red,' he said, and the dog obeyed.

'Red?'

'Yeah, Jenny's youngest daughter named her, so Red she is.' He watched me, eyebrows raised. 'Are you getting in?'

Holding onto the door, I swung one foot onto the running rail and hauled myself up and into the seat and onto an old blanket that must have been there for the dog and that would no doubt leave my pants even muckier. To shut the door, I had to reach out of the cabin and pull it heavily towards me, hoping I didn't fall out in the process. With the doors shut, it was suddenly quiet. I remembered another afternoon in the front of Angus's car – not this one, of course, but an older ute. I glanced across at him. Was he remembering too? He clenched his teeth, the movement causing his jaw to square and pulse. No, I'd wager it was another more painful memory he was recalling.

'Buckle up,' He dipped his head towards the seatbelt.

I did as instructed.

'How is Jenny?' I asked. His younger sister used to be my best friend. 'I imagine she's married now?'

'Yep.' Drops of water were sliding down the planes of his face.

'You said before that her youngest daughter named your dog, does that mean she has more children?'

'Yep.'

When he didn't elaborate, I took the hint and turned my head to look out the window. The road into town was as I recalled, but then it hadn't changed in decades, so why would I expect it to now? As we got closer, I noticed some fields had been turned from grazing to grape, and a scattering of new project-style homes, remarkable only for their predictable bland-ness, stood where previously none had. Otherwise, it was as if time had stood still.

I snuck another glance at Angus; while some grey peppered his thick hair – so dark it was almost black – the years had been kind to him. He'd been the hottest boy in town when we were growing up; now he'd filled out in all the right places – that was evident from the way his checked shirt hugged his body and the way his jeans clung to his thighs, tensing powerfully as he stepped on the clutch to change gear. The action caused my focus to shift to his forearm, brown from a life spent outdoors, his hands wide and capable, rough-ened, no doubt, from work. In comparison, Otis's arms were lean, his hands pale and soft, his fingers long and elegant, his nails filed and cared for. A memory of how Angus's hands had used to feel when they stroked my soft skin snuck through. Would they feel any differ-ently now? An involuntary shiver ran down my spine.

Shaking my head to dislodge the thought, I turned back to the window, again wiping away the condensa-tion from our breath.

'It all looks the same.' It was a mundane statement to break the silence more than anything else.

'So you expected that you'd go away and everything would stand still just as it was until you decided to grace us with your presence again?' It was the longest sentence he'd said, the words almost bitten out.

'I didn't mean anything by it,' I turned back. The rain was falling harder, the windscreen wipers battling to keep up. 'It was just something to say ...'

'The road might look the same, but things have changed.' He might as well have said that *he'd* changed.

I searched his profile for something of the twenty-two-year-old man I'd known – and loved – and found nothing. Angus had indeed changed. Where once those eyes had been filled with love – for me – now it was quite the opposite. If I'd thought that with time and absence might come forgiveness, I was very much mistaken. There was no doubt about it – Angus hated me.

I didn't blame him – I hadn't forgiven myself. I doubted I ever would.

Neither of us spoke for the rest of the journey. So focussed on his stillness and the uncomfortable silence meant I paid no further attention to the landscape – it was all one wet, grey blur.

When he pulled up out the front of the Royal Hotel – or the middle pub as the locals called it – I came to with a start.

'Here you go,' he said, both hands gripping the steering wheel, the muscles of his forearms like steel cables.

'Thanks.' I reached for the door handle. 'Um ...'

'What?'

'Can you please get my bags out of the back?' When he turned to glare at me, I forced myself to glare right back. 'I'd do it myself but can't reach.'

With a snort that was more like a grunt, he unclipped his seatbelt, signalled to Red to stay where she was and slid out of the cabin.

With much more awkwardness, I climbed down without twisting my ankle. By the time I'd reached the footpath, both suitcases were waiting, water dripping down their sides; Angus was climbing back into the ute.

'Thanks,' I called as his door slammed shut.

But he was already gone.

SEVEN

I took a deep breath and wheeled my suitcases out of the rain, scanning the building before me. Here was something that hadn't altered. The Royal, which had stood proudly in the middle of Mannus Ridge's high street since the gold rush in the 1870s, was as it had always been – well, at least since the exterior was last renovated way back before the First World War. Double-storey and constructed of brick – the front of which had been painted in a yellowed-cream – with a sloping heritage green tin roof and the same heritage green on the timber trims of the balcony (which itself acted as a long narrow awning), the Royal looked like most other country pubs in southern New South Wales or northern Victoria. It had been in the family since my great-great-great-(great?)-grandfather built it

– the original structure being a cobbled-together timber shed, somewhere for the miners to have a drink. My sister and I might've been born in the local hospital, but my father was born upstairs in the owner's residence, his mother was born here, her father was born here … You get the idea. I didn't like to think what would happen once my parents could no longer operate it. If neither Jacinta nor I were inclined to take it over, I supposed it would need to be sold, yet Mannus Ridge wouldn't be the same without a St James behind the bar of the Royal Hotel.

I checked my watch – it was just past four in the afternoon, which meant the bar would be filling with the usual Friday afternoon crew; on the upside, that meant my parents would (hopefully) be too busy to fuss over me, not yet anyway.

After another deep breath, I raised the handles on my suitcases and wheeled them to the heavy double-fronted doors, pausing again before turning to push them open with my bum. Once inside, I stood for a beat, my eyes closed, allowing the bar's sounds and smells to wash over me. While the scent of cigarettes I associated with my early childhood was now (thankfully) long gone, ever-present was the faint whiff of spilled beer that was part of the multi-coloured carpet. I remember being able to smell it even when Dad replaced the old carpet with a slightly more tasteful multicoloured carpet about twenty years ago, so it must've seeped into the walls and the floors over the years. This was a different multicoloured carpet – marginally more tasteful than the last – and I wondered when they'd had that fitted.

There was the chatter and clink of glasses from the bar, the competing sounds of the football replays and the races from the sports bar off to the left and the faint melody from the poker machines in the gaming room. And above it all was the cheerful voice of my mother. 'Hello, love, will that be your usual?'

It was the soundtrack to my childhood and, until now, I hadn't realised just how much I'd missed it. And then, as if a switch had been flicked, the voices went quiet.

'Lee, is that really you?'

My eyes snapped open at my mother's voice, surprise and a slight break in it.

'Jeff, it's Lee! She came!' Mum seemed frozen behind the bar, hands poised, ready to fill the empty schooner glass.

'What's that, Lizzie love?' My father turned from the back of the bar where he'd been stacking glasses fresh from the dishwasher. As he saw me, his eyes widened, but they both stood rooted behind the still-silent bar.

My faint smile and half shrug broke the spell, and Mum lifted the hatch and hurried towards me, her arms outstretched. Dad was slower, deliberately wiping his hands on a towel before following her.

The warmth of my mother's arms and the way my head still fit in the crook of her neck almost undid me again, and when Dad joined her, his embrace enfolding us, the tears ran down my face for the second time today.

The sound of a voice broke the spell. 'Oy, Lizzie! Where's my beer? Still brewin', is it?'

Mum wiped her eyes and the three of us disentangled. 'Put a sock in it, Macca,' she called back, her clear blue eyes not leaving me. 'You won't die of thirst in the next few minutes.'

Gripping my hands, she stepped back and ran her eyes over my dishevelled self. 'You look half drowned, you poor thing. What were you thinking being out in that weather? You're hardly wearing anything – you must be cold through.'

Mum hadn't changed much over the years. Her slim figure was, perhaps, a little fuller, the line of her jaw softer than it used to be, the once blonde hair now short and wavy, the greys blending through the ash-blonde. Up close, she appeared drained, lines and shadows under her blue eyes showing the strain of the long hours she and Dad had always put into the business. If Jacinta was right, the lines had deepened due to worry over Dad.

'It's good to see you, love,' said Dad. 'Jazz said you'd try and come for the party, but I have to say, I don't think she believed it.' He said the last with a wry smile that told me he hadn't either. 'Although your mother did hope ...'

'Well, I'm here now.' Suddenly defensive my words were more clipped than I'd intended. 'Jacinta said you hadn't been well ...'

'It's nothing you need to worry about.' He waved my concern away, not quite meeting my eyes. When he grinned, the action smoothed the lines on his forehead, which he always said had been caused by Jacinta and my demands as teenagers, the 'you want what?' lines. 'It's a bugger to be getting old.' It was the same line he'd been saying for as long as I could remember. 'Now, let's get you settled.' He raised an eyebrow at the sight of the two large bags but said nothing and wheeled them through to the bar. 'And tell me, how did you come to be wet through?'

'I had a flat tyre.' I followed Dad, wincing as the

straps rubbed the sores on my little toes. 'About ten kays out of town.'

'And you fixed it yourself?' Mum asked. 'No wonder you're soaked, you poor thing.'

'No, I got a lift into town.' I ducked my head, the wet strands of hair curtaining my face.

'Who with?' Mum lifted the hatch and walked back behind the bar. 'Hold your horses, Macca,' she said. 'I'll get your beer as soon as I get something to warm Lee up.'

'Don't worry about me, Mum. We can't have Macca going thirsty now, can we?' I plastered a fake smile and squared my chin, ready for the onslaught.

'So it's you then?' asked Macca, who'd been a fixture on this particular bar stool for the last six decades. Heaven forbid anyone who attempted to sit there. 'Welcome home, girl. It's about time you showed your face around here.' Macca's tone was gruff, but his eyes were soft.

'Thanks, Macca,' I planted a kiss on the old man's whiskered cheek.

'Oh, be off with you,' he said, rubbing at where I'd kissed. 'You'll have all those other buggers wanting a kiss too.'

'There you go, Macca.' Mum slid a schooner of beer across to him. 'That'll keep you quiet while I see to Lee. Now'—she turned to me— 'you were telling me who gave you a lift into town.'

Inwardly I grimaced, having hoped she'd forgotten the conversation. 'Ummm, Angus came by,' I muttered.

The chatter suddenly stopped again, about a dozen faces turning to stare at me. Well, that guaranteed I'd be the talk of the town tonight.

'Angus?' Mum said. 'Not Angus McGuire?'

I nodded. 'Yes, he was kind enough to offer me a lift.'

'I'll bet he was happy about that,' muttered someone a few stools from Macca. It was a voice I remembered well – Dean (Spider) Webb. I cringed as a few chuckles were uttered in response.

'That'll be enough from you, Spider,' said Mum firmly. 'That was very nice of him,' she said to me. 'How was he?'

I ignored the mutterings along the bar, which stopped when Mum turned her glare on the perpetrators – Spider and his mates. 'He seemed well. Didn't have much to say, though.'

'I don't suppose he would have,' said Macca with a straight face.

'So where's your car now?' asked Dad, still gripping the suitcases.

'I had to leave it there. Angus said he didn't have

time to change the tyre. I guess he thought we could sort it out when I got here.'

'Yes, I'm sure that was what he was thinking,' said Dad, who didn't sound as though he believed that at all. 'Do you have a spare tyre?'

I nodded. 'Yes.'

'Is it one of those space-saver tyres?'

'Angus asked me that too – I think so. Does it matter?'

He idly scratched behind his head. 'Only that you'll be limited in speed and will need to get it replaced as soon as possible – those things are designed to only last long enough to get you out of trouble.'

'Oh. Okay.' I nodded as if I understood.

'I'll leave your bags in the office, and we'll head out now and get it. We'll be back before it gets too busy in here.'

'Are you going to let Lee get dried off and tidied up before you drag her back out again?' Mum's frown mirrored the concern in her voice. Dad disappeared into the room behind the bar he used as an office.

'I'm fine, Mum. I'm probably only going to get wet again. I'll put a jacket on, though,' I said, aware of how little I was wearing. It had been fine for a warm December morning in Melbourne, but I'd forgotten how quickly things cooled down here in the mountains once a southerly change came through – even in summer.

As I went to unzip my suitcase, Dad reappeared with two rain jackets. 'Here you go, Lee.' He handed me a mottled Driza-Bone. 'That'll stop you from getting any wetter. And here'—he pulled a pair of puddle boots and thick red Explorer socks from under his arm— 'these'll save your toes.'

The jacket swamped me. It was, however, warm and covered the parts of me that were beginning to attract attention from some of the men in the bar. The boots were a size too big but much more practical and warm.

'We shouldn't be too long, Lizzie,' he said.

'I'll be fine here,' she replied.

I followed Dad down the timber-lined hall, past the stairs that led upstairs to the family rooms (the guest rooms being accessible from stairs at the opposite end of the bar), and past the restaurant with its blackboard menu and functional white wipeable tables, out the back door to the car park.

He led the way to a dark grey four-wheel drive and opened the passenger door for me.

'I see you're still not locking your car,' I said derisively.

'It's Mannus Ridge, love, not Melbourne.'

'True.'

It had stopped raining, and this time, I paid more attention as we drove over the bridge, the water flowing fast in the creek that had been dry when I last saw it, and up the hill past the hospital; the oak trees that would be brilliantly coloured during autumn now in their summer wardrobe.

'It's greener than when I saw it last,' I commented. 'I thought the fires might've caused more damage ...'

'They did,' he replied soberly. 'The country's come back well, though, and the rain this year has helped. A couple of years ago, though ...' He shook his head sadly. 'It was so dry. It was a hard time – harder for some than others, but we did what we always do and pulled together as a town.' He hesitated and then said, 'Did Angus mention they've taken on the winery – the old Talbot place?'

'No, he didn't mention it.' I wrinkled my nose. 'But I know the one – adjacent to their property on the old Millers Creek Road. The Talbots were one of the first families to plant grapes, weren't they?'

He nodded sagely. 'That's the one, and yes, they were. They expanded about ten years back and built a cellar door maybe five years ago.' He cleared his throat. 'Apparently got into a bit of debt in the process. Bob was an ideas man but not so big on the practicalities of business. Anyway, they were hit hard by the drought, and the fires got so close they took out the house garden and the machinery shed. We have no idea how the house or the winery escaped – or the grapes. It was like that, though – the fire. It was the last straw for poor old Bob, though, and when he died, the kids didn't want anything to do with the business. Marjorie wanted to move to the city to be nearer to them, and the banks were circling, so Angus stepped in and took it off their hands.'

'I would've thought Angus's father would've had something to say about that,' I said, a cynical twist to my mouth. 'Mr McGuire was always quite vocal about the incomers turning good grazing land into grapes.'

'Maybe he would have, but he's been gone for a while now, and Angus is running the show. He has someone managing the wine part of the business so he can concentrate on the farm, but he's still involved. Did your mother not mention it?'

'Not that I recall.' Had she mentioned it? Perhaps I hadn't been listening.

'And Angus didn't say?'

'He didn't say very much at all,' I said wryly.

'Well,' Dad said slowly. 'You can't blame him, I suppose. Things like that take a bit of getting over.'

'It's been nearly fifteen years.' I rolled my eyes and let out a little snort of frustration.

'Even so.' When I didn't reply, he said gently, 'Go easy on him, love. He'll come around. You left and had a career; he had to stay on here and take on some big responsibilities running Balloch Estate. It's been different for him.'

What he didn't say was that Angus had stayed while I'd escaped. He didn't need to.

'I couldn't help but notice how much luggage you brought for a couple of nights, love.' When I couldn't get my words past the lump in my throat, he added, 'Are you in some sort of trouble?'

I nodded bleakly.

He reached out and patted my arm lightly. 'You can tell us when you're ready,' he said. 'And you can stay as long as you need. We'll be glad to have you.'

My eyes burning, I managed, 'Thanks, Dad.'

'Is that your car up ahead? The red BMW?' Dad's voice broke the moment.

When I answered in the affirmative, he made a U-turn and pulled up in front of it. 'Let's get this tyre changed and get back into town. We'll get you a new tyre fitted tomorrow.'

BACK IN TOWN, Mum had already been busy on the phone as Jacinta was waiting for us in the car park. Jazz had never been still as a child, and things had not changed as she shifted her weight from leg to leg. Where I had Mum's petite stature and colouring, Jacinta was the opposite and had inherited her restless energy, her build – tall and lean – and her colouring – hazel eyes, and thick chestnut-brown hair – from Dad.

'You came,' she said, a hesitant smile on her face warring with insecurity.

'Yeah, I did.' I lifted one shoulder. 'You did say it was important ...' I sent her a teasing grin.

'It is.' She finally moved forward to kiss my cheek before throwing her arms around me. 'I'm glad you're back. We need you,' she added so quietly I had to strain to hear her.

'What's going on, Jazz?' My empty stomach was churning again.

'I'll take your bags up to your old room, Lee,' said Dad, stopping to kiss Jacinta's cheek. 'Then you'd better get in and cleaned up.'

'Yeah, you had,' Jazz agreed. 'You look like shit. What is that outfit anyway?' Her eyes raked down my bedraggled form, the loose-hanging Driza-Bone over the mud-spattered clinging pink top, the capris that I doubted would ever be white again, and the ghastly black gum boots. Without waiting for an answer, she continued, 'Mum said Angus gave you a lift into town – I would've loved to be a fly on that wall. You know he's seeing Georgia Tyson, don't you?'

'No, he didn't mention it,' I muttered, pushing aside a brief pang of, what, regret?

'Yeah, Jenny's not happy about it – you two never liked Georgia, did you? Anyway, it is what it is. You know Jenny's married? She finally said yes to Dave when he asked her for about the tenth time. I don't think he believed it for a while when she said yes. And then—'

'Jacinta St James,' Mum yelled from the doorway. 'Let your sister come inside. You've got plenty of time to catch up later!'

When Mum went back inside, I grabbed Jacinta's arm. 'What did you mean before? When you said I was needed here?'

She waved it away. 'I'll tell you later. It'll keep. Mum said you've come with a couple of suitcases – does that mean you're staying for longer than the week-end? Or are you so important these days you travel with five changes of clothes every day?' As I would've bristled, her cheeky grin told me she'd been joking. 'You'd better do what Mum says and get cleaned up,' she said. 'She'll be wanting to show you off to the town.'

My old room hadn't changed from when I'd left it that last summer and couldn't be more different from the slick, neutral apartment I'd left in Melbourne. Against the white timber-clad walls, accents of fuchsia and aqua stood out boldly. On my double bed was a mandala-inspired cover in those colours, with silk cushions in similar shades. There was the old 'tallboy' set of drawers that Jenny had helped me paint white and to which I'd affixed mismatching ceramic knobs in all different colours and patterns. On the wall, the Backstreet Boys and Westlife posters from my teenage years had been replaced with abstract art prints. It was the room of a young woman full of hope for the future, not someone whose colour had seeped out of her bit by bit until all that remained was a stylish husk with no substance.

I lifted the first of my suitcases onto the bed and began emptying it into the tallboy. These were clothes fit for the office, not for Mannus Ridge. Beautiful clothes, expensive clothes, but completely out of place here. As for my shoes? I cringed again at the thought of how much money I'd spent on shoes over the years.

Unzipping the second suitcase, I pulled out dresses and coats and, with an armful of them, opened the doors to my wardrobe. And there it was, still in the clear plastic bag I'd brought it home in from Canberra – my wedding dress.

The clothes slid from my arms and crumpled in a pile on the floor as I reached for the dress and carefully lifted the plastic covering away, displaying the dress it had been protecting for the past fifteen years. I'd almost forgotten how beautiful it was – and how all four of us, Mum, Jacinta, Jenny McGuire and I, had cried when I'd tried it on the first time.

Simple in style, the ivory silk dress was strapless, a champagne satin sash encircling my waist, the skirt falling to the floor in an A-line. It was the most beautiful dress I'd ever seen. As I'd gazed at myself in the mirror that day, I didn't see the bridal store I was standing in, but rather the old white timbered church on the hill in Mannus Ridge, Angus waiting for me at the end of the aisle, afternoon light pouring through the stained glass above the altar casting a warm glow over the proceedings.

'It's a beautiful dress,' Mum said, having snuck into the room without me noticing. 'You would've made a beautiful bride.' With care, she took the dress from my hands and replaced the plastic, hanging it back in the wardrobe. I slumped back on the bed as she picked up the dresses from the floor and hung them up. 'You have some lovely things,' she said.

'None which will be of much use here, I'm afraid,' I said wryly, leaning back on my elbows as she worked. 'What possessed me to bring winter coats?'

'I suppose that depends on how long you're here for.' She sent me a questioning look. 'Your father said you could be here for a little while.'

'Is that a problem?' After all the rejections of the past fortnight, I couldn't have borne another from my family – although after virtually ignoring them for so long, they had more right than anyone else not to welcome me with open arms.

'Of course it isn't.' Mum turned away from her task, a small smile playing at the corner of her mouth. 'You stay as long as you need.' When I opened my mouth to thank her, she added, 'I know when one of my girls is hurting, and you have been for a very long time – perhaps longer than you think.' My eyes filled again. 'Now, go and get yourself cleaned up. I'll finish here. Come down when you're ready.'

AFTER A QUICK SHOWER, my hair back in its usual tight bun and dressed in the only pair of denim jeans I owned and a navy easy-fit knit top, the look completed with a pair of shiny black designer riding boots that had never seen either a horse or dirt, I headed downstairs.

Jazz was behind the bar with Dad and another younger woman, who Jazz introduced as Chelsea. Ignoring curious eyes, I settled on a barstool next to Macca and sipped at the white wine Dad pushed across to me on a cardboard coaster. 'Where's Mum?' I asked Jazz when she was between customers.

'In the restaurant – Mark will be here soon with the kids, so she thought it would be nice to have a family dinner.'

'What about the bar?' I looked around the room, which had filled up since earlier this afternoon.

'Oh, don't worry about that – Nicky will be here soon to help. She still does a few hours on a Friday and Saturday night when things are busy.' Nicky Murphy was one of Mum's closest friends and had been working behind the bar for as long as I could remember. Jazz leant closer. 'Sometimes I don't think Mum needs the help – not now we have Chelsea and a couple of other local girls to call on – but I think the little bit of money comes in handy for Nicky.'

I nodded in understanding. Nicky and her husband (the kids had long since moved to the city) had a property about ten kilometres out of town. I imagined that with the long years of drought they, like many other farmers, would've struggled over recent years – it was just like my parents to help in this way.

When Nicky arrived, she wrapped her arms around me tightly and squeezed until I thought there was no breath left to squeeze out. 'You're a sight for sore eyes, Lee.' Then she held me at arm's length and shook her head sadly. 'Why did you stay away for so long?'

My eyes filled yet again, and I blinked to keep the tears in. 'I knew I'd disappointed and hurt everyone,' I finally managed. 'I didn't think anyone would want me here after what I did.'

'Oh, Lee.' She pulled me in for another bear hug. 'We've all missed you. But you're here now and everything will be alright again.' She pulled away, patted me quickly on the cheek and blinked her tears away. 'I'd better get behind that bar and relieve Jazz.'

Nicky was physically the opposite of my mother, yet so similar in temperament. She'd always been Mum's support structure – and vice versa – but it sounded as though there was more going on with my parents than even she could help with. Perhaps it was just relief that I'd finally come home, but my instincts told me it was more than that. Just how sick was my father? When we were in the car together, I'd examined his face for signs of illness. Like Mum, the bags under his eyes seemed heavier, more pronounced, his smile not quite reaching his eyes, and he'd lost a little weight since I'd last seen him; he appeared tired but otherwise tanned and healthy. My heart skipped as I contemplated all the potentially serious illnesses that didn't show on the outside.

My ponderings were interrupted by the arrival of Jacinta's husband, Mark, and their three children. After greeting Jazz, Mark hung back for the briefest of seconds before giving me a hesitant peck on the cheek, his smile tight, his eyes not quite meeting mine. I couldn't blame him, really; he was, after all, Angus's younger brother. While I'd seen him from time to time over the years when they'd come to Sydney, he'd avoided my company as much as possible – in deference to his brother's feelings, I supposed – and I'd been fine with that. Now, though, under Jazz's watchful eye, I smiled widely and said, 'It's good to see you, Mark.' If he was surprised by my unusually enthusiastic greeting, he didn't let on.

'And these are Hayley, Jackson and Cody,' said Jazz, pushing her children forward.

The two boys – who Mum had told me were now eight and six respectively – shuffled forward, their eyes on the ground.

'Hey there,' I said a little awkwardly, ruffling their hair rather than embarrassing them with a kiss from an aunt they barely knew.

Hayley, gangly and almost thirteen, hung back, obviously torn between curiosity and a typical almost-teenager disdain for showing that. She lifted her head and half smiled, pink flushing her cheeks, before lowering her head again. When she looked up again, I smiled gently and moved forward to kiss her cheek. 'It's so good to see you again, Hayley.'

Even through her shyness, she reminded me so much of Jacinta at the same age – tanned and lanky, with a single thick chestnut ponytail hanging halfway down her back.

'You remind me so much of your mother.' I tucked some stray hairs behind her ear. 'I've often wondered how she won the genetic lottery with her height and that lovely thick hair and skin that tans rather than burns, and now I see you've scored it too. You're taller than me already; I'll need to remember to wear heels next time!' She giggled at the rueful smile on my face. 'Your mum tells me you're a swimmer – we'll have to catch up while I'm here and you can tell me all about it.'

She grinned and nodded. 'Okay.'

'Your Aunty Lee used to swim too,' said Jazz, 'and ride horses.' She gave me a sideways glance, a conspiratorial smile behind it. 'You two will have a lot to talk about – just wait till you see her shoes!'

I couldn't help chuckling at that. 'How do you know I brought them with me?'

'You had two suitcases with you, Lee – you're hardly travelling lightly.'

THE RESTAURANT WAS EMPTIER than I remembered, especially for a Friday night. Aside from our table, only a few others were occupied. When I commented as such, my parents exchanged glances, with Mum saying, 'Oh, I don't know darling, it is out of season.'

'Since when is it "in season"? Mannus Ridge isn't exactly tourist central,' I retorted. 'Even in the depth of winter, the bistro used to be busy. What's happened? Has another restaurant opened? Don't tell me the Imperial has started doing meals?'

The 'top' pub – so called because it was at the top of the high street – had only ever done a bar menu, preferring to offer more space to gaming machines. It had always been an unspoken agreement that the Royal did meals, and if you wanted to play the pokies, the Imperial had a much wider range.

'We don't need to be talking about that at the moment,' Mum said quickly, shooting another cryptic glance at Dad. 'Not on your first night back. In fact,' she said, 'we wanted to talk to you about tomorrow night.'

'Dad's party? I'm so sorry, Dad, I didn't bring you anything – I hadn't exactly planned ... and then I got covid and ...' I didn't want to admit that finding a present for my hard-to-buy-for father had been the last thing on my mind.

Dad waved my explanations away. 'Just having you home is present enough, Lee.'

'Okay, so what are the arrangements for tomorrow night?' I asked.

'Obviously, it's here,' said Jazz. 'We're closing the pub for the night, but then all the regulars are invited anyway, but'—Mark put his arm around her, and she looked up into his face in a way that made my heart hurt with envy— 'Mark and I have asked Dad if he minds sharing his birthday with our surprise wedding.'

I choked on the sip of wine I'd taken. 'Your surprise wedding? I thought ... well, that is, I assumed ...'

'That we'd decided never to get married?' Jazz finished for me with a wry smile. 'We've been together so long I think we wondered whether we needed to – especially after ...' She dropped her eyes, but I knew what she'd almost said – especially after Angus and I hadn't quite made it down the aisle.

'But you're not wearing an engagement ring ...?'

'That's because I haven't officially proposed yet,' said Mark with a cheeky grin. 'I'm intending on doing that tomorrow night too.'

'The surprise wedding at an engagement party has been done to death,' said Jazz, sounding much more world-weary than I knew she was.

'But the wedding at a proposal thing'—Mark picked up her hand and kissed her palm— 'is new.'

'Well,' I said brightly, 'I think it's a lovely idea. I'm glad I packed something nice to wear.'

'By the look of those suitcases, I'd say you brought your entire wardrobe,' Jazz said, laughing. 'Maybe I should be raiding your closet for something nice to wear. Just how long are you staying anyway?'

'I'm not sure. Maybe a couple of weeks.' I raised a questioning brow in Mum's direction.

'It's almost December now – you'd be mad to go back before Christmas,' said Mum.

Jacinta laughed out loud. 'As if Lee could be away from work for that long. You never take holidays! Then there's your boyfriend – what was his name again? Otis? He'd miss you if you were here that long – don't you usually spend Christmas with him? You always loved Christmas more than anyone else I know.'

I cringed as I recalled all the lies I'd told my family over the years – how I couldn't come home for Christmas because I needed to spend the day with Otis. No, he couldn't come with me because he had children from a previous relationship he needed to see. Yes, I knew it was bad luck, but that was just the way things were. And yes, it was unfortunate that he came with baggage, but honestly, Mum, most men his age these days came with some. Besides, there was no way I could take any time other than the public holidays off work.

In reality, I'd volunteer to work through so others could take leave. As for spending time with Otis on Christmas Day, I'd usually sit at home alone, waiting for that moment during the afternoon when he could escape his family for long enough to phone me. Looking back, I couldn't believe how little self-respect I'd had where he was concerned, but still, my heart ached for him – although, I had to admit, less than I'd expected it to, eviction being an excellent cure for heartbreak.

'Christmas is a long way away,' I said, 'but I'm well overdue for some time off, so I thought I'd stay here for a little longer.' I forced a laugh into my voice. 'Work and Otis can do without me for a couple of weeks.'

'Well, we're glad you came home, aren't we, Mark?' Jacinta squeezed her husband-to-be's arm, but his smile appeared forced.

'The thing is,' Jacinta began, 'I'd like you to be my bridesmaid.' She almost blurted the words out as if she was expecting me to say no.

'Oh.' The lump that hadn't been far from my throat today made its way back. 'I'd be honoured. Who else are you having?'

'Well'—she flicked a glance to Mark— 'no one knows we're doing this yet. We told Mum and Dad, and that's it – just family. We're not even telling the kids until tomorrow morning. Mark will tell Angus in the morning, too.' Her smile faltered. 'It's why I was desperately hoping you'd be home so I could have you.'

My eyes burned, and I pressed a knuckle into the corner of my eye to keep the tears at bay. It really had been important to her that I was here. How many more times over the years had she wanted me here and I hadn't been? Worse than that, I bumped her calls and rarely phoned her without her having called me (several times) first. When I think of how close Jazz and I had been growing up and how she'd looked up to me, I felt small and mean. I rested my hand on hers.

'I'm sorry,' I choked, unable to say more.

Expression sympathetic, she nodded, her eyes as full as mine. 'You're here now; the rest doesn't matter.' Jacinta and Mark exchanged glances, put their heads together and whispered something. Jazz's mouth widened to a smile. 'Do you think?' she said, just loud enough for me to hear.

'It can't hurt to ask' Mark whispered back, a furtive glance to where our parents now stood talking to patrons.

'What are you two muttering about?' I asked, taking a sip of wine.

'Well,' began Jazz, 'if you're staying around for a little while, would you mind looking after the kids for a few days? Mark and I are going to the Sunshine Coast for a sort-of honeymoon, and Mum was going to move in, but if you're here ... It would take the pressure off Mum ...'

The horror must have shown on my face. Trusting me with her children? I had no idea what to do with kids – I didn't even really know these. After dinner, Hayley had left our table to see a friend on the other side of the room. She must've sensed my gaze on her and looked up and grinned. As for the boys, they'd spent dinner bickering so much that they'd had to be separated and were now in the corner of the room doing goodness knows what. What on earth was I going to do with three kids?

'It'll be easy,' said Jacinta. 'They're at school each day, and we'll be home for the end-of-term things. All you need to do is make sure they're dropped off, picked up, bathed occasionally and fed. Too easy.' When I still couldn't seem to get a response past my lips, she said, 'It's okay; I know it's a big thing to drop on you when you've just arrived home and Mum had already said she'd move in. I just thought—'

Her sideways glance at Mum reminded me of how tired she'd looked and what Jazz had told me about Dad's health. Suddenly I felt very selfish indeed. She'd been here the whole time, helping when needed, and I hadn't. Besides, it was only a few days and if I needed her, Mum wasn't far away, and I'd already missed so much of their growing up. If I was to ever have a relationship with them – especially with Hayley – that window of opportunity was closing fast.

'No problems.' I waved her protests away and plastered a smile I hoped reached my eyes. 'Of course I'll help out. Mum will need to help me with the cooking, though; I'm hopeless these days.'

'Don't worry,' said Jacinta. 'So am I, so the kids don't have great expectations.'

'You used to be a good cook, Lee,' Mum said, sitting back down at the table. 'Entering cakes and scones and goodness knows what else into the show each year. Don't you cook for yourself in Melbourne?'

'I haven't baked in years,' I said. 'Probably not since I left. At home, I mostly eat out or order in; by the time I get home from work, it's usually too late for anything much.'

'You work too hard,' said Mum. 'And you don't look like you eat enough to keep a sparrow alive, love. You're even thinner than the last time we saw you.'

'I'm fine, Mum,' I rubbed my hands on my arms. 'I was sick for a couple of weeks and completely lost my appetite. That's all.' The truth was, I hadn't had an appetite for anything – other than wine – in a very long time.

'Hmmm,' said Mum, her eyes on the roast lamb and vegetables I'd barely touched. 'It doesn't look like it's back yet. If you're not careful, you'll make yourself sick again.'

'Good country air and some long walks will do the trick,' said Dad, winking at me and handing me a fresh glass of wine. 'The old Lee will be back with us before we know it.'

I gave a half-hearted smile and said that would probably be the case, but the truth was, I had no idea how to find the old Lee, and even if I did, wasn't she better left behind? My future, Ainsley's future, was in the city and Lee from Mannus Ridge had no place there.

EIGHT

What was that noise? I opened my eyes – and closed them almost immediately against the sun blazing through my open window. There it was again. Rolling onto my back, I opened my eyes once more, this time taking in my surroundings. I hadn't dreamt it; I really was in Mannus Ridge and in my old bedroom. And, if I wasn't mistaken, that carolling that had woken me was the morning song of a country magpie. Something else I hadn't realised I'd missed.

Stretching, I reached over for my phone and sat bolt upright. It was well after nine; I couldn't remember the last time I'd slept this long and this deeply – without having resorted to a sleeping tablet to do so, that is. And my head was fog-free, thanks to just a few glasses of wine last night. Maybe a few weeks at home would be just the thing to get my head into the right space to figure out what came next. Plus, I wouldn't need to delve too far into my savings. It was looking to be a win-win.

There was a soft knock at the door, and Mum came into the room carrying a tray with a cup of coffee and a plate of food.

'I thought you'd probably be awake by now,' she said with a smile. 'I also figured you might be hungry.'

As I was about to open my mouth to say that coffee was all I usually had, the toasty, buttery smell of fried bread hit my nose and my tummy growled in response. 'Is that Dad's eggy bread?' I asked hopefully, wriggling into a seated position and piling pillows behind me.

Dad's eggy bread – squares of torn-up white bread, soaked in a little milk before having eggs stirred through it and then cooked in butter like an eggy-bready omelette – was a childhood treat. Jazz and I always used to argue over who would get to tear up the bread.

'It certainly is.' She placed the coffee on the bedside table and the tray on my lap. 'And before you tell me you don't eat carbs or fat or whatever else these days—'

'I need fattening up?' I finished, dipping my finger

into the brown sauce and licking it off, relishing the sweet yet tangy taste on my tongue.

'Not what I would've said, but yes.' She grinned and sat on the edge of the bed, watching as I cut into the first piece of fried eggy bread, the crusty bits knobbly and buttery. 'This is so good.' I closed my eyes briefly in comfort-food bliss.

'I'm glad. I'm also glad you're home.' She patted my leg under the doona. 'Now, don't feel you need to look after the children while Jacinta and Mark are away – she did rather spring that on you. I'm fine to do it if it's too much for you.'

I shook my head. 'I'm sure I'll be fine, and if I'm not, you're not far away. I just haven't had much to do with kids – especially not these – but I'm realising I've missed out on so much with them.'

Mum nodded sagely. 'Maybe.'

She shut her mouth quickly as though she'd been about to say something else and then thought better of it. 'What?' I asked.

She inhaled deeply. 'Your father said you were in trouble.'

'Aaah.' I wiped my mouth with the paper napkin on the tray. 'And you're wondering what kind of trouble?'

She nodded. 'Not that it matters – we're here for you regardless.'

'Thank you, but it's not that sort of trouble.' I placed my knife and fork back on the plate, reached for my coffee mug and took a sip. 'It's more that ... well, I've completely stuffed up my life.' Still cradling the mug, I searched for the words. 'I lied to you last night – I'm not needed back at work because ... well, I've lost my job.' Ignoring her indrawn breath, I continued. 'And Otis won't miss me because he's broken up with me and returned to his wife – not that he'd ever left her. And, to make a bad situation even worse, he owns the apartment I've been renting and has kicked me out. So, I'm not here because Jazz asked me to come; I'm back because I have no job, no boyfriend, nowhere to live and I own nothing except my car and way too many expensive clothes and shoes that I no longer have use for. I've been on a great salary for the last few years and spent almost all of it – on said car, apartment, clothes and shoes – so if it wasn't for the payout I received from work, I'd have no money either.' I pressed my lips into a tight line, then sighed. 'I've managed to either ignore or piss off every friend I ever had, so I have one left – and he's in Bali on his honey-moon – so in short, I'm thirty-five years old and have nothing to show for it. I've made a complete mess of everything and have absolutely no idea what I want to do next.'

Feeling both shame at my situation and relief for finally dropping the pretence, I slumped back against the pillows, unable to meet Mum's eyes.

'Well,' she finally said. 'That's quite the predicament.'

'I'm sorry,' I muttered.

'What on earth for?'

Even though I couldn't look at her, she sounded genuinely surprised. 'Where do I start?' I laughed ruefully. 'For not marrying Angus when I should have, for leaving here to go to uni, for never coming home, for ruining every opportunity I've had, for falling in love with a married man. All of it.' My voice rose the longer I spoke, and I ended my little speech with a swing of the arm that almost dislodged the tray from my knee. 'I've disappointed everyone in town. Mostly, though, I'm sorry for disappointing you.'

'Oh Lee ...' She shook her head sadly. 'Your father and I aren't disappointed in you. You've always wanted more from life, and we were worried when you and Angus became so serious so young that it would lead to trouble. Even if you had married Angus, there would've come a time when you felt as though you'd missed out on something. Perhaps if you'd gone away to uni straight out of school rather than staying ...' She pursed her lips. 'No, there's no point in wondering what might've been. What I am disappointed about is that you stayed away for so long thinking you couldn't come home. We've all missed you.'

Tears that hadn't been far from the surface filled my eyes. 'I knew everyone hated me because I left so close to the wedding. That was wrong of me.'

'It's no one else's business,' Mum said firmly. 'They would've had as much to say if the pair of you had been divorced too – especially if there were children involved. As for the job and the boyfriend, all I can say is maybe they weren't that good for you if it's got you into this state. How long has it been?'

'The job or Otis? Seven years – for both. I didn't know at the start – that he was married. And when I did ... well, he was so persistent and persuasive, and I'd been so lonely for so long after Angus. I have no excuses, though. I knew he'd never leave his wife, but I couldn't seem to find the strength to leave him. And every time I thought I did, he helped me get promoted, so I owed my career to him, I suppose.'

'But it didn't make you happy,' she guessed.

'No.' I sighed. 'It didn't. To be honest, after what I'd done to Angus, part of me didn't feel as though I deserved to be happy. And then one day, I woke up and realised that I'd given away so much of myself – my integrity, my friends, my family – and for what? A job I didn't feel good about and a man I had only part-time.' The tears flowed freely, and I made no effort to stop them. 'None of it has turned out the way I thought it would, and I've hurt so many people along the way.' With the back of my hand, I wiped my eyes. 'I don't know what to do next. I know my life is in Melbourne or Sydney – and so is my next job – but ...' I shrugged miserably and reached for a tissue from the box on my bedside table.

'Darling girl ...' Mum moved the tray onto the floor and hugged me. 'You don't need to have all the answers just yet. Use these next few weeks to take it easy and find yourself again. You can stay here as long as you want.'

'Thanks, Mum. I know you'll tell Dad, but do you mind if I don't say anything to Jazz yet? I don't want her to know I'm only back because I couldn't see I had any other choice – even though'—I smiled through my tears— 'here is probably exactly where I need to be.' As I said the words, I believed them to be true.

'It's our secret, Lee. Now,' she said, standing and retrieving the tray and coffee mug, 'we've got plenty to be getting on with to get ready for tonight, so how about you get out of bed and get moving?'

'Just give me the list and I'm on it!'

For the first time, I think that losing it all might just have been a blessing in disguise.

AFTER WISHING Dad a happy birthday and getting my tyre replaced, the rest of Saturday was spent setting up for the party. While the pub opened for lunch, it would close early, enabling everyone to attend the birthday bash slash wedding. After helping with the styling of the dining room, I volunteered to drive to Millers Creek, the neighbouring town, to pick up the flowers Jazz had ordered.

'I would normally have used Jenny – you know she gave away hairdressing and has turned the old station house into a plant nursery and florist, didn't you?' When I shook my head, Jazz continued. 'She's got it looking great, but this was supposed to be a surprise, so Millers Creek it is.'

When I returned, Mum was waiting for me to relieve her behind the bar. 'You'll be the talk of the town anyway, Lee,' she said, 'so you may as well get behind the bar and get it all over and done with.'

It wasn't as confronting as I'd been afraid it would be – aside from a few snide looks and comments, the old-timers were mostly welcoming, and the few unfamiliar faces had no knowledge of my history anyway. As much as I hadn't been able to wait to get out of town and away from the pub, it all came back quickly, and before I knew it, I'd settled into a rhythm of greeting patrons, pulling beers, pouring wines, dispensing spirits and even exchanging the odd bit of banter with the regulars who'd been drinking here forever. Mum was right about people moving on.

Later in the afternoon, I left Dad to close up and went upstairs to help Jazz and Hayley get ready. The kids had been told this morning and Hayley would be joining me as a bridesmaid.

For her surprise wedding, Jazz had chosen an aqua halter-neck dress that left her toned, tanned arms bare and fell almost to her ankles in an asymmetrical ruffle hem. Strappy nude heels completed the look.

'Oh, Jazzy,' I said, choking up, 'you look beautiful.'

Mum seemed lost for words and had her hand on her chest as if to keep the emotion at bay.

'I don't know what to do with my hair, though,' she said, lifting the heavy mass off her shoulders. 'And you've always been better with make-up than I am.'

I stood back and took it all in. 'I reckon we put it up. Lucky Mark is as tall as he is because in those heels and with the hair I'm about to give you, you'll be eye to eye with him.' I chuckled. 'Which is how it should be!'

It didn't take me long to do her face and put her hair up into an elegant up-do, and when she spied herself in the mirror, she gave a little clap. 'I look quite pretty,' she said as if surprised she could be so.

'It's perfect,' said Mum.

'You're perfect,' I said, linking arms with my sister.

'Thank you, Lee.' Jazz's voice hitched a little.

'You're welcome,' I said, my voice thick. Turning my attention to Hayley, I said, 'For someone who only knew they were helping their mother get married a few hours ago, you're looking fabulous too.'

Hayley was wearing a strappy ink-blue hanky dress that Mum had told me she'd worn to her year six formal the previous week.

'Thanks.' She lowered her eyes, an embarrassed flush on her cheeks, before raising them again and asking in a small voice, 'Do you think you could do my hair and make-up too?'

My eyes flew to Jazz, who nodded, her eyes suspiciously bright. 'Absolutely,' I said. 'Okay, let me look at you properly ...' While I'd seen the resemblance to Jazz immediately, it wasn't until I really looked at her eyes that I noticed she had the McGuire grey eyes – the same as Mark and Angus. 'I think we'll leave your hair out because the colour is amazing. Maybe a little eyeshadow – silvery blue to bring out the grey in your eyes – a touch of mascara and a shimmery lip gloss?'

When she nodded enthusiastically, I got to work.

'Oh, Hayles,' Jazz breathed when I'd finished, giving her daughter a quick hug, admiring their joint reflections in the mirror.

'Thank you, Aunty Lee,' said Hayley, seemingly unable to turn her attention from the mirror.

'You're welcome, gorgeous,' I said.

'Now we just need to find something in your wardrobe for you to wear,' said Jazz.

'Oh, but ...' I began to protest.

She shook her head. 'Before you say you're perfectly capable of choosing something, I am not having you turn up to my surprise wedding in something navy or neutral so you can blend into the background. You're back and everyone needs to know it.' She held my hands and looked closely at me. 'You have nothing to be ashamed of, and tonight you'll be showing Mannus Ridge – and Angus McGuire – exactly that.'

My tummy dipped as I realised that, of course, he'd be there. As would Jenny and her husband Dave and those of our old gang who hadn't left town.

As if she knew what was going through my head,

Jazz said, 'Let's show them the real Lee – the fabulous, confident, smart woman that you are.' She tilted her head to the side. 'What do you say?'

'What can I say?' I said, leading her and Hayley into my room.

'Fake it until you make it is what you always said to me,' she said with a laugh. 'So let's find something to fake it in.' She moved across to the wardrobe and began rifling through clothes while I sat on the bed and watched her. If only she knew how much I really would be faking it.

'Oh my god, Lee,' she exclaimed, 'you have some gorgeous clothes. Hayles, check out these shoes! I hate to think how much some of these cost.' She pulled out a Max Mara shift dress and grimaced. 'The price of this could probably pay my mortgage for a month!' Shaking her head in horror, she continued examining the closet and missed the heat of shame flash across my cheeks.

'This one!' Triumphantly she held up a wide-legged jumpsuit, a dramatic navy floral swirl print adding luxe to the ivory background. 'It has the same neckline and keyhole detail as mine, but with a wrap waist, and the print is almost the same colour as Hayley's dress. When did you last wear this?'

I stood and walked across to the wardrobe, feeling the silky texture of the fabric between my fingers. 'I bought it for the Top Team conference in Fiji last spring.'

I'd bought the outfit with such high hopes for the conference – a whole week where Otis and I could be disinterested colleagues during the day, and lovers at night. It hadn't turned out that way, though, as Tiffany Samuels had resigned abruptly in the airport lounge, leaving me to explain her absence to JC and causing Otis to berate me. I'd later heard on the grapevine that instead of coming to Top Team in Fiji, she'd boarded a flight to Hong Kong and was now travelling the world with her travel writer boyfriend taking photos. I'd always envied the respect she had from her colleagues and the capable way she did her job, and now I envied her bravery for walking away from the toxic environment I'd helped create. Maybe she should be thanking me? No, she'd never do that. She would, however, probably laugh if she knew the way things had turned out for me.

'Lee?' Jazz must have asked me a question. 'Are you okay?'

I nodded. 'Yes, I'm fine. Just remembering and ...'

'You'd be worried about seeing Angus, I suppose,' she said. 'Especially with him being best man and all, but ...'

Whatever else she had to say whirred into white

noise. Angus as best man. How the hell was I going to stand up there and help Jazz get married, with Angus as best man, all the while knowing that once upon a time it was supposed to be he and I getting married with them – and his sister Jenny, and best mate Dave, as our attendants. I squirmed inside. Yes, I needed to be as fabulous as possible, and the jumpsuit was exactly the outfit.

'You're right,' I said. 'I'll wear this and these shoes, I think.' I pulled out a pair of strappy heels in the same ivory as the jumpsuit.

As I started to pull my hair into a tighter version of the up-do I'd given Jacinta, Hayley sprang from her position on the bed to stop me. 'No, Aunty Lee, wear it down.'

'But I always wear it up.' I bundle it in a ball on top of my head. 'It feels more ...'

'In control?' Jazz finished for me. When I gave a little half nod, she said softly, 'You don't need that here.'

I frowned as our eyes met in the mirror, the colour of her dress making hers appear almost green. 'I don't know what you mean.'

'Don't think I can't see it, Lee, the mask you wear. You're home now; you don't need to pretend to be anyone else.' Standing beside me, she rested her head against mine, and for a second, our roles were reversed and she was the older sister, the one with the answers, the one I looked up to. 'They'll need to get used to you being around,' she said. 'Angus, Jenny and Dave, that is; no one else counts.'

'What about Mark?' I asked quietly. 'How does he feel about me being back?'

'He's happy for my sake – for all our sakes.' There it was again, that hint that something was going on. 'As for that business between you and Angus, well, Angus has moved on and so have you. We're all older and wiser now.' She flashed me a bright smile. 'Now you're home, everything will be fine.'

I almost asked her again – to tell me what no one seemed to want to tell me. As I opened my mouth, she gave a little shake, followed by a broad smile, almost as if she was reminding herself that today was about being happy. 'Yes,' she said again, 'now you're home, everything will be fine.'

NINE

Just as it had done yesterday, the crowded bar fell silent when Jacinta, Hayley and I entered. Jazz flicked her eyes to me and giggled. 'They don't usually shut up when they see Hayles and me, so I think this is for you.'

I placed a shaking hand on her arm and plastered on a smile that was as fake as my nails and said, 'I don't know, how long has it been since they saw you scrubbed up this well?'

She considered that for a half beat. 'There is that. Yes, you're right, the silence is about me and has nothing to do with the prodigal's return.' Flashing me a grin designed to put me at my ease, she added, 'Okay, it's showtime.'

I grabbed a glass of white wine from the tray on the counter and picked my way through the crowd to where Mum was talking to Jenny Taylor. Taking a long mouthful, I waited while the alcohol coursed through me, settling my nerves. While meeting Angus had been awkward enough, it was this meeting with his sister and my ex best-friend that had been filling me with dread.

I'd tried to explain to Jenny why I was leaving Angus and Mannus Ridge, but she hadn't wanted to hear. We were upstairs in my bedroom; I was sitting cross-legged on the bed and she'd perched on the cushioned window seat.

'If I don't go now, I never will,' I'd said. 'It's not forever – I'll do my degree and come back. We can get married then. It's not that I don't love Angus,' I'd said, my voice catching with tears, 'it's just that I think I'll always regret not going to uni like I'd always planned.'

If I closed my eyes, I could still hear the sneer in her voice. 'If you really loved him, you wouldn't want to leave.'

'If he really loved me, he'd give me the space to do this,' I'd shot back. 'He'd support me – you both would.'

'It's because he loves you that he wants you to stay with him. You know he can't leave Balloch Estate – it's his birthright and where his life is. There's been a McGuire at Balloch for nearly two hundred years; Mannus Ridge is where he belongs.' Angus's great-

great-great-grandfather had put down his bag in what would become Mannus Ridge at much the same time as mine.

'Well,' I'd said quietly, 'Maybe it's not where I belong.'

'I thought you said you belong with Angus, and this is where he is, so if you love him, this is where you should be.' Her chin was tilted obstinately, anger making the little flecks of gold in her hazel eyes blaze.

'If I don't do this now, I think I'll always wonder, and one day – maybe not for years – I'll wish that I had and that will destroy us.' Tears were coursing down my cheeks, and I made no effort to stop the flow. I'd lain awake, turning the decision over in my head every night since receiving the offer of a place at the University of Sydney five weeks earlier. 'I won't get this chance again.' I was desperate to make her understand.

'I don't understand why you applied in the first place.' Jenny stood and stalked around the room, stopping by my dressing table and picking up a lipstick. 'I thought you'd given up on the idea after you weren't accepted when we finished school.' Unclipping the top, she wound the lipstick up to its full height and then wound it back down again, the fuchsia pink bright and happy.

'I had,' I said. 'But then we broke up, and I thought

it was a sign that maybe I should try again. Remember – you told me I should.'

'Yes, but I always knew you would get back together again.' She turned away briefly, but not before I saw the truth in her eyes.

'And you never thought I'd get in.' I waited for her confirmation.

'You're right,' she said eventually. 'I never thought you'd get in and you two would get back together and we'd all be as we should be – you with Angus, me with Dave. Our kids would grow up together and be best friends like we've been.'

That's when I understood that in pursuing my dream, I was destroying hers. It was almost enough to make me stay – that and the thought of hurting Angus, of living without him. The sight of my wedding dress hanging on the outside of the wardrobe – the dress I was due to wear in just over a month – mocked me. For a second, I allowed myself the fantasy of walking down the aisle in it towards Angus, the light of love in his eyes. What would any of it be worth if he wasn't with me?

'If you do this,' she said slowly, unable to meet my eyes, 'I'll never speak to you again; no one in this town will speak to you again.'

'You don't mean that,' I said desperately.

'I do.' She flipped the cap back onto the lipstick with a little click. 'If you do this, you're not just turning your back on Angus and me, you might as well be telling every single person in Mannus Ridge that they're not good enough for you, that Ainsley St James is far too ambitious and important to be buried in a boring little nothing town like this one.'

'That's not what this is about,' I wailed.

'Isn't it?' She narrowed her eyes, her stare piercing my heart. 'Georgia Tyson was right about you. She's always said that you think you're better than us.'

'I don't think that – I never have.' I was on my feet, my hands pleading with her to understand that this was about me, not her, not Angus, and not Mannus Ridge. I needed to know if there was anything else out there.

'Really? Well, you're certainly acting like it now.' She shook her head sadly. 'I'm done trying to reason with you, Lee – although I suppose in your new life, you'll want to be known by your full name.' She exhaled loudly. 'If you go, don't bother to say goodbye; I won't care. You do this and you're dead to me. Don't bother coming back.'

When she left, I curled up into a ball on my bed and cried for hours – it had been harder than the conversation I'd had with Angus the previous night when I'd told him I couldn't marry him and why. When I'd asked him to wait for me.

When the tears had stopped, I packed my bag, and when the sun was finally up, crawled out of bed and left, leaving just a note for my parents and Jacinta. I vowed I wouldn't return until I'd made something with my life that would show them all it had been worth it. Until a couple of weeks ago, I hadn't cried since.

From a distance, Jenny looked much the same – a little rounder from behind, maybe. She'd cut her hair too. Instead of bunched up in a thick ponytail, she wore her dark brown hair in a short, straight bob, the caramel tints hitting the light as she nodded emphatically to something Mum was telling her. As if sensing my presence, she turned to face me. Releasing the breath I'd been holding, I summoned a smile to my lips and animation to my voice. 'Jenny, how nice to see you. You look great!'

For a heart-stopping moment, I thought she might ignore me and continue the conversation she'd been having before I interrupted her.

'Lee,' she said, no answering smile on her face. 'I heard you were back.'

'It was such a lovely surprise,' said Mum, her glance darting between us, rushing to fill the silence. 'When Jacinta said Lee was thinking about coming, I don't think any of us quite believed it.' She laughed uncomfortably. 'But then yesterday, there she was.'

'I'm surprised you could spare us the time from your important job and your important boyfriend in the city,' Jenny drawled, no trace of the laughing girl who for so many years was my partner in adventures. There was a time I thought we'd be friends for life, that nothing could break us apart. I'd been wrong.

'It was no bother.' I waved the words away but the hurt lingered. 'They can all do without me for a little while. Jazz said you finally married Dave.'

She nodded, her eyes restlessly casting around the room. 'Yep.'

'And you have children?'

'Uh-huh, two – Ethan and Ivy.' I waited for her to expand on that (doesn't everyone want to talk about their children?), but she didn't.

Still, I persisted. 'How old are they?'

'The same as Jacinta's two youngest. Listen, Lee, I —'

I don't know what she would've said as Dad dinged the bell above the bar for attention.

Once the chatter had quietened down, he began to speak. 'We'll get the formal part of tonight over and done with before you buggers get too settled in, so thanks to you all for coming to help me celebrate my sixtieth birthday.' When he mentioned his age, he covered his mouth in a mock-cough. As the age-related jibes came from the floor, he held his hands up. 'Yeah, yeah, I know. Enough of the old jokes. As I was saying, thanks to everyone for coming out – although I know you're here for the free beer.' That comment earned him a cheer. He raised his glass in my direction. 'Mostly though, I want to thank Lee for coming home for the occasion. We've missed you, Lee, and I'm sure everyone here will make her welcome.' My cheeks burned at the sound of the claps around the room – more than I expected, although I noticed Jenny's hands didn't move. 'Before we go any further, though, Mark here wants to say a few words.' He cast his eyes around the crowd for Mark. 'Come on, mate; it's your turn.'

As Mark took his place beside Dad, Dad clapped him on the back. 'Over to you, son.'

Mark shuffled in his place, hands in his pockets, shoulders hunched.

'Get on with it,' yelled Macca. 'Some of us are getting thirsty.'

'Pipe down, Macca,' said Angus. 'Let him speak.' Angus had been leaning against the bar, one hand in the pocket of his jeans, the other nursing a schooner of beer. His navy blue short-sleeved shirt made his hair look darker; he ran his hands through the thick waves.

Dragging my attention from Angus, I shot a look at Jenny. Her brow was furrowed and her eyes narrowed. 'Do you know what's going on?' she asked.

'Ahem.' Mark cleared his throat. After another little pause, he said, 'Okay, everyone here knows how long Jazz and I have been together.'

'Forever,' yelled Spider. 'You get less time for murder!'

'Yeah, yeah, we've been together forever, but ...' He cleared his throat again. 'Jazz, baby, you know how much I love you, and I know we've done everything the wrong way about, but I couldn't think of anyone else I'd want to do life the wrong way about with.'

'That just about covers your sex life,' Spider yelled.

'Shut up, Spider!' said Macca.

Mark's face was deep red, but he bravely continued. 'The thing is, Jazz, will you marry me?'

Jacinta had been walking towards him as he spoke and reached for his hands, her eyes holding his. 'On one condition, Mark McGuire,' she said, beaming.

'Name it.'

'That we do it now.' By the look on her face, they'd practiced this part of the proposal.

'Now? Like right now?' Mark played his part well.

'Uh-huh. I'm not giving you any opportunity to change your mind,' said Jazz.

Jenny looked at me and muttered under her breath, 'It's not the McGuires changing their mind that you need to be worried about.'

I pretended not to hear her and moved away, ducking behind the bar to watch proceedings from there.

'Besides,' Jazz was saying, 'it would be a shame to waste this dress ...'

The crowd took up a chant of 'do it, do it, do it'.

Mark held his hands up for silence. 'Well, it doesn't appear I've got much of a choice,' he said, a note of resignation creeping into his voice. 'Is there anyone in this fine establishment who can legally marry us?'

'I'll do it,' said Nicky, stepping forward. 'I'm a qualified celebrant, so it will all be legal.'

'Aaah, but we don't have any flowers for the bride,' Mark said, unable to hide his grin. 'Jazz can't get married without flowers.'

That was my cue. 'What about these?' I asked with my best innocent look on my face, producing the flowers I'd stashed under the bar.

'So,' said Jazz slowly. 'We have a celebrant and flowers, but what about rings? Does anyone have any rings we could use?'

'Will these do?' asked Angus, stepping forward.

That was when the crowd knew for sure the whole

thing had been a set-up, and a cheer rang around the bar and everyone wanted to slap Mark on the back and kiss Jazz and exchange 'did you knows?'

As the crowd surged forward, Angus and I were left standing on our own. He didn't look at me and while my eyes kept darting in his direction, I tried not to look at him. Jenny had been one of the first to rush across and congratulate the happy couple, but beside her was Georgia Tyson. If I thought the look Jenny had sent me was decidedly unfriendly, Georgia's could have turned me to stone.

ANGUS and I managed to get through the entire ceremony without exchanging words, yet every single nerve was conscious of him. When his arm brushed mine as we signed the marriage certificate, a line of goosebumps rushed to the point of contact before scattering throughout my body. For that moment, he was close enough for me to inhale his scent – not his cologne, but that underlying spicy, leathery aroma that was pure Angus. I reminded myself that it had only been two weeks since I'd broken up with Otis, that officially I was supposed to still be heartbroken, but it made no difference. My heart and hormones were operating on memory, and there was no arguing with them.

Because it wasn't a traditional wedding, there were no bridal tables, and the food had been all finger food and set out on trays on the bar counter, but immediately after signing the register, Jazz grabbed the deejay's microphone and called for quiet.

'Oy! You lot! Shut it!' Once the chatter had died down, she tapped the microphone a couple of times before speaking. 'I know Dad said there'd be no more speeches, but there's been a wedding, so you'll need to put up with me for a few minutes.' She held out her hand, and Mark moved to take it, their smiles full of hope and happiness. 'This is an upside-down wedding, so you'll be hearing from me and – don't worry, Macca, you won't go thirsty.' Macca held up his schooner in a silent toast. 'When we first decided to do this, I said I wouldn't do it without my big sister being here.' As she sought me out, my eyes burned and my nose twitched. 'But I didn't want her to feel she had to come home – I wanted her to want to come home ... and she has and I'm so happy for that. Lee, I know you've been worried about coming back, but it wouldn't have been the same without you. It hasn't been the same here without you.' She held her hand out towards me, and through moist eyes, I blew her a kiss. 'So, I'd like to raise a toast to my beautiful bridesmaids – my gorgeous daughter Hayley and my equally gorgeous sister.' She held up her glass in a toast.

I knew exactly what she was doing – and I loved her for it. In publicly acknowledging me like this, she was announcing to Mannus Ridge that I'd been forgiven – that my family had forgiven me and that Angus's brother had also forgiven me – even though I knew he wasn't *quite* there yet. Now, finally married to my sister, Mark was obviously prepared to go along with whatever statement she wanted to make.

'Now, if you'll excuse me, my husband and I have a dance to dance – and then the formal bit of the night is over!'

The opening chords of Ed Sheeran's 'Thinking Out Loud' played and Jazz and Mark took to the floor. When the music changed to Ellie Goulding's version of Elton John's 'Your Song', Angus was in front of me, holding his hand out. 'It's tradition,' he said, not quite meeting my eyes.

I nodded once and allowed him to draw me into his arms, his body moving stiffly, making no effort to disguise the fact that I was the last person he wanted to be up close and personal with. Sadly, my hormones didn't care whether he was a willing partic-ipant, and I closed my eyes and imagined it was our first dance for the wedding we didn't have and he was looking at me the way his brother was now looking at my sister. What would our song have been? I couldn't remember if we'd decided; he'd wanted 'I Need You' by some country singer I'd never heard of, and I told him that if he had that, I'd choose '2 Hearts' by Kylie Minogue, who he'd never really liked. What had begun as an argument had ended with us making love – as most of our arguments had.

'How long are you staying?' His gravelly words broke the spell I'd slipped under.

I shrugged. 'I'm not sure, but a few weeks, I think. I'm looking after Jazz and Mark's kids next week. We'll see what happens after that.' When he made no reply, I said, 'Dad mentioned that your father had passed away … I'm sorry for your loss.'

'Thanks. It was a while ago now.'

I risked a look up into his face. His chin was firm, his jaw square as if he was clenching his teeth, his eyes focused on the other side of the dance floor. As if he felt my gaze, he glanced down and for a heartbeat, our eyes held and everything else stood still as we whirled back in time to when I was twenty and he was twenty-two and we were so deeply in love we'd thought nothing would ever come between us. My breath came faster; he swallowed, then Georgia was beside us, and the moment was gone.

'You don't mind, do you, Lee?' she asked sweetly.

I shook my head and stepped away. 'Not at all. He's all yours, Georgia.'

'Yes, he is, isn't he?' she said smugly, sliding a possessive hand up his arm before moving easily into his arms.

Forcing a half smile, I turned away and headed to the bar.

'Wow, that was awkward.' Jenny must've been watching us dance.

'A little,' I said, eyes drawn to Angus and Georgia on the dance floor. The music had changed to something more upbeat, and he was self-consciously shuffling around the makeshift dance floor. I smiled to myself; some things never changed. On a horse, Angus was at home, almost at one with the animal, but dancing had never fallen within his comfort zone. Sure enough, as the music changed, Angus murmured to Georgia and led her from the floor back to where Spider and a few other people stood nursing drinks.

'I'm surprised you haven't been back before this,' said Jenny, taking a sip of her wine and eyeing me over the top of the glass. 'But I suppose it's better late than never.'

'It's not every day your father turns sixty and your sister gets married,' I said, watching a giggling Hayley take to the dance floor with some other girls. It didn't seem that long ago that those giggling girls were Jenny and me screeching, 'Oh my god, I LOVE this song!'

Jenny lifted a shoulder and said, 'Well, you've got to hand it to your parents, they certainly know how to throw a farewell bash.'

My tummy fell as her words filtered into my brain. 'Sorry?'

She turned to look at me, her eyes wide, mouth hanging open. 'You really don't know?'

'Know what?' A horrible feeling of foreboding pricked my skin.

'They didn't tell you?' Jenny's eyes darted around, looking for a way out. 'God, Lee, I'm so sorry. I thought you knew – and that was why you'd come back.' In her horror at having spoken out of turn, her tone was gentler.

'I still don't know what you're talking about.' I shook my head slowly and raised my palms, encouraging her to spill the beans. Suddenly what Jacinta had said on the phone about Dad's health, the fatigue I'd seen on my parent's faces, the tests Jazz said Dad had been having – the ones they'd tried to fob off as being routine – and the way everyone had been so relieved I was home. My heart skipped a beat. 'Is it Dad?'

'I don't think it's my place ...' Jenny began, her eyes on the floor, her hand sweeping away a lock of hair that had fallen over her face.

With an exasperated snort, I left her standing there and stalked over to where Mum was sitting, chatting to a group of old friends – one of which included Kerry Tyson, Georgia's mother.

'Doesn't Jacinta look happy?' Kerry directed her question towards me. 'She and Mark certainly make a lovely couple.'

'They certainly do,' I said, trying to catch my mother's eye.

'It's lovely that you've come home,' she continued. 'It must be such a relief to your parents.'

'I'm beginning to understand that.' Mum seemed to be deliberately ignoring me.

'Of course a lot has changed since you were last here.' Kerry seemed oblivious to my attempts to capture Mum's attention.

'Uh-huh.'

'You'd know that my Georgia is with Angus now. We're all hoping to hear more wedding bells before too long – although I'm sure Georgia will want to get married in a church rather than a pub.' She turned to Mum. 'No offence, of course.'

Mum smiled tolerantly. 'None taken.'

'Although Angus is a little marriage-shy, but you can't blame him for that, can you?' The last was said with an arch look.

I smiled tightly. 'No, you can't. Ladies, do you mind if I steal my mother for a minute?'

Without waiting for her response, I grabbed Mum's hand and led her to the office behind the bar. 'Okay,' I said. 'What's going on?'

'Nothing you need to worry about tonight,' Mum said, pivoting on her black pumps to head back out to the party.

I moved to stand in the doorway, barring her exit. 'Jenny said this would be a farewell party.' I crossed my arms. 'What did she mean by that?'

Mum sighed heavily. 'Lee, darling, do we need to talk about this tonight?'

'I think we do before someone else tells me what you or Dad should have.'

At first, I thought she would brazen it out, but when her shoulders slumped, I knew I had her. 'We're selling the pub, Lee.'

My tummy flip-flopped. 'Why?' Then, before she could answer, I said, 'Is it Dad? Is he sick?' My hand flew to my chest, palm pressing my sternum. 'He is, isn't he? Oh god, you should have told me!' Beneath my hand, my heart was beating its way out of my chest.

Mum laid a soothing hand on my arm. 'No darling, your father's not sick. It's nothing like that. It's just ... it's time.'

'But ...'

'No, Lee,' she said gently. 'Not now. We'll talk about it tomorrow, I promise, but let's not ruin tonight. Okay?' Her eyes were pleading with me to understand, to let them have this last big party with all their friends.

I nodded slowly, reluctantly. 'Okay. But we are having that talk tomorrow.'

'We will,' she said. 'I promise.'

TEN

Despite the late night – by the time everyone had gone and we'd cleaned up, it had been well after midnight – I was awake not much after six. Unable to sleep any longer, I dressed in workout gear and headed for a run.

A warm morning with the promise of a hot day, I passed the showground and sale yards, the soft early morning light filtering golden through the leaves of the poplars that lined both sides of the road.

Heading out of town, the road climbed steadily, and before too long, my lungs were burning and I was grateful for the water bottle I'd grabbed on the way out. I might've worked out every morning in Melbourne, but it had been way too long since I'd run outdoors. If I was going to stay for a few weeks, though, without access to a gym, it was something I'd need to get used to.

A couple of kilometres out of town, I crossed over into the pine forest and followed one of the fire trails that crisscrossed through the trees.

I hadn't been able to get information out of anyone else last night. Mum had refused to talk any further on the subject, Dad made sure he was surrounded by friends each time I caught his eye, and while I was tempted to drag Jazz away and demand she told me the truth, I didn't want to risk ruining her evening.

While I mightn't have been able to talk to my father, I watched him closely for any signs of illness or fatigue, but he seemed in good spirits, even if it was all for the benefit of the crowd. I couldn't imagine him selling the pub and being happy about the decision, so it must've been all for appearances. One last hurrah, so to speak.

But what would they do without the pub? While I was struggling with the same question regarding my job, the pub was different – it was in their veins; it was their heritage, home and livelihood. Being publicans was more than what they did; it was who they were. They couldn't easily walk away from it; there had to be a reason, but if it wasn't ill health, then what?

And if they were selling, who were they selling to? What did the town think of that?

With so many questions running through my head, I suddenly realised I'd run further than intended. Stopping, I doubled over, my hands on my thighs, sucking in the breath. Leaning against a tree trunk, I took a large swig from my water bottle, wiping the drips away with the back of my hand. As my breathing settled, I tipped my head back, the tops of the pines all seeming to angle upwards, little patches of blue sky visible between the canopy. That was another thing I'd forgotten, how silent it was here, yet at the same time, how alive the trees sounded; they creaked and groaned almost as if they were talking.

I smiled ruefully at the fanciful idea that trees could talk, but when I was little, that's exactly what I thought – that the birds and the trees and the wind all communicated with each other and that if I sat quietly at the base of a tree, my back against it and my eyes closed, they might just let me in on the secret. It's why I never felt frightened to be in this forest alone and often cycled out here when I needed to get away from things; when the noise, the expectations became too much, the trees welcomed and protected me. When had I stopped believing in that sort of magic?

I sank to sit cross-legged on the needled ground,

rested my back against the gnarly trunk and closed my eyes, my breathing regulating, my heartbeat slowing, and let the tree magic work its way back into my soul. Maybe I didn't need to have all the answers just yet – maybe I wasn't meant to. In fact, maybe all this was supposed to happen so I could be here for Jazz's wedding, get to know her kids and help Mum and Dad with whatever was happening with the pub. Maybe I was meant to come back, slow down, switch off and do all those things that normal people with a real life do. Maybe I was meant to come back to find myself again, and then everything else would slot into place and I'd be able to return to the city with a plan and a new job.

The truth was, I'd barely thought about Otis since I'd been here. I missed him, of course I did, but I didn't miss what went along with loving him – the absences, the silences, the secrets, the lies, the birthdays and Christmases and Easters and holidays spent alone. Had any of that been worth the stolen moments we had together, or had I just gotten so used to the sacrifices and the compromises that it had all become part of the deal?

I scoffed at the thought of what my ex-colleagues would say if they could see me now; if they knew what was going on inside my head they'd think I'd completely gone mad. Otis would look perturbed and say, 'Where's Ainsley and what have you done with her?' Yet sitting here listening to what the birds and the trees and the wind had to say seemed to be the sanest thing I'd done in years. I felt more like me than I'd done in years. More Lee and less Ainsley.

'I don't see you in fifteen years, and now suddenly you're everywhere I go.'

At first I thought the deep voice was the trees talking to me, but they'd never sound so wry. My eyes snapped open. Angus was mounted on a bay mare. I squinted as I looked up at him, the sun flashing through the cracks in the canopy blinding me.

'Or maybe it's you being everywhere I go,' I returned, scrambling to my feet and wiping the pine needles and dirt from my bum.

'Talking to the trees again?' he asked, and then before I could answer, added, 'Not that I expect you need advice on anything anymore.'

'What's that supposed to mean?'

He shrugged. 'Nothing.' A brief silence. 'How did you get out here?'

'I ran.' I waved my hand in the direction of my trainers.

'Quite a run.'

I lifted a shoulder to indicate it wasn't that far.

'Especially after last night.'

I didn't know what he wanted me to say to that; the fact that he was talking to me at all was confusing enough. I searched his face for a sign, but his hat shadowed it, the same weather-worn Akubra he'd been wearing on Friday.

'You had a late night too.' I wiped some sweat off my top lip with the back of my knuckle.

'But I'm used to early mornings.' His implication was, of course, that as a soft city girl, I wasn't.

Before I could bite out a 'me too' and have the discussion descend into a petty argument over who slept in the longest, he swung effortlessly out of the saddle and led the mare closer to where I was standing. Unable to resist, I stretched out a hand and stroked her velvety neck, loving the musky animal smell of sweaty horse. She pushed her head into my belly, snuffling into my tank top, causing me to chuckle softly.

'I don't have anything for you,' I said to the horse. 'What's her name?'

'Jane.' His mouth quirked at the corner.

'Let me guess, Jenny's youngest named her?'

He nodded and almost smiled before remembering that he wasn't meant to smile at me. For that brief nanosecond, though, I was reminded of the Angus I'd fallen in love with and had missed so desperately. I was also made aware of just how close he was.

'Well, Jane, you're a beauty.' I tickled the horse's mouth and grinned as she puckered in response.

'Did you know about the wedding?' he asked, watching me crooning to his horse.

I shook my head. 'Not until Friday night. Jazz said she wanted me to come home because I wanted to, not because she'd guilted me into it.' I smiled wryly, remembering the conversation we'd had the day I lost my job. 'Although she sort of did that anyway.'

More silence.

I risked a sideways glance at him and was surprised by a look of ... what? Regret? Whatever it was, it was gone in an instant.

He dropped Jane's reins and walked off a few steps, toeing the soft ground with his boots before turning back. 'Jenny said you didn't know about the pub being sold.'

I shook my head and buried it into the horse's soft neck, wrinkling my nose as her mane tickled it, feeling Angus's eyes boring into my back. Reluctantly, I lifted my head and turned to face him, Jane nudging the back of my legs.

'Do you know the details?' When he hesitated, I said, 'Please, Angus, no one will tell me anything.'

His teeth latched onto his lower lip, and he tilted his head back, lifting his eyes to the sky, the knuckle of his forefinger tapping against his chin as if he was waiting for a sign or guidance. 'There's not a lot I can tell you,' he finally said, his focus now on the forest floor and the little hole he'd dug with his boot.

I sighed, more from exasperation than anything else. In this town where everyone knew everything about everybody – and liked to make sure that the knowledge was passed around – why was no one telling me anything?

'Do you know who they're selling to?' When he shook his head, I tried again. 'Do you know if it's a done deal?' Another head shake. 'Do you know why they're selling?'

He raised his head, tipping his hat back so our eyes could meet. A shiver of remembered sensation ran through me, and I had a sudden urge to wrap my arms around myself.

'I think,' he began before another brief pause. 'I think there's some trouble with the bank and they've been made an offer that's difficult to refuse in the circumstances.' His voice sounded stilted, the phrasing unnatural, as if he was choosing his words carefully. 'But I haven't heard that from your parents so can't know for sure.'

I nodded slowly, my brain turning the information around. Trouble with the bank? The hotel had been in the family forever and, as far as I knew, the only mortgage on it was to cover the overdraft facility. Maybe they'd taken out a loan to renovate, but other than the new carpet in the bar, everything seemed much the same as it had been. Unless they'd had to increase the overdraft to see them through covid lockdowns? If this had been weighing over their heads, no wonder Dad was having health problems and Mum looked so worried.

'You should have been here,' he said quietly. 'They needed you.'

'I didn't know ... They never said.' I handed Jane's reins back to Angus and bent to pick up my water bottle from where it sat at the base of the tree. 'But I'm here now.'

'For how long?' The words came out hard, sarcastically. He might as well have said, 'You're too late to do anything, and this is all your fault for not being here and now that you know, are you going to run away again?'

'As long as I need to be,' I said simply. I sucked in a ragged breath. 'As long as it takes for me to sort this mess out for them.'

He placed his foot in a stirrup and hoisted himself back into the saddle. 'What can you do about it?'

'I have no idea, but I have to try.'

And then I lifted a hand in farewell as I began the run back into town. When I paused a little way along the trail and looked back, he was still sitting on his horse, motionless, watching me.

———

WHEN I FINALLY PUSHED THROUGH the back door and ran up the stairs into the family kitchen, I was drenched with sweat. While I'd been in the forest talking with Angus, I'd been sheltered from the sun, but back out in the open, it was blazing.

My parents were sitting at the old oak table that had sat in this kitchen for generations. Both were nursing coffees, and from his peaky expression, Dad was also nursing a hangover.

Mum looked up in surprise as I appeared, dripping, in the doorway. 'We thought you must still be in bed,' she said, frowning as she took in my appearance. 'Don't tell me you've been out running in this heat?'

I nodded, still puffing. 'I was awake early and needed to get rid of the cobwebs.'

Dad raised a couple of fingers in an approximation of a greeting. His head must be bad.

'The forest?' guessed Mum, shaking her head ruefully at Dad.

'Yeah.' I hovered in the doorway, deciding whether to tell them what Angus had told me.

'Have you eaten?' Mum was already up, moving towards the fridge.

'No, I'll shower first. Don't worry about making me anything; I'll sort something out.'

'It's no bother. I'm about to make your father and me a bacon and egg sandwich – it's no hassle to put on another.'

I almost said that I don't touch white bread, bacon, butter, tomato sauce, or, indeed, usually breakfast, but somehow said, 'Thanks. I'll just get changed and be back in five.'

By the time I was back, clean and smelling decidedly more fragrant than I had been, Mum was plating up breakfast. I accepted the sandwich and the coffee gratefully.

'It's no wonder you're so skinny if you go running in heat like that every day.' The combination of egg, bacon and simple carbohydrates finished the coffee's work and restored Dad's power of speech.

'I don't normally run in heat like that,' I quipped, wiping some drippy egg from my plate. 'It was shady in the forest, and I didn't realise how hot the sun was until I was out and back on the road.'

'You always did like it in there,' Mum said.

'I saw Angus in there this morning.' I pulled a stray piece of bacon from my sandwich and chewed on it. How had I forgotten how good bacon tasted? 'He was out riding.'

'I remember you and Angus used to go riding there too.' Mum said it almost as a way of filling the ensuing silence. 'You used to enjoy riding.'

I was glad to have the excuse of exercise to explain my suddenly flaming cheeks – there was a lot we used to enjoy in that forest. I placed what was left of my sandwich on the plate and took a mouthful of coffee.

'I asked him what he'd heard about the sale of the pub.' I tried and failed to meet the eyes of first Mum and then Dad. 'He said he heard there was some trouble with the bank.'

'It's nothing for you to be worrying about Lee,' Dad muttered.

'If it means that the pub is being sold, I think it is something I need to be worrying about,' I said firmly. 'Who knows, I might even be able to help. It's not like I haven't worked in one bank or another for the last decade.'

'Maybe now isn't the time to discuss it.' Mum rolled her eyes in Dad's direction. 'We're all a little tired this morning, and you'll be needing to head over to Jazz's place so they can be on their way.'

While it was obvious that Mum was trying to delay what must be an awkward conversation, I had to admit that while they were both tired and, especially in Dad's case, a little seedy from the night before, now probably wasn't the best time. Although if I was to have any chance of doing anything about the situation, it wasn't a conversation that could be put off much longer.

'Does Jazz know?'

'We told her some of it the other day,' conceded Dad. 'Just that we've got ourselves into some money troubles and that the pub needs to be sold. She wouldn't understand the ins and outs of it, though, so we haven't bothered her with it.'

It seemed like they hadn't thought to bother anyone with it.

'I understand you don't want to discuss it now, but we are talking about it. Tomorrow morning – after I drop the kids off and before you open. Okay?'

Both dropped their heads as if I'd scolded them – and truly, I wanted to scold them. At the same time, though, I understood why they hadn't felt able to tell me. Why would they? I hadn't been around; I'd been too busy wrapping myself up in my own self-impor-tance and had made it clear I wanted nothing to do with Mannus Ridge or anyone who lived here. I'd effectively exiled myself for fifteen years as punishment for the decision I'd made and hadn't thought about what that had meant for my parents or Jazz, and now here we were – with my parents about to lose everything they had.

No, that wasn't going to happen. I mightn't be able to make up for fifteen years of absence and neglect, but I could start by helping them save the pub.

ELEVEN

While I hadn't expected to sleep well in Jazz's spare room, I'd been out like a light almost the minute my head hit the pillow and woke naturally when the sun peeked through the cracks in the curtains, the magpies carolling their good morning, a rooster crowing in the background.

After dressing in my exercise gear, I whistled softly for Bella, the family's kelpie cross, and set off for a quick run. Jazz had said the kids usually woke around seven, so I'd be back in plenty of time.

The sun was already warm against my back as I ran past the homestead where Angus would be sleeping. Would Georgia be there beside him? I quickened my pace to drive the thought from my head. Whatever Angus and Georgia did was no business of mine.

When I agreed to look after the kids, I'd forgotten that Jazz and Mark lived in what had probably been a stockman's cottage on Balloch Estate, the McGuire's land. 'It's just until we finish building our house in town,' Jazz had said. 'But I'm married to a builder, and our house is so far down his priorities. At least the rent is good, so we can afford to pay extra into the mortgage – and I'm close to work.' Jazz worked in the cellar door at Talbots Wines.

Knowing that she lived here and understanding that meant I'd be able to see the wrap-around verandah of the McGuire homestead from Jazz's verandah were, though, two different things.

As if she guessed the direction of my thoughts, Jazz had inclined her head towards Angus's house and said, 'Is that going to be a problem?'

'No,' I'd said quickly. 'Of course it won't be.'

With the Talbot's vines on my right and a herd of Angus cattle grazing in the paddock to my left, I paused and leant against the paddock gate and watched the cows until Bella barked at me to keep moving. 'Okay.' I ruffled her head. 'You're right; we need to be getting back.'

Back home, I let the chooks out of their yard and checked their water, collecting a couple of still-warm eggs from the nests; Jazz had warned me that I'd need to check a couple of times during the day at this time of the year. I toed my shoes off on the deck and put them on the rack left for that purpose – remembering to tip them upside down the way I'd been taught when I was a child to guard against anything crawling inside.

There was no movement in the house, so I opened the door first to the room Jackson and Cody shared, pushing aside the curtains to fill the room with light, and then to Hayley's. While the boys were awake and almost immediately up and running to the kitchen, Hayley groaned and turned over in bed, mumbling something incomprehensible.

'It's time you were up, Hayles,' I called. Bella, seeing the open door, took the opportunity to rush in and leap onto the bed, snuffling her way into Hayley's face.

'Get her off me!' Hayley said, giggling. I walked away and left them to it.

Jazz had already laid out uniforms before she left, so all I needed to do was make sure they made it to school dressed and fed. Jackson and Cody gulped their cereal down and rushed off, racing each other to their bedroom. Hayley loitered at the table, seemingly unable to decide between cereal or toast.

'Can I get you anything?' I asked, my brain

working its way through potential breakfast alternatives.

'No thanks, Aunty Lee,' she sighed. 'I'm not sure that I'm really into breakfast these days.' Then she hesitated and plastered a worldlier than almost thirteen look on her face. 'It's the refined carbs, you see. Mum doesn't understand. Do you eat carbs, Aunty Lee?'

Sighing inwardly, I grappled with the question. In truth, I'd consumed more carbs over the last couple of days than I had in months back in Melbourne, but the last thing I wanted was for the Melbourne version of me to be a role model for Hayley.

'Not all carbs are created equal,' I said. 'And everything is fine in moderation.' I crossed my fingers behind my back and hoped that was the right thing to say to a body-conscious teen. How did Jazz deal with situations like these?

'What are you eating for breakfast?' she asked, an arch smile on her face.

While I'd been either going to skip it or delay it until after the kids had gone to school, now I said, 'I spied some wholegrain bread in the freezer, and I thought I might have a boiled egg and soldiers.' I paused and smiled at her. 'Do you want me to make one for you too?'

Her face lit up, and suddenly she was twelve,

almost thirteen again instead of twelve, almost sixteen.

Once the breakfast things were cleaned away, I ducked down the hall for a quick shower and change, deliberating for more minutes than I had over what to wear. None of my clothes – all designer brands, the most casual of which were fine for shopping or lunch in the city – seemed to suit life here. As a priority, I'd need to go online and buy another pair of jeans, some basic cotton tees, shorts and flip-flops – at least. I might only be staying for a few weeks, but city clothes made me look more of an outsider than I already felt I was. Actually, I mused, I probably should buy as much as I could in town – otherwise people might think I thought I was too good for the shops in town. Man, this was a minefield to negotiate.

Dressing in camel capris with a navy tee and my Ted Baker white sandshoes, I went to put my hair up in its trademark bun but decided at the last minute to make do with a high ponytail. Reaching automatically for my usual make-up, I opted instead for a tinted moisturiser. Even after a few days, the bags under my eyes had diminished, and I had more colour in my cheeks.

I quickly glanced at my watch and realised we were on the verge of being late – on our first morning.

'Okay, kids, let's go,' I called. 'What happens with Bella? Does she stay or go?' I asked Hayley.

'She stays. Cody, can you get Bella a biscuit?'

Cody nodded, but Jackson said, 'I want to give Bella her biscuit this morning.' And they were off and running again.

'Is it always like this?' I had no idea how Jazz did it every morning.

Hayley rolled her eyes in a very teenager way and said, 'Pretty much.' Then, after a little pause, 'Ummm, Aunty Lee, you've forgotten to make us lunch.'

I pressed the back of my palm to my forehead. 'Your mother gave me two jobs – to keep you fed and get you to school – and I've failed on the first day. I don't suppose there's still a canteen at school?'

She grinned conspiratorially. 'A lunch order will be a real treat.'

'Great. Where do you keep the paper bags?'

'What paper bags?' Hayley's grin had turned into a frown.

'To write the lunch orders on.' I rolled my eyes at her question.

This time it was Hayley's turn to roll her eyes. 'We do it on an app these days,' she said. 'It's covid-safe.'

All kids finally piled into Jazz's large four-wheel drive; I set off down the dirt road, pulling off to the side when I saw Angus's ute coming towards us, Red's head out the window barking enthusiastically. I raised a single finger from the steering wheel in the traditional country greeting way, and once he'd passed, drove the short distance to town.

———

KIDS SAFELY AT SCHOOL, I stopped off at the bakery on my way to the hotel.

Mrs Wilson was behind the counter as she had been every day since before I was born. Once upon a time, the teenager helping her would have been me – and Jenny McGuire. Our first casual jobs were in the bakery.

Knowing we were best friends at school, Mrs Wilson had hired us both on the basis that at least she knew we'd get along and there'd be no mean girl business behind the counter.

'I won't stand for any slacking off to talk and giggle, though,' she'd warned.

I'd kept the job at the bakery even after I turned eighteen and could legally serve in the bar – although I'd been working evenings in the hotel restaurant for a couple of years before that. At the time, I was desperate for money, saving up to get enough behind me to go to Sydney and attend uni, so was working every possible hour I had – in the bakery after school and on Saturday and Sunday mornings, in the hotel in the evenings – cramming in my school work whenever I could. And I'd done it – saved enough money to cover my expenses for at least the first six months in the unlikely event that I couldn't get a casual job to pay the rent upon arriving in Sydney.

I'd been devastated when I missed the required mark to get into my course by just one point – perhaps I would've been better placed to have worked less and studied more. Jenny got an apprenticeship at the local hairdresser's, and Mrs Wilson gave me her shifts. 'Just until you can apply again,' she'd said. 'It's a waste for a brain like yours to be working here.'

Between working at the bakery and behind the bar, I was busy, occupied and, most importantly, earning money, but I was getting nowhere. My dream had always been to go to uni in the city and become someone important in the world of business – to break glass ceilings and show everyone that a girl from Mannus Ridge who hadn't been to the right schools could do anything she put her mind to – and I wasn't letting go of that.

But when Angus and I began dating, I put all that on hold. We were young, in love and mad for each other. I loved him with the same single-mindedness that, only months before, I'd used to chase my city dream. And for the next year, I didn't think about leaving town – at least not until we had the argument that broke us up briefly. Then I thought about it again.

It was after the football one Saturday afternoon – the sort of winter day where the sun doesn't ever really come out properly, where the horse hair tangled on the fencing wire is stiff with frost, where even in town, we'd have to run the hot water slowly until the pipes warmed up, when ice would need to be scraped off windscreens with a credit card. One of those days when the damp and the cold gets so far into your bones that there's no warming up from it.

Mannus Ridge had been playing a team from Millers Creek and, after a spiteful game, had come away victorious. Angus had been instrumental in the victory – having scored two tries, setting up the plays that led to another three, and had kicked five goals. As he walked off the field, covered in mud and scrapes and despite the cold, I wanted nothing more than to get him alone. The wave of desire that flooded through me when our eyes met was like nothing I'd ever felt before. I wanted him so much it made me shake and quiver inside. I wanted him hard and fast and dirty. I wanted all of him. And I knew in that instant that he wanted me in the same way.

On his walk back to the change rooms, he ignored

all the well-wishers and 'good onya mates' and headed straight to me, cupped my face and kissed me hard on the lips. It was almost as though he was branding me for all to see, and I loved it, relished it. 'Later,' he promised gruffly before heading into the sheds.

I have no idea how long I sat there, a stupid look on my face, tasting the dirt his lips had left behind, goose-bumps rippling across my chest at the thought of what 'later' meant.

'The poor cow doesn't know.' The comment, too loud to have been whispered, too soft to have been intended for hearing, came from Julie Pritchard, one of Georgia's posse, sitting a few rows behind me in the stand.

'What do you mean?' Her companion was Lou Ingalls, the daughter of the local bank manager and new in town.

'Angus and Georgia used to date, you know,' Julie was saying, now not even worrying about keeping her voice down. 'According to Georgia, they're just on a break. She was trying to make him jealous with Spider Webb, and Angus caught her with him. He still loves her, though.'

'But I've heard it's serious between him and Lee St James – did you see that kiss just then?'

It sounded as though Lou was almost swooning

from the romance of it all, but Julie was having none of it. 'Oh, that? That was for Georgia's benefit. Didn't you see him look at her before heading to Lee? No, Lee is just a rebound girl, and Angus and Georgia will be back together soon. In fact,' she paused dramatically, 'they never really stopped seeing each other ... if you know what I mean ... They'll be officially back together by the end of the football season – you heard it here first.' Julie ended her prediction with a knowing giggle.

I didn't stay to hear more; instead, I gathered my bag, zipped up my coat and wound my scarf tighter around my neck. What Julie had said was spiteful rubbish, but that didn't stop the green-eyed monster from whispering in my ear, 'How can you be sure?'

That night at the pub, I drank and laughed and snuggled into Angus's side as I always did, but I couldn't stop from watching Georgia closely – the way her eyes darted to his at every opportunity, the way she flicked her streaked blonde hair about, the way her boobs wiggled in her t-shirt, the tight top leaving very little to the imagination. When she left with Spider, I thought I saw Angus frown, but if I did, it was gone quickly.

'How long has that been going on for?' I asked, inclining my head in the direction they'd left.

'Who knows?' Angus's reply had a tone of 'and

who cares?' to it that should've been enough warning for me to leave it alone, but at nineteen, in love and full of a bitter jealousy I'd never felt before, I couldn't.

'I thought she was still hooked on you,' I said. 'In fact'—I forced a laugh into my voice— 'I'd heard they were only together because she wanted to make you jealous.'

I held my breath and waited for his answer. 'Well, if that was the case, it certainly backfired on her then,' he said. Wrapping his arms around me, he pulled me in towards his body so he could nuzzle in behind my neck, his touch reawakening the desire I'd felt earlier. 'Now,' he murmured, 'are we going to get out of here?'

While my parents knew I stayed over at Angus's house from time to time, they didn't want him sleeping over at the hotel. While part of me understood that – their house, their rules, and a younger sister under the same roof – it certainly complicated things at moments like these.

Turning in his arms, I reached up, my thumb brushing his lower lip lightly. 'Jazz is staying over at Emily's tonight,' I said, knowing that even now she was probably in the back seat of Mark's car somewhere, 'and the pub is still open for another hour or so, and if we're quiet, we can probably make it upstairs without Mum or Dad knowing ...'

His eyes darkened to stormy grey, the tilt to his mouth wicked. 'What are we waiting for then?'

It was only later, lying in his arms, my heart slowly returning to normal, that the overheard conversation came back into my head and out of my mouth.

'Julie Pritchard said I was your rebound from Georgia, that you were still seeing her behind my back.' He stiffened but I kept my head on his chest, loving the tickle of his hair against my cheek and the slightly musky, earthy smell that was pure eau de Angus after sex.

'Babe?' he said. 'What's this about?'

'Nothing,' I mumbled.

'It sounds like more than nothing to me,' he said. 'Where's this coming from?'

There was an edge to his voice I couldn't describe but didn't like. 'I overheard a conversation today,' I said. 'Between Julie and Lou Ingalls.'

'And you trust them more than me?' He pulled away and swung his legs out of bed.

'Where are you going?' I asked tremulously.

'Where do you think? Home, of course – unless you're going to accuse me of going to see Georgia.' His back was straight as he pulled on his clothes, steel in his voice.

'I didn't say I believed it,' I cried.

'Then why bring it up?' He turned to face me, shook his head and shrugged his leather jacket on.

'I don't know,' I mumbled miserably.

'Maybe it's because you're jealous of Georgia and Spider.' His lip curled into a sneer as he said it.

'Don't be ridiculous,' I snapped, suddenly more angry than upset.

'Is it? If we're talking about listening to gossip and, let's face it, there's plenty of it in this town, I got mine straight from the horse's mouth.'

'What are you talking about?'

'You and Spider. He told me how you came on to him and how upset you were when he called an end to it. He also said you were still intending on going to the city and would forget all about me when you did.'

'*He* called an end to it?' Even as I was holding the sheet around my nakedness, I couldn't stop my mouth from dropping open. 'There was nothing to end. I went out on one date with him after we left school. One! He took me to the RSL Club at Millers Creek, and we had Chinese at the restaurant there – one dish for him and one for me. The guy doesn't even share his Chinese food! Then he took me home and tried making out with me in the car park even though I'd said no. Then he called me a prick tease and told me he was only going out with me because Georgia was seeing you and she was the one he wanted. As far as I'm concerned, Georgia is welcome to him.'

'That's not how he tells it,' Angus mumbled.

'And you have the hide to stand there and have a go at me for not trusting you? Have a listen to yourself!'

I swung out of bed and dressed in my pyjamas. 'Just go, Angus,' I said wearily.

'Go as in leave now or go as in that's it, we're over?' His hands were clenching and unclenching, and he couldn't meet my eyes. 'Or is this your way of getting me to break up with you so you can shoot through to Sydney like you'd planned?'

I shook my head in a combination of exasperation, disappointment that he could even be thinking the way he was and a pain in my heart I had no other way of expressing except through tears – and I wasn't going to let him see me cry.

'Yep, that's obviously what I was planning all along.' Sarcasm dripped from every word. 'No doubt Spider told you that too.' I strutted across to the bedroom door and held it open. 'Good night Angus.'

He looked between the door and me and then, without another word, slammed the door on his way out.

I'd cried myself to sleep that night, and the next morning in the bakery, Mrs Wilson took me aside. 'I've heard, love,' she said. 'If you're meant to be together, he'll come back; if not, there'll be someone else out there. Just promise me one thing – you won't put your life on hold while you wait for him to come to his senses.' She patted my cheek and smiled, a kind and wise smile that came with years of dealing with people. 'Right, you get yourself a sausage roll and a cuppa and sit out the back with Ed for a bit. I'll take care of the counter.'

So that's what I did. Mr Wilson and I chatted about nothing very much as he mixed, kneaded and rolled dough. After a finger bun with a slather of butter in the middle, I headed back to the counter and dealt with the curious eyes – good news really did travel fast in this town – and then I went home and reapplied to university.

Angus and I were only apart for a few weeks, and not long after that – on my twentieth birthday – he proposed and I very happily accepted and began planning our wedding. All was fine until the letter came from Sydney with my university acceptance – and it was Mrs Wilson I turned to then, too. I waited until after we'd closed for the day before hitting her with my problem.

'You didn't tell him that you'd applied?' she asked.

'I did, but I don't think either of us thought I'd get

in, so we both dismissed it, and now ...' I wrung my hands as I grappled with the decision I had to make – the one that would affect the rest of my life.

'I can't tell you what to do, Lee,' she'd said, 'but you're young – you both are – and maybe waiting a few years while you get your education isn't a bad thing.'

'Angus said he doesn't want to wait and that if I really loved him, I wouldn't ask him to, but can't I love him and get my degree? Why does it have to be one or the other?'

'Did you tell him that?' she asked, not looking up as she placed the neenish tarts that hadn't sold into little cardboard boxes.

'Yes, but he said if he let me go, he knew I wouldn't come back, and I said that if I didn't go, I was afraid that I'd regret it one day and resent him every time we had a big argument.'

Mrs Wilson's face held the same expression it did when she was deep in thought. 'Very true, that. What do your parents say?'

'I haven't talked it over with them. They're so excited about the wedding – I even have the dress hanging in my wardrobe. I know they've already spent money on deposits for the photographer and catering ... I can't disappoint them. And what if I choose uni and Angus calls my bluff and I hate it in Sydney?'

'Lee, your parents love you and will support you whatever your decision. As for the rest, you can ask what-ifs until the cows come home. Your parents can't tell you what to do, Angus can't tell you, and I certainly can't.' She straightened from behind the cabinet and took my hands in hers. 'This is your life, Lee, live it your way. Now'—she released my hands and handed me a box of tarts— 'take these home with you.'

All of that played in my head like a movie, as clear as if it had been yesterday. Mrs Wilson handed her customer their change and turned her attention to me. 'What can I help you with today?' I smiled and her eyes widened. 'Well, if it isn't Lee St James,' she said. 'I'd heard talk that you were back.' To the teenager on the counter, she said, 'Lee started here just like you.'

The girl cast me a quick grin and rushed to serve the next customer.

'Have you got time for a quick cuppa, Lee?' Mrs Wilson was already untying the apron from her generous waist. These days she was almost as wide as she was tall, and her short pixie-cut hair was now completely grey, but when she smiled the years slipped away and I was a teenager again – in love for the first time and so unsure about what the future held. Without waiting for my response, she led the way to the kitchen and flicked on the kettle.

I glanced at my watch. 'Yes, but it will need to be a quick one – I need to talk to my parents before the pub opens this morning.'

She nodded in understanding. 'Aaah, the business about the sale. I wondered if that was what had brought you back.'

'Would you believe I had no idea until Saturday night?'

She smiled briefly and placed teabags in mugs, then cut a sausage roll in half, placing it on a paper plate in front of me.

'Oh, but ...' I protested.

'No buts,' she said. 'You don't look like you eat enough to keep a fly alive. Now, get stuck into that.'

Sighing gracefully, I bit into the sausage roll, the savoury, peppery filling reminding me more than anything else of the hours I spent here as a girl.

'I was sorry to hear about Mr Wilson,' I said. Mum had told me the old baker had passed away after a brief battle with cancer two years ago.

Sadness washed over her face as she passed me my tea. 'Thank you, Lee, and thank you for the flowers you sent. It's not the same without him.'

'But you've kept up the bakery – who's doing your baking now? Has your son come into the business?'

Ed junior lived in Sydney with his wife and

daughter and, to the best of my knowledge, had never shown any inclination to become involved in the business.

'No, he's not interested. I have a new boy – although he'd hate for me to call him a boy given that he's in his thirties – doing the baking. An English boy – was over here when the borders closed and got stuck. Thankfully, he's decided to stay – for now, anyway.'

'Well'—I licked a blob of tomato sauce from my thumb— 'his sausage rolls are certainly up to scratch.'

'He had to drive to Canberra this morning for supplies, but hopefully you'll meet him next time you're in.' She eyed me keenly over her mug. 'How long are you staying for?'

'I'm not sure,' I said, brushing away some flaky crumbs that had landed on my pants. 'It depends on what's going on with my parents.'

Mrs Wilson cleared her throat before taking a sip of tea. 'I know they wanted to tell you earlier, but ...'

She didn't need to finish her sentence; they had wanted to tell me, but I'd given no indication that I was prepared to listen, let alone help them.

'I'm here now,' I said, wondering how many more times I'd need to say that before it made me feel any better.

TWELVE

When I arrived at the hotel, I accepted Mum's offer of yet another coffee but refused to have it in the kitchen. 'No,' I said firmly, 'we'll have it downstairs in the office.' While they exchanged the kinds of glances with each other that Jazz and I would've once done when we'd been in trouble, they didn't argue with me.

Dad seated himself in the chair behind the desk, Mum and I took the two opposite.

'What's the story?' Straight to the point. I was in no mood to be fobbed off. 'I didn't think you had any loans outstanding.'

Dad's eyes flickered to Mum's and when she gave a tiny nod, he exhaled loudly and ran his finger under the collar of his polo shirt as if the fabric was irritating him.

'Dad?' I prompted.

'There's always been a mortgage on the hotel, Lee,' he said. 'It's just that in the past, we've only ever run the working overdraft through it – enough to pay suppliers and employees each week. Nothing more than that.' He flashed Mum another quick look. 'Then we got talking to someone in the bar one night – he was a consultant from the tourist board here to speak to the council about promoting the wineries, the rail trail and some of the winter tourism. He suggested we spend a bit of money and bring the pub up to date to market ourselves as a boutique hotel.' Some of the doubt I felt must've shown on my face when Dad said, 'I know what you're thinking – the locals want the pub to stay as it is, but the travellers want something more. We thought we could do both, so we borrowed some extra money and renovated the guest rooms upstairs – reduced the number of them and added ensuites. It looks pretty good,' he said as an aside. 'You should have a look.'

'How were you going to pay it back, though? Surely the bank would've wanted a cashflow forecast and a business plan?' My mind was busy adding up the amount they must've borrowed against the turnover I assumed was coming in – and finding a massive hole in the calculations.

'Yes, but the consultant helped us with that too. We only get a few travellers staying overnight, so the income from that has always not been much, but with the improvements we planned for the restaurant, some advertisement of the guest rooms and the projections of wine tourism alone, we were convinced we'd be fine.' He pushed his chair back from the desk to open the drawer under it. 'I've got the numbers here somewhere.'

'Good, I'd like to go through them later.' I reached behind my head to pull at my ponytail to tighten it. 'I take it you didn't complete the changes to the restaurant?'

'No. We were about to, but we had the fires,' Mum said. 'We weren't planning on doing a lot in there, just some fresh paint, brighten it up, modernise it a little.'

'And then covid hit'—Dad shrugged— 'and everything shut and we went into lockdown. Tourism stopped completely, and the income dried up.'

'Which bank are you with?' Alarm bells were ringing in my head.

'Yours, of course. When the broker asked who we preferred, we said we'd stay where we were, thank you very much, because our daughter works there.' Mum seemed almost offended I'd ask such a question. 'He didn't know you, though,' she added.

'I'm not surprised; CP employs thousands of people. You should've been able to apply for hardship, though – that would've delayed your payments for a while.' My brain was whirring through the hardship policy that had come across my desk the last time it needed buy-in from my team.

'Yes, we did that, but it also coincided with us coming off interest-only onto a principle and interest payment, so the payments went up, and before you knew it, we were behind by three months and they were phoning us and sending legal papers.' Dad passed me the stack of correspondence held together with a large bulldog clip.

'Riiiight ...' I said, leafing through the notices. 'Did you make payment arrangements? Normally that's enough to hold off action – if you maintain those arrangements.'

'Yes,' said Mum, 'but obviously it was nowhere near catching the arrears.' She pushed her chair back and stood. 'Anyone else for another coffee?'

'Thank you,' I said absently, still reading the documents, my eyes widening when I came to the balance owed. I let out a low whistle and shot Dad a look. 'This is more than I thought it would be.' He dropped his gaze, and pink flushed across his cheeks. 'Okay, well, there's no going back, so now we need to work out how we get you out of this.' I reverted to all-business mode. 'Do you have the business case and projections there?'

'Yes,' he said, handing them over. 'It's why we're selling, love; your mother and I can't see any other way out.' His shoulders slumped, and a grey and drawn face replaced his earlier embarrassment. How long had they been sitting on this?

'Do you have a buyer? Everyone is talking as though it's a done deal.' I reached for a pen on the desk and made some notes in the margin of the cashflow. Whoever had drawn these up had certainly made some broad and optimistic projections.

His nod was filled with sadness and resignation. 'Yes. We've been approached by a company from Sydney – I'm not sure exactly who's behind it, but their representative has been down a couple of times over the last few months, and it was only last week that we decided we had no choice but to agree to terms. It is,' he said dejectedly, 'the only way we can see that we'll have something to leave you two. As it is, the debts will be cleared and we'll have a little something to fund our retirement as well.'

'I can't understand why you didn't tell me you were putting it on the market,' I said. Something was missing in this story that I couldn't quite put my finger on. It had to be in these numbers somewhere.

'That's the thing, we didn't have it on the market,' said Mum, coming back into the office with mugs of coffee and a plate of gingersnaps. 'It was quite fortuitous – we'd only received the demand notice the day before and there he was. At first, we were sure we'd be able to keep to our payment arrangements and chip into the arrears through normal trade recommencing, so we told him we weren't interested, but he was back just a couple of weeks later and we began to think about it.'

'Don't look like that, Lee,' said Dad. 'Don't feel sorry for us – we were always going to sell at some time or another. Jazz isn't cut out for business, and there was a time we hoped ...'

'That I'd come back from the city with my business degree ready to take over?' I finished his sentence.

He pursed his lips. 'Something like that. But as the years went by, it became clear you'd never come back to Mannus Ridge to stay – and that's still the case, isn't it? Even with what's happened – and yes, your mother filled me in – you're still planning on returning to the city, aren't you?'

I pushed my middle finger into my temple; there was no easy way to say it. 'Yes, that's where my life is – and where my next job is.'

Dad lifted his shoulder. 'So we sell now rather than later.'

'No,' I said, 'You're both still too young to retire – what would you do with yourself?' When he shrugged, I added, 'Let's not rush into this. Have you signed anything with these people yet?'

He shook his head. 'There's a document here that sets out all the terms. We were going to sign it now the wedding is done.' He handed me the document.

'This is a Heads of Agreement, Dad. It's almost the same as a contract, but it means that if you pull out of the agreement, you'll be liable for some costs.' I scanned the document. 'This amount they're offering doesn't sound enough – it barely covers the value of the gaming permits. Have you had the pub valued?'

'No, we didn't think we'd need to, and the deposit will get the bank off our backs immediately. They've already talked about evicting us – in which case we'll have no options but will have to wait to see what price they can get.' Dad leant forward, his hands on his thighs as he made his point. 'The agent says we're running out of time – he's pushing us to sign.'

My teeth gripped my top lip as I read. 'No'—I flipped to the next page and scanned the words— 'that makes no sense at all. If you're keeping to a payment arrangement and the arrears aren't increasing, they can't move to the next stage, not unless there's no other way out. Have you told the bank you're selling?' When Dad nodded, I said, 'How long have they given you to sell?'

'Well,' said Dad, 'that's the problem – we've been barely able to keep to the repayments and haven't managed to make the extra required, so they gave us three months – that means we have until the end of the month to clear the arrears or have a contract for sale.' Mum's worried gaze rested on my father. 'Otherwise they said they'd move to obtain possession.'

'When did they tell you this?'

It was very unusual for CP to give a final date that fell over a major holiday period. Normally, they'd extend it to the end of January or February to avoid potential bad publicity around Christmas. Especially for a hotel that was the centre of the community in a town like this, which had been hard hit by drought and natural disasters, not to mention the impact of the pandemic on hospitality. Plus, as far as I could work out, they were only four payments behind. This didn't make sense. Was there anyone I knew in that part of the bank I could ask? My eyes closed briefly ... It fell under Otis's domain. There was something else that was lurking around my brain.

'The dining room was almost empty on Friday

night,' I said. 'That used to be one of the busiest nights of the week for you.' When neither of them spoke, I added, 'Is there anything happening there I need to know about?'

'Things have been quiet since the hotel in Millers Creek changed hands,' said Mum. 'It was bought by a group from Sydney, and they've been offering two-for-one meals to Mannus Ridge locals to eat there.' She shrugged. 'We can't compete with that. We had to let Tilly, our head chef, go at the beginning of the pandemic when we stopped serving meals – we only did simple takeaway for all of that time – and they grabbed her. It left us with a part-time cook who has a limited range and is only staying on until we can get someone permanent. We were just beginning to get back on our feet and that was the end of it. Now,' her voice caught, 'we're just getting further and further behind. Why will people come here for a drink if they have to get in their car to go to Millers Creek for dinner? And why would they come to us when they're going to get the same old roast of the day and pay extra for it?'

'How long ago did that happen?' An unwelcome thought flitted through my brain.

'It was ...' Realisation flickered across Mum's face.

'It was just after we received the first offer.' She glanced at her watch.

'It's okay, Mum, I know you need to get ready to open. If you can get me access to the accounts and all the documentation you have, I'll see what I can find out. No promises, but if there's a way out of this that doesn't involve you needing to sell the hotel, I'll try to find it. Okay?'

Mum gave me a grateful hug.

'You said Jazz knows some of it?' I asked.

Mum shook her head and exchanged glances with Dad. 'Only when we decided to sell. Before that, we told her your father was having some routine tests that we didn't want her to worry about.'

'Well, it's obvious she did worry because that was what she used to guilt me into coming here. What sort of tests are we talking about?'

Dad waved my concern away. 'My blood pressure was up, so just the usual for my age.' His cheeks tinged with colour. 'It was easier to let Jacinta think there was something wrong with me than to explain what was really going on.'

My eyebrows raised at this. 'She thought you were going to die, Dad. She was worried – we both were.' He dropped his eyes from mine as he understood how concerned we'd been. 'What about the sale? That seems to be general knowledge?'

'I told most people that we were retiring,' Mum said simply, rising from her chair. 'Although I did mention trouble with the bank to Kerry ...'

'Which is how that story got around town.'

I forced a smile I hoped was reassuring, and they went to open up.

What if they'd spoken to me before now? Would I have taken the time to look into it, or would I have brushed them off, too busy to spare the time for my family? I was very much afraid that the answer would've been the latter – and that left me feeling selfish, small and more than a little ashamed.

WHEN MUM DROPPED in with a salad sandwich for lunch, I thanked her but continued to work as I ate, filling the bank statements and accounts with notations and the writing pad with questions.

The original projections used to substantiate the loan weren't constructed with any firm data behind them. I'd been trained to apply a sensitivity analysis to all my proposals – a best-case scenario, a worst-case scenario and something in the middle. I wouldn't have expected my parents to know about that, but I would've assumed that the professional who had brokered the loan for them would have. There was, however, no point in going back to problems with the origination process, so I concentrated my efforts on the cashflow forecasts and determined quickly that the current turnover was insufficient to pay the minimum required payments going forward, let alone the arranged amount to catch up the arrears. Plus, with interest rates increasing as well as supplier costs, the debt would cripple them unless they could reduce it, regain the customers they'd lost to Millers Creek, and attract the travellers they had done the renovations for. Their decision to continue employing staff they could no longer afford wasn't helping, but they couldn't manage the work on their own. I wasn't surprised Dad's health was suffering. The wonder was that he hadn't had a heart attack already – they must both be exhausted.

While the expense had been irresponsible considering their financial situation, I completely understood why they'd wanted to throw the weekend's party – it had been their way of saying goodbye and thank you to the community.

At three, Mum ducked her head around the door to the office. 'Do you want me to get the kids for you?'

I looked up from my work. 'Is that the time?' I groaned and buried my face in my hands, pushing against my forehead with my fingers as if that could alleviate the vague headache lurking. 'No, it's okay, I'll get them.'

I stretched my arms above my head and rolled my shoulders to ease the stiffness I hadn't noticed while I'd buried my head in figures.

'How have you gone?' Mum asked hesitantly.

'I have some ideas,' I said carefully. 'But give me another day to answer some questions I have.'

She shifted her weight from one foot to the other. 'Thank you, Lee – for all of this.'

'Don't thank me yet, Mum, besides,' I added with a grimace, 'I can't help but feel at least partly responsible – if I hadn't been so wound up in myself and my own dramas, you might've felt as though you could confide in me.'

'What's done is done, Lee, and you're here now. Now, what are you making the kids for dinner?'

'I think I can just about remember how to make spag bol.' I grinned. 'How far wrong can I go?'

THIRTEEN

Once home and fed afternoon tea – crackers with vegemite and cheese – the two youngest took off outside with a football and the dog.

'What happens now?' I asked Hayley with a conspiratorial grin.

'Well,' she mused, 'now you tell me I need to get my homework done, and I'll lie and tell you I don't have any and you'll throw your hands up in despair. And then you look in the fridge and the freezer for dinner inspiration, mutter under your breath and yell at the boys to come in for a shower. Then you start cooking and yell at them again because they haven't come in and they may as well lock the chooks in.'

The adult look on her face made me laugh out loud.

'Here's an idea then,' I suggested. 'How about you get the homework you say you haven't got and do it out here? That way, you can talk to me while I'm cooking.'

'And the boys?' she asked guilelessly.

'We can take it in turns to yell at them.'

'See, Aunty Lee, it's only day one and you've got the hang of this. All you need to master now is the packed lunch thing.'

When I picked up the tea towel and made to flick it at her, she squealed and ran off giggling.

I gathered the ingredients I'd bought in town and set them all on the kitchen counter.

'Do you know what you're doing with that?' Hayley emerged from her room with a pencil case and a workbook and sat at the kitchen table.

'It's been a while,' I said, 'but I'll have you know I used to make the best spag bol the St James family had ever seen.'

'It would have to be better than Mum's,' she said with a laugh. 'Anyway, Gran's told us how you used to win prizes at the show for your baking.'

I chuckled. 'I hope you're not expecting anything like that. I've hardly cooked a thing since I left uni. When I was in share houses, I used to do all the cooking, but since I've been living on my own ...' I lifted a shoulder. 'It's been a while. Now, let's see if I can work out how this oven works.'

'Don't you live with your boyfriend?' Hayley padded to the fridge for a glass of water and held up another glass in silent question. At my nod, she handed it to me.

'No,' I said. 'He lives in Sydney and I'm in Melbourne, so I don't see him very often.' I placed the beef mince into a colander and rinsed it with cold water to separate it into smaller pieces. 'In fact, we've broken up.' I patted the beef dry with kitchen paper and tipped it into a roasting pan.

'That's sad,' she said, pulling her knees up to hug them. 'Are you sad?'

I put the roasting tin into the oven while I pondered her question. 'I was,' I finally said. 'But I don't think I am anymore, not really. My heart will live to fight another day.' I flashed her a quick smile and began chopping vegetables.

'Cody doesn't like celery,' Hayley pointed out.

'Well, it's a good thing he won't know it's in there then,' I said, cutting it as fine as I could. 'Every spag bol needs onion, celery and carrot.'

'Not Mum's. Mum's just has meat, onion and tomato soup.'

'Okay, well, this *definitely* isn't your Mum's spag

bol then.' I turned to her and rolled my eyes. I held up some mushrooms. 'Do you think I'll get away with these?'

She thought for a second. 'Let's give it a go.'

'Aunty Lee ...' Hayley began hesitantly after a few minutes when the only noise was the rhythmic sound of the knife hitting the chopping board.

'Yeeeees.' I added diced carrots to the celery and started chopping an onion.

'Did you and Uncle Angus really used to be together?'

I took a breath and flashed her a quick smile. 'Yes, we did. Why do you ask?'

She shrugged.

'You've heard things, I suppose.' When she nodded, I gave my attention back to the onions. 'Yes, we were together, but it didn't work out.' I wiped my eyes. 'Don't worry, it's just onions ...'

She giggled, then her face turned serious. 'I thought I'd ask because I hear things, but no one wants to talk about it.'

'That's okay, it was a long time ago, and a lot has changed since then.' I tipped the onions in with the other veg and checked on the meat, breaking up some of the little clumps with a fork.

'Why are you doing that?' she asked. 'Cooking the meat in the oven?'

I paused. 'You know, I can't remember? Roasting it intensifies the flavour, and I think I read something years ago about how doing it this way helps it absorb the sauce better.'

She seemed to accept that answer and said nothing more as I concentrated on chopping some bacon.

'To save me rummaging through everything, where will I find a big frypan?'

Hayley uncurled herself and retrieved a battered sauté pan from one of the cupboards. 'Mum uses this one.'

'So will I then.' I placed it over medium heat, added some oil and began frying the bacon.

'Did you love Uncle Angus?' Hayley asked quietly, almost as if she were afraid I'd snap and tell her to mind her own business.

'Yes, I did. Very much. It's why it hurt so much to leave,' I said honestly. 'It's okay, you know'—I turned to face her briefly— 'you can talk to me about these things. I remember wanting to know things when I was your age, and while it seemed everyone was talking, no one was saying anything to me.'

Her face lit up. 'That's exactly how I feel!'

'Well, then,' I said, my attention back on the pan

and the vegetables I was about to toss into it. 'Ask away.'

'Okay ... how did you know you were in love?'

'With Angus?' I pulled the roasted mince from the oven and drained off the fat. 'I fell in love with your uncle when I was about your age – although, of course, it was just a crush then.' I tipped the meat into the pan and poured in a tin of crushed tomatoes, stock, and the mushrooms. 'He was two years ahead of me at school, and I thought he was the hottest boy that ever walked the earth – and I suspect he knew it too. I was always here because of Jenny and used to see him a lot – although I was best friends with Jenny before I had a crush on her brother. I could never tell anyone, though – Jenny and Mark would've teased me too much.' The memory made me chuckle. Young love, first love, the fantasies I'd woven around it had all been so innocent. I tasted the meat sauce and added some red wine vinegar and oregano. 'We didn't start dating until after I finished school, though, and then I really fell in love with him.'

'But how did you know?'

I pursed my lips and ceased stirring the sauce. 'People say that when you know, you'll know – and that's true. It's not just about thinking about the other person all the time; it's more than that.' I reduced the heat to a simmer and popped the lid on the sauce. 'You would've heard that I left before we could get married?' Hayley nodded. 'Well, I know people would say I did that because I didn't love him. The truth is, I did that *because* I loved him. Somehow, I knew we were too young, and it wouldn't have worked. I would've blamed him for what I didn't get to do, and he would've known that.' I filled my water glass up from the tap and drank most of it in one big gulp. 'That probably makes no sense at all.'

'Not really,' she said, shaking her head. 'Is that why Aunty Jenny doesn't talk to you anymore? Because you left Uncle Angus?'

I nodded. 'Yes, but also because when I left Angus, I also left her – our friendship. Anyway'—I forced a wide smile— 'it's all worked out for the best, and Angus is now with Georgia.'

'She's such a cow,' muttered Hayley, pouting. 'And don't try telling me I shouldn't say things like that.'

I smiled at how quickly one could go from worldly teenager to sulky child at this age. 'I'd never tell you that,' I said with a cheeky grin. 'Because I happen to think so too – but that's our little secret.'

She made a gesture as if she was locking her lips shut with a key. 'It's in the vault, Aunty Lee.'

'Excellent. Now, while this sauce is doing its thing,

I'm going to do the chook thing and yell for your brothers, so if you want a shower, now would be the time to do it.'

'Jackson, Cody,' I called when I stepped onto the verandah. 'Shower time.'

'In a minute,' Jackson yelled back.

'Now!'

As the boys ran towards the house, Bella streaked ahead of them, coming to trot beside me as I scattered some kitchen scraps for the chooks, checked their water, collected more eggs, and did a quick count to make sure all were present and accounted for before locking them in for the night.

As I walked back to the house, admiring the pinks and oranges of the sunset behind the vines in the adjacent field, Red tore up the path and jumped all over me. I held the basket of eggs above my head with one hand and used the other to pat the dog.

'Red!' Angus's voice drifted across from the big house, the dog immediately responding. I lifted a hand in greeting, and after a brief pause, he returned the gesture before turning to go inside.

AFTER THE KIDS were in bed following a dinner where no one complained about hidden vegetables, lunches made for the following day and the kitchen tidied, I poured a glass of wine (my first and only for the day) and wandered out to sit on the old rocking chair on the verandah.

It was just after nine, so not long dark, but there were already some stars out and I raised my glass in a silent toast and took my first sip of the fruity wine, feeling my body and mind relax. Aaaah. How on earth did people hold down jobs and manage a family? I was exhausted!

What I couldn't deny, though, was just how much I'd enjoyed it all – from chatting this afternoon with Hayley to the good-natured bickering of the boys and their pleasure at the special 'let's not tell Mum' treat of ice cream with Milo, to the contented clucking of the chooks as they pecked around for the scraps I'd thrown them, their feathers ruffling in the slight breeze. It had been a nice day.

I'd even enjoyed going through the numbers at the hotel earlier, getting a handle on where things had gone wrong and what needed to be done to fix it. There was a route through this; I just needed to find it. The way I figured it, the immediate issue was the repayment of arrears – that would keep the bank off their back and buy some time. Unless the debt itself was reduced or turnover increased, though, it was only a matter of time before they were back in the same position. While I had a few ideas floating around as to how they could reduce some costs and increase income, it wasn't going to be easy and would depend on several variables falling on the right side of the ledger. Debt reduction had to be their key goal, but how to do that?

Once we cleared the arrears and looked at the strategy, if my parents then decided they wanted to sell, they could do so on their terms and in their timeframe – and would have the space to get a proper valuation done of the pub. The deal that was presently on the table felt too low and rushed. It was also too convenient. Who were these buyers and how did they just happen upon the hotel at Mannus Ridge? More to the point, how did they know to approach just as the bank was issuing a demand for payment? Had someone within CP breached privacy? Surely not.

As for the hotel at Millers Creek, was there any relationship between the new owners and the company seeking to purchase the Royal? And, to take that one step further, why had the previous owners sold up in the first place?

Tomorrow I'd head into town to buy a few clothes,

then drive to Millers Creek and see what I could find out. It couldn't hurt.

With that decided, I finished my glass of wine. As I stood to go inside, a shadow moved on the verandah of the homestead, the door opened, and the light inside turned off. Had he known I was sitting out here? No matter. I went back inside, rinsed out my wine glass, switched off the lights and collapsed into bed.

FOURTEEN

This morning when I set off with Bella for my run, Red joined us too, the two dogs keeping me company as I pounded the dirt track that ran along the perimeter of the vineyard. As I jogged back to the cottage, Red headed up to the homestead where Angus was on the verandah, leaning casually against one of the wooden posts, a mug in his hand. I waved tentatively, and he seemed to hesitate before walking down the stairs and across to where I stood puffing and sweaty.

'Morning,' he said gruffly. 'This running is a thing with you then?'

'Not really.' I lifted my heel towards my bum and held it there with my hand to stretch my quad. 'I'm used to getting up early and going to the gym, and I can't do that here, so ...' I lifted the other leg. 'It's a nice change to be exercising outside, though.'

'Not so nice in winter,' he said, a quirk to his mouth.

'No, it wouldn't be.'

'Not that you're likely to be here by then ...' He sipped from his mug, his gaze disconcerting, the silence making me feel awkward.

'How ...'

'What ...'

We spoke at the same time. 'You first,' I offered.

'I was just wondering how you're going with the kids. If you need any help with them ...' As he made his offer, he turned and tossed the last of his coffee onto the ground. 'I mean ... I'm just there, you know.'

'So far, so good,' I said. 'Although I had a failure of the lunch kind yesterday – but I think they were happier with the money for a lunch order than they would've been with a vegemite and cheese sandwich.' He relaxed enough to smile at that. 'They're great kids – exhausting, though! I don't know how Jazz does it.'

'I guess it's whatever you're used to.' Another short silence. 'Did you have that talk with your parents?'

I nodded shortly. 'Yeah.'

'So, what now? Will you return to the city when Jazz and Mark are back?'

Again, he didn't look at me as he asked, so I couldn't tell whether he hoped I'd go back or hoped I'd stay around. It shouldn't have mattered either way, but it did.

'I think I'll stay around for a bit – at least until I can sort this out for Mum and Dad.'

'Do you think it can be fixed?'

'Yeah, I do. Something's not quite right, which has me thinking ...' Bella nuzzled against my leg, and I reached down and scratched behind her ears. 'Let's just say I have a few questions.' I paused and rested my foot on the rim of a plant pot to stretch my hamstring, enough time to debate how much I wanted to share. 'Do you know anything about the hotel at Millers Creek?'

His head tipped to one side at my change of subject. 'Which one? The Commercial?' I nodded. 'Only that it changed hands about six months back and that they're offering good meal deals for Mannus Ridge residents – two for one, I think.'

'Have you been?'

'No. Georgia wants to go over there and try it, but it seems disloyal to your parents somehow ...' His voice trailed off and his eyes narrowed. 'You think that's tied in with the downturn at the Royal?'

'I do. Have you heard whether the previous owners were in financial trouble?'

'After the last few years, isn't everyone?' When I lifted a shoulder in acknowledgement, he added, 'But yeah, I had heard something. Jenny might know – she used to work in the salon over there and still knows a few people. It could be worth talking to her.'

I lowered my eyes. 'I'm the last person she wants to speak to.' A familiar pain pierced my heart. When would that stop hurting?

'Maybe, but if she knows you're serious about staying around to help?' I didn't attempt to hide the hope on my face. 'I'll call her.'

'Thanks.' I glanced at my watch. 'Oh, look at the time. I better keep moving or we'll all be late. There are chooks and breakfasts to be taken care of and ...' I reached out and grazed his arm. 'Thanks, Angus.'

He nodded once in acknowledgement, whistled for Red and headed back to the big house. For a few seconds, I seemed unable to move or shift my attention from his retreating figure but gave myself a little shake.

WITH THE KIDS dropped off and after a quick drop-in at the hotel to see my parents, next on my list that morning was some more appropriate clothes, yet the only boutique in town was run by Kerry Tyson. While I was all for supporting local businesses, the idea of supporting this particular business set my teeth on edge. Yet, it had to be done, so I took a deep breath and pushed open the door.

'Lee St James! I would've thought our humble little shop was below your designer tastes.'

Great, Georgia was on the counter; Mum had warned me that Georgia, the town beautician, sometimes manned the shop when her salon was closed. I'd picked the wrong day to go shopping.

'What was it you were wearing the other night? Ted Baker? From Ted Baker to Tysons is quite the comedown.'

'I'm happy to take my money to Millers Creek if that would suit you better,' I said, holding onto my temper with the most tenuous of grips. 'I thought, though, it was all about locals supporting locals these days. I didn't realise Tysons was doing so well that you could afford to turn people away.'

'Well,' she drawled, 'not every business in town is struggling, and besides, you're hardly local, are you?'

'No problems.' I casually turned to leave, hand resting on the door handle. 'I'll see you around, Georgia.'

'Not if I can help it,' she said, her lips curled into a snarl. 'It's not like you'll be around for long.'

I smiled thinly. 'It's been a while since I last had a proper break, so I'm thinking of staying around for a bit.'

'People haven't forgotten what you did, you know.'

'Oh, I don't know,' I said, more breezily than I felt. Unable to resist stirring her up, I added, 'Everyone has been very welcoming, and Angus didn't seem to mind when I spoke to him about it early this morning.' Somehow, I hid my grin as the barb hit home.

As I pulled the door open, Kerry Tyson was on her way in. 'Lee! How lovely to see you,' she trilled. 'Your mother said you might call in – that you needed quite a few things to tide you over. So nice of you to consider supporting a local business when we know you usually favour more high-end brands.' Then, noting my empty hands, her smile slipped. 'Didn't we have anything to suit?'

'I'm not sure, Mrs Tyson,' I said.

'Oh, Kerry, please ...'

'Okay, Kerry. I didn't get a chance to look around; before I could, Georgia assured me you'd have nothing here to my taste, and as I was heading over to Millers Creek, I thought I might try there instead.' I suppressed a smile. 'Bye.'

Kerry struggled to hold her smile in place while shooting daggers at her daughter. 'Well, maybe we might see you in here another day,' she said. 'Let me know when you're coming by and I'll be sure to serve you personally.'

As I left, Kerry scolded Georgia. 'Just because you don't like the woman is no reason to turn away good custom ...'

My next stop was Jenny's nursery in what used to be the old railway station house. On a spur line to the main Sydney-Melbourne route, the last train to stop at Mannus Ridge was back in the seventies, and the stone station house had sat vacant ever since. Jenny had, so Jazz had told me, taken it over a few years ago and transformed the old platform into a home for plants and the station house into a florist with a small café attached.

When I arrived, Jenny, dressed in a knee-length denim skirt and t-shirt, was loading bunches of Australian native flowers into the buckets at the entrance. 'Angus said you might drop by,' she said before disappearing back inside for more bunches.

'Can I help?' I asked.

'Be my guest,' she said briskly.

Between the two of us, we had the buckets all filled quickly.

Wiping my hands against the bum of my navy capris, I said, 'Did he tell you why I wanted to see you?'

She nodded. 'He seems to think you'll stay around long enough to see it through – is he right?' With her hands on her hips, she added, 'You've disappointed people here before, so don't start something you're not prepared to finish.'

From anyone else, her words would've made me bristle, but from her, it was understandable. I swallowed my instinct to bite back with 'is that a warning?' and instead said, 'I know ... and I won't.'

Her stare was long and hard, but I held it until she dropped her eyes first. 'If you say so,' she said, but despite the disbelief in her words, her jaw relaxed, and her hands dropped from her hips. 'You better come in for a coffee and tell me what you're thinking.'

Where I'd chosen my words carefully with Angus this morning, I knew that nothing less than the complete story would be enough for Jenny – so as she made coffee, I filled her in on the situation and my suspicions.

Coffees made, she led the way to one of the wrought iron round tables at the rear of the house.

'I remember how drab this place was,' I said, gazing around at the whitewashed walls filled with, the labels told me, paintings by local artists. 'But you've really transformed it.'

A long timber shelf made from repurposed railway sleepers held a selection of jams, preserves, mustards and sauces, while another was home to a selection of pottery and ceramics. An oak bookcase stood in another corner, filled with a selection of both practical and decorative garden and landscaping books and country-style cookbooks for sale.

'Thanks.' I didn't think she was going to say more but after taking a sip of her coffee added, 'Remember when we used to come up here on our bikes? This part was always boarded closed, but we'd still ride up the ramps and pretend we were catching the train somewhere that sounded so glamourous – places like Paris and London ...'

I smiled as my mind took me back. As Jazz grew older, she sometimes tagged along, but it was always Jenny and me. 'I remember.'

'You've probably been there now,' she said. 'For real, I mean.'

I nodded but didn't elaborate.

'What are you hoping to get from all of this, Lee?' There was a hardness in her tone, which I was beginning to realise, was a protection for her and a warning for me not to get close enough to hurt her again.

Although if she thought I could hurt her again, some-where under that shell, she must still care.

'Initially to stop the sale of the Royal,' I said. 'It's not just my parent's livelihood, but also their home, and I can't imagine them without it.'

'But what if your parents really have had enough and want to sell? It's not like you or Jazz are inclined to take it over.' She cradled her mug in both hands and blew softly across the top.

My shoulders slumped as I acknowledged the truth of her words. 'True, but I don't want them to sell it like this – under pressure from the bank, without having the time to decide if it's what they really want. If they do decide to sell, I'll support that – of course I will – but we'll get a proper valuation done and they can choose who they want to sell it to. After all these years and all their work, it's not fair to watch them be pushed or bullied out. Besides, it's important for this town that it goes to someone who will be part of the community like they have been – not some consortium from Sydney or wherever that wants another country pub to add to their portfolio.'

She leant forward, her eyes narrowed. 'Hang on, this bank that's hassling them – isn't it the same bank you work for? How does that sit with you?'

I took a breath and decided to trust her; honesty

after all these years had to be the best policy. 'I no longer work for them – which is why I can stay as long as I need.'

'So that's the only reason you're back then?' She laughed scornfully and sat back in her chair.

'It was the reason I came back.' My eyes held hers again. 'But it's not the reason I'm staying.'

'Really?' Everything about the stiffness of her posture to the tone of her voice told me she didn't believe me, but there was something in her eyes that said she desperately wanted to.

'Really. I'm staying because I should never have left it as long as I did to come back, and if I'd stopped running for half a second, I might've realised my parents were in trouble and been able to help before things got out of hand. I'm staying because I want to try and make up for that even though I know that I can't, not really, but there's a possibility I can still make things *right*. I'm staying because I've realised how much I've missed my family – *really* missed them and how great Jazz's kids are and how I want to get to know them better. And I'm staying because I'd forgotten what I loved about Mannus Ridge and how good it feels to be back – even though I resisted coming back for so long for reasons I see now were all in my head. And I'm staying because I missed you and desperately want to tell you how sorry I am – not just for what happened with Angus and me, but how leaving him and leaving here cost me my best friend in the world, too.'

By the time I finished my little speech, my throat was thick and my eyes full. I dabbed at them with the back of my hand and rummaged in my handbag for a tissue.

When I looked up again, Jenny's eyes were suspiciously bright, and she pressed the knuckle of her middle finger to her nose and sniffed. 'I missed you too.' She blinked a few times. 'If we're being really honest, I think I was angrier on my own behalf than Angus's when you left; I hated you for a long time because of that. It's only in the last few years that I've realised you probably did the right thing for both your sakes – and I know that while he'd never admit it, I think Angus regrets not giving you the room you needed back then. If he had, you might still be together now.'

My smile was grateful. 'Who knows? We were both so young and sure we knew what was right ...'

'Why did you stay away so long?' When I didn't reply immediately, she exhaled. 'It was because of us, wasn't it? Angus and me and what I said?'

My shoulders slumped and I nodded. 'Partly. I

knew I'd hurt you and you hated me, and I couldn't face that – or the fact that I'd disappointed so many people.' I let out a rueful puff of air. 'I told myself I wasn't going to come home until I could show everyone how far I'd come – as if that would make it worth all the hurt. But look at me now; I'm back and out of work and in the lowest place I've been since I left. It's so ironic how things work out.' I chuckled mirthlessly. 'But I'm glad they did; I needed a reason to come home.' I tilted my head to the side, my smile tentative. 'Do you think we can ever be friends again?'

Her nod was equally tentative. 'Yeah, I reckon. What I can't ever forgive you for, though'—the smile fell from my face— 'is leaving that bitch Georgia Tyson to get her claws stuck into Angus.'

I couldn't help the laughter that burst from me. 'She's not that bad ...' I attempted to keep a straight face as I told the lie.

'Not that bad? She's worse than that! What he sees in her is beyond me. Actually, that's a lie too – I know exactly what he sees in her. To be honest, though, I think he just got tired of evading her and gave in. Hopefully, he'll come to his senses soon.' The look she gave me was part speculative and part crafty, as if an idea she'd previously dismissed was suddenly possible.

'Don't,' I warned.

'Why not? I know you've got a boyfriend in the city, but you can't tell me you've ever completely gotten over Angus ...'

I made myself laugh again to show her how ridiculous the idea was. 'That's a no to the boyfriend in the city – his wife found out about us, and he broke up with me the same day my job broke up with me.'

'A wife?'

'It's a long story – and one for a glass or three of wine – but I didn't know there was a wife when we began dating.'

'Hey,' she said, her palms facing me. 'No judgement, but I notice you didn't answer my question about getting over my brother.'

My face was flaming hot. 'I don't think I'll ever be over Angus, but he'd never trust me again – and I don't blame him for that. Plus, no matter what happens now with the hotel, I'll have to return to the city at some point.'

'Do you, though?'

I nodded. 'I mightn't have a job at the moment, but the city is where my work will be, when I find some. This time, though, I'll be back more regularly – and I'll stay in touch.'

Jenny's sly smile was back, and it reminded me of how we used to tease each other about boys when we were teenagers. 'If we're trading secrets, I don't think he's ever properly gotten over you either.'

'Well,' I said, pressing my cool hands on my still-hot cheeks, 'I'm heading over to Millers Creek, and if I want to be back before school breaks up, I'd better get moving.'

'No worries. I'll see what I can find out about the sale of the Commercial and if you need help with the kids this week – for pick-ups or whatever – give me a bell.'

We swapped numbers, and before climbing back into my car, I hugged her quickly. More importantly, she hugged me back.

FIFTEEN

All three kids had swimming lessons after school, so by the time I got them home, the younger two were fractious and wrangling them was more of a challenge than it had been yesterday.

Tonight, when I took my wine out onto the verandah and saw the shadow moving in the almost dark of the homestead, I knew that while last night he might've been prepared to sit in the dark and watch me, this time Angus was letting me know he was there.

While he mightn't be able to see me completely, I figured he'd be able to see the movement, so before I could think twice, I waved and beckoned him over. At first, I thought he was going to ignore me, but when he stood, it was clear he was coming over. Too late I remembered that after I'd showered, I'd changed into the singlet top and shorts I'd bought today in Millers Creek. Whatever – it was late, it was hot, and he probably didn't care.

'Hey,' he said. He'd changed after the workday and was dressed in football shorts (that fitted closely enough that my hormones jumped up and paid attention) and a black AC/DC band t-shirt that had seen better days.

'Hey yourself. Would you like a glass?' I held up the bottle of red I'd been drinking.

'Thanks – especially since it's one of ours.' His smile was cheeky and sent a rush of warmth through my body.

'Is it?' I looked more closely at the label. 'Why didn't I know that?'

'I have no idea,' he said wryly.

'The Talbot Pinot Noir ...' I looked up at him. 'That should've given it away; Dad told me you'd bought their business.' A germ of an idea was forming in my mind. 'It's good, though.'

'I'm glad you think so. We're hoping to give Central Otago pinots a run for their money.' As I moved to stand and get him a glass, his hand grazed my arm. 'Don't get up; I know where the glasses are.'

While he was gone, I settled back in the chair, drawing my legs up to sit cross-legged. Pouring himself a glass, he sat in the chair beside me. We clinked glasses and sipped. In the quiet of post dusk, it was the most comfortable we'd been in each other's company since I'd returned; at the same time, I was acutely aware of his nearness, the heat carrying the faint scent of freshly showered Angus and gently teasing me with it.

'How did you go today?' He finally broke the silence.

'Good – although I started the day with a run-in with your girlfriend.' I smirked as I recalled the scene and the scolding she would've received from her mother for letting good business walk out the door.

'I heard.' His voice sounded like he was smiling, and a quick sideways glance confirmed it.

'I thought you might have.' I shrugged to let him know I didn't care what Georgia had said about me. 'I might possibly have encouraged her – just a little,' I held my thumb and forefinger close together to show just how little. 'Kerry was not pleased when I left without buying anything, though; I had to leave before I laughed out loud. And yes, I know that makes me sound super bitchy, but I don't care. I won't, however, be going to Georgia's salon for a leg wax any time soon.'

His chuckle rumbled around me. 'I reckon you can hold your own these days where Georgia is concerned.'

'Yeah, I reckon I can. Anyway, I went into Millers Creek and got some of what I needed – I'll go back and see Kerry another day when her bitch of a daughter isn't there.' I sent him a cheeky grin. 'Sorry.'

He returned it. 'No, you're not.'

'You're right; I'm not. I used my time in the fitting rooms at the boutique in Millers Creek wisely, though – I discovered the new owner of the Commercial Hotel is a company named Emano Holdings– and that just happens to be the same company who's looking to purchase the Royal from Mum and Dad.' I paused, my nail tapping against the stem of my wine glass. 'I haven't yet worked out who's behind it, so I'll do a company search over the next few days, but there's definitely something not quite kosher going on.'

'What are you going to do about it?'

'The first thing I need to do is take the pressure off my parents so they can decline the offer of sale without the bank stepping in to enforce it – while there are arrears outstanding that aren't reducing, the bank can force them to sell, even if they don't have possession. I've worked in banking long enough to know that enforcement is the last way out, so clearing the arrears is the only way to buy themselves time.'

'What do you mean by way out?' He was leaning forward in his chair, listening intently.

'When it comes to credit, an ability to repay is always the first way out; when you fall behind, it's about arrangements that will catch things up so you can continue to repay as normal or refinancing to reduce the payments. If that's not possible, the bank would prefer that the customer makes the decision to sell to repay the debt – and they can and will put enough pressure on the customer to "encourage" that decision – and the last way out is when the bank needs to enforce that themselves. It really is the last option, though – and there's always the possibility of adverse publicity, so it isn't something they do lightly.'

'But if your parents could clear the arrears, wouldn't they have already done that?'

I hesitated before answering. I'd spent most of the drive home going through the options, and while this would eat up a good chunk of my savings, it was the only viable one I'd come up with. 'No, they can't, but I can,' I said quietly.

'How much is it?'

I told him, and he gave a low whistle. 'Do you have that sort of savings?' There was surprise in his voice. 'Jenny said you'd lost your job; won't you need that money?'

I wasn't surprised Jenny had confided in him, yet instinctively I knew she wouldn't spread that knowledge any further. Despite what had happened between us, I'd always been able to trust her – and Angus with my secrets.

'Yes, but they were generous when I left.'

'Isn't that supposed to tide you over until you can get another job?'

'Yes, it just means I have less time up my sleeve before I have to do that.' I turned to face him. 'I've thought it through and can't see another way out of this, Angus. Besides, there's a strange sort of symmetry in me using CP keep-quiet money for this purpose.'

'Keep-quiet money? What would they give you that for?' He reached over and topped our glasses up.

'Thanks.' I took a sip and thought about giving him a glib half response before deciding against it. 'I stuffed up at work so deserved to lose my job, but the man I've been seeing is an executive running for the top job.' I lowered my eyes to my glass. 'A married executive.'

'I see. And you reckon they were worried you'd say it was harassment.' He sounded flat and judgey.

'Something like that.' I placed my wineglass on the little table and straightened my legs; out of the side of my eye, I saw his gaze swing in their direction, and the knowledge sent a thrill through me. 'The thing is, I didn't know he was married at first, but that doesn't excuse me, so go ahead and judge away.'

'Did I say I was judging you?' He raised his eyebrows as he waited for a response.

'No,' I finally said, 'but I wouldn't blame you if you did.'

'It's none of my business,' he said, and inwardly I flinched. 'In any case, it sounds as though you've spent long enough judging yourself.'

'Maybe.'

Another silence. 'If you pay out the arrears, does that mean you'll go back to the city after that? You said this morning that you would once they were sorted.'

'Are you that keen to get rid of me?'

In the filtered light coming through from the screen door his cheeks turned a delightful shade of pink, and he dropped his eyes. 'No, I'm getting used to the idea of you being around again – although Georgia can't wait to see the back of you.' He added the last with a grin.

'Well, she'll be disappointed because paying the arrears off is just the first step – after that, I need to work out how they can keep up with their payments or we'll be right back where we are now within a few months. So that means I'll be around until everything is sorted out properly.' I searched his face for a reaction, but he remained impassive. 'That might be until we work out how to restructure the debt or restructure the way the pub works, or it could be until they sell the pub to someone of their choosing.'

As I spoke, I thought I saw the beginnings of a smile play around his mouth, but it was gone as quickly as it had appeared.

'In that case, I'll see you around,' he said, drained his glass and stood to go, towering over me, taking up all the room and all my breath. 'You're doing a good thing, Lee.' He said it so gently it was like a whisper, and my heart rose into my throat.

Unable to answer, I nodded. He smiled briefly, held his hand up in a wave and walked down the stairs and across the grass to the homestead. I watched the torch on his phone flickering along the path until he was on his verandah and opening the door to his house. He stood in the doorway, silhouetted against the light from inside and held his hand up again before disappearing.

WHILE RED JOINED Bella and me as we pounded down the lane again this morning, I'd been slightly disappointed when Angus didn't appear after we'd finished.

After I let the chooks out, I leant against the

wooden support of the coop for a few minutes and watched them clucking and scratching contentedly, the rooster calling to his girls each time he found something tasty or interesting. If someone had told me a month ago that I'd be taking pleasure from something as simple as this, I would've laughed at them.

If I'd been in the city now, I'd already be on my second or third coffee for the morning, my stomach churning with anxiety about the day to come. This early in December we'd be on the rundown to Christmas with the end-of-quarter deadlines fast approaching and adding to the pressure. The office Christmas party would've been held last weekend, and I would've suffered through that wishing that Otis had attended and knowing that none of my colleagues wanted me there. I would've left at the earliest opportunity, leaving them all to get on with the frivolity they would still be talking and laughing about now – frivolity I would have had no part of.

Would I have done anything differently if I'd had my time over again? It was pointless to wonder.

I hadn't always been a bitch to work for or with – until I went to CP. While I'd worked hard and been single-minded in my ambition, I hadn't been in a situation where I'd needed to choose between that ambition and my integrity. I'd been good at what I did and had gotten on well with my colleagues. Rather than being promoted internally, I'd moved through the ranks by changing companies every few years, and in doing so, hadn't upset anyone I worked with.

One of the red hens pecked around my feet, and I bent to pick her up. She flapped a little at first but soon settled into my arms as I absent-mindedly stroked her soft feathers, the light turning them into a thousand shades of autumn.

In hindsight, it hadn't been CP that changed me, but Otis. Otis taught me about managing up while keeping an eye on who was coming up behind me. It was Otis who'd promoted me out of my analyst role into an HR position completely out of my skill set and, from that, my most recent role. From discomfort came insecurity, and from that, paranoia that eventually someone would find me out, find us out, and it would all be gone.

I inhaled deeply, allowing the early warmth of the sun to run through my body, the smell of the morning dew and the silky softness of the hen's feathers calming me. I hadn't realised how much stress I'd been under – to perform at work, to keep Otis happy – until it was gone. While I'd been beating myself up for not being as perfect as I knew I should be, I'd also been punishing my body with caffeine and alcohol, excessive exercise, and poor nutrition. Yet in a few short days, everything had changed.

I still exercised, but it felt more like a reward than a chore; I'd cut down my coffee and alcohol without thinking about it, and I was eating better – three meals a day, mostly. In my old life, I avoided breakfast and lunch and would never have even looked at pasta – let alone eat it two nights in a row. Last night's pumpkin macaroni cheese had gone down as well with the kids (no one complained about the pumpkin) as Monday's spag bol had. And I was already feeling better for it.

While the kids and I were settling into a routine of sorts, I was resisting my urge to obsess over my to-do list and was enjoying having a routine and the knowledge that it was flexible and, in most cases, the world wouldn't end if something wasn't done. The challenge would be translating that to my new work life when I finally returned to the city and started a new job. I didn't, however, need to think about that now.

Mostly, though, it was the company I was enjoying. Back in Melbourne, I spent the day with people I knew actively disliked me and most evenings on my own. While I usually worked weekends, occasionally I'd catch up with Benji and Brendan, and if Otis was in town, my time would be his. Other than that, I hadn't made friends there. I even spent my birthday back in

October alone; Otis had been planning to be in town, but had, at the last minute, cancelled. I could've phoned Benji but had been too embarrassed. I'd been lonely but hadn't wanted to admit it.

Here, though, it was different. I'd expected to be treated as a pariah or, at the very least, with suspicion. Instead, I'd been generously welcomed by most. So much so that I already knew it would be a wrench to leave – when that time came, as it would. This time it would, however, be different.

Placing the hen back on the ground, and with one last glance towards the homestead, I headed back into the cottage, calling as I entered the door, 'If you're not up yet, you should be!'

SIXTEEN

'How are you coping with the cooking?' Mum asked as she folded the washing.

'Better than I expected,' I admitted. 'It's coming back to me, but I'm going back through what I used to cook for Jazz and me. We've had pasta two nights in a row, and tonight I'll do salmon patties, but after that, I'm running out of ideas. And yes,' I added with a laugh, 'It's only been two nights.'

'And they're behaving themselves?'

'Mostly – Jackson's feeling comfortable enough now to try the occasional backchat, though. You know what he said this morning when I asked if he'd done his reading homework?' I chuckled at the memory of the exchange. 'With a completely deadpan face, he said, "I would have, Aunty Lee, but it would've taken me over an hour and that wouldn't have been a good use of my time." I know I'm not supposed to encourage him, but I couldn't help but laugh. And, as you know, where Jackson goes, Cody follows.'

Mum paused, a pile of folded tea towels in her arms, a reflective smile on her face. 'I do know – it reminds me a lot of you and Jazz when you were growing up. And what of Hayley? How are you two getting on?'

'She's just gorgeous – she's good company and has been chatting while I cook each night and helping me with the boys too.'

'It will be good for her to have you here,' said Mum. 'Jazz doesn't have time to give her the one-on-one attention she needs from time to time, and Jenny is busy with the shop and her kids. Even when you go back, it will be good for her to call you and talk if she needs to.'

'Or even spend holidays with me.' It was something I'd been thinking about the previous evening but wouldn't mention to Hayley until after I'd spoken to Jazz.

'I think she'd like that,' said Mum softly.

'Do you want a cuppa while we wait for Dad?' I asked, feeling suddenly emotional again.

'Yes, please. Pop the kettle on while I put these away.'

She was soon back, and when she went to make the coffee, I waved her away. 'You sit for a change and let me do it.'

'Kerry told me you called by yesterday ...' she began. 'And even though I'm guessing that skirt and top or those sandals didn't come out of your suitcase, they didn't come from Tysons either.'

'Aaaah, yes ...' I handed her a mug of coffee. 'I'm afraid I let Georgia get under my skin. I bought these at Millers Creek.' I was wearing a printed cotton skirt that sat just above the knees, a bright pink tee and tan sandals. 'It's more colour than I'd usually wear, but ...'

'It looks good on you – you always used to wear such a lot of colour ...' She didn't need to finish her sentence. My suitcase had been full of neutral clothes – just as my apartment had been completely neutral. After taking a sip of her coffee, she added, 'I know Georgia can be difficult, but it would be nice if you need anything else that you give Kerry another chance.'

'As long as she doesn't go on and on again about how happy she is to see Georgia and Angus together and whether or not there'll be wedding bells soon.' I rolled my eyes.

'Ainsley ...' warned Mum, and I shrugged to let her

know I accepted her censure. 'Besides,' she continued, 'you made your choice in that regard a long time ago, and it's all water under the bridge.' She narrowed her eyes at me across the top of her mug. 'Isn't it?'

'Yes, of course,' I blurted. 'That doesn't mean I have to be happy about him being with *her*.' I sounded like a sullen, jealous teenager – well, I was one of those things. 'I'll never forgive her for how she and her friends broke us up the first time.'

'They didn't do anything that wasn't ripe to be done,' said Mum enigmatically.

I sighed, pursed my lips, and decided to leave the subject alone.

Mum, however, obviously wasn't done with it. 'Have you seen anything of him since you've been at Jazz's?'

'Who? Angus?' When Mum raised her eyes to the ceiling in silent exasperation, I relented. 'Yes, a bit. Actually ... he came over for a quick drink last night. I hadn't realised that Talbots Wines was his – although, given I knew he bought their property, I should've made the connection. I wonder if he has time to even breathe, what with the farm and the winery.'

Not to be distracted, Mum picked up only the first part of my reply. 'So, you two are friendly again?'

'Not yet, but we're getting there.' As a speculative

gleam came into her eye, I said, 'And not like that either, so don't go thinking it.'

'Not like what?' Dad came into the room, automatically flicking the kettle on.

'Lee was just saying how she's been seeing a bit of Angus over the last couple of days,' Mum said innocently.

'And I was just saying that it's not like she's thinking,' I cut in.

'How was I thinking, Lee?'

I shook my head. 'To change the subject'—I sent a mock glare to Mum, who smiled benignly— 'I discovered yesterday that the same company who wants to buy the Royal bought the Commercial in Millers Creek.'

'Go on,' said Dad, stirring a teaspoon of sugar into his mug.

'I'm not sure who's behind it yet or under what circumstances the Commercial was sold, but I'll send an email this morning to the broker who's been negotiating the deal for the hotel and let him know you won't be selling the Royal to the company he represents. If they want it badly enough, they'll come back with a better offer, but you don't have to sell to them if you don't want to – at least not until you know what sort of hotel they intend to run.'

'But what about the bank?' said Dad, sounding puzzled. 'We have to clear the arrears or have a signed sale contract by the end of the month.'

I took a deep breath. 'I know you're not going to like this,' I said, 'but it's too late; I've already done it – I've transferred enough money to clear your arrears and cover this month's payment.'

They seemed struck mute at this. Mum was the first to recover. 'We can't ask you to do this, Lee. Your savings are your savings – you'll need that money for a rental bond or a deposit or whatever it is you're going to do when you go back.'

'You *didn't* ask me to do it, and I still have some money left from my payout, but what better use of my money than to make sure you guys are okay?'

His eyes bright, Dad seemed overcome by emotion and struggling for words. 'Lee love,' he finally managed, 'you didn't have to do this; when you said you'd look into it, we didn't expect—'

I laid a calming hand on his arm. 'I know you didn't, Dad. I'm doing it because I want to and for no other reason, okay? There's no catch. I'm not going to tell you how to run your business, and if you want to sell, you still can. I just want to ensure that whatever you decide, it's your decision and you're not rushed into it. That's all.'

Dad nodded slowly. 'Thank you, Lee; your mother and I truly appreciate the gesture. Does that mean you'll be going back to Melbourne now?'

There it was again, the expectation that I couldn't wait to leave. 'No, I'm in no hurry to go back, and while I said I'm not going to tell you what to do, I still want to make sure the best financial structure is in place for you to manage the payments going forward. If, at that point, you decide to sell, I'll help you with that. Plus, I want to find out who was behind this purchase – and the one in Millers Creek – even if it is just for my own curiosity.' I smiled gently. 'So, if it's all the same to you, I'll stay around for a bit longer – maybe until Christmas.'

Mum's eyes had filled with tears, and she dabbed at them with a tissue. 'Stay as long as you like, Lee. It's been too long since we were all together for Christmas.'

'It has been,' I said quietly. What I didn't say was that it had been almost as long since I spent Christmas with anyone I loved.

LIFE SETTLED INTO A PATTERN. I'd go for a run each morning, Bella and Red by my side. Some mornings Angus, already dressed for a day of work on the land, watched us return and some days he didn't. Then it would be time to tend to the chooks, tend to the kids, and do the school drop-off. The routine felt like a soft mattress I could fall into, and I relished the simplicity and order of my days. I even enjoyed cooking each night for the kids and had tried my hand at baking again, enjoying that too. Although the kids gave me rave reviews, I doubted my efforts would win any prizes just yet.

During the day, I'd either attend to the accounts at the hotel or help behind the bar until it was time to reverse it all and pick the kids up, head home to tend to the chooks and cook dinner. Every evening after the children had gone to bed and everything was packed away, I'd pour a glass of wine and take it onto the verandah where Angus would join me. Some nights we'd chat lightly for an hour or so; others, we'd sit quietly and watch the stars. While I knew I'd fallen back in love with him – although not so much fallen as easily slipped – it felt different from how it used to be. I still wanted him as much as I'd always done – no amount of trying to rationalise with my hormones could deny that – but this time, there was another layer to the wanting. Every night our conversation became easier and our silences more comfortable. Neither of us had mentioned the past, and I didn't want to risk our new-found friendship by doing so.

While I'd seen his glance wander to my bare legs every so often, other than that, there was no indication from his side that he felt the same flames every time our eyes met or the same shiver of desire whenever his hand brushed against mine. Besides, I reminded myself, he was with Georgia and I would be going back to the city after Christmas.

I'd made the promised visit to Tysons on Wednesday morning; Kerry had obviously been told by Mum that I'd helped them out and was staying until Christmas and was full of gratitude on their behalf. In turn, Kerry must've told Georgia enough to send her tearing out to the homestead as soon as the salon closed, as I saw a small blue car with her at the wheel heading up the drive when I was putting the chooks away. It had gone again when I ventured out with my evening wine, and when Angus came over to join me, neither of us mentioned it.

Jazz and Mark were having such a great time on the Sunny Coast that they asked if I minded staying on for longer, and I was having such a great time being here with the kids and the chooks, and the dogs and Angus that I quickly agreed.

On Thursday, Jenny called and offered to pick the

kids up from school and bring them home. I'd made a Milo cake for afternoon tea that the kids had wolfed down, and afterwards, Ethan took off outside with Jackson and Cody, and Ivy, who had a massive case of hero worship when it came to her cousin, disappeared down the hall with Hayley.

Jenny and I took our tea out onto the verandah where we could chat and still keep an eye on the boys.

'Angus was saying he's been seeing a bit of you over the last few days,' she said, that same dancing, speculative gleam she had in her eye the last time we spoke of this.

'A little, yes,' I said. 'He drops around in the evening for a glass of wine. That's all.' When her eyebrows raised in disbelief, I reiterated it. 'It really is all there is to it.'

'But you'd like there to be more?' she guessed.

'Maybe,' I admitted, 'but he's with Georgia, and I'm heading to the city after Christmas.'

If I kept telling myself this, it wouldn't hurt so much when the time came – or so I convinced myself.

'Why don't you stay?' she said, reaching for another slice of Milo cake.

'And do what? There's no job here for me. Besides,' I admitted, 'I couldn't stay and watch Angus marry

Georgia – and yes, I know I had my chance and threw it away, but I just couldn't.'

I watched her face as the pieces came together in her head. 'You've fully fallen for him again, haven't you?'

I nodded miserably. 'Yeah. It happened so easily; I don't think I ever really stopped loving him. Please don't say anything though – this friendship, or whatever it is, is nice and I don't want him to feel uncomfortable.'

'Your secret's safe with me, but if you did get back together, would you stay this time?' Even though her face remained impassive as she asked the question, her back stiffened and I knew just how important my answer was.

'Yes,' I finally said after a short silence. 'I think I would.' And then, when I saw the hope in her eyes, I added, 'But we're never going to get back together, so the question won't come up.'

Her mouth curved into a small, satisfied smile. 'No, of course it won't, but if it did, you'd need to find something to keep you occupied, so I don't see why you can't think about that now.' She wore such a 'so there' expression that I couldn't help but laugh.

'So, tell me,' I said, 'what have your sources told you about the Commercial?'

'Now there's an obvious change of subject if ever I heard one.' She brushed some stray cake crumbs off her jeans. 'You were right, though, the Nielsons, who were the previous owners, fell into financial trouble during covid and the bank instructed them to sell, and lo and behold, a broker turned up and made them an offer just days later.'

'Wow, that's almost the same situation as Mum and Dad.'

'Pretty much. They accepted the offer quickly, and the sale went through about six months ago. According to my friend, they're devastated by what's happening to the pub. It's being run by a licensee, some guy from Sydney, and they've updated all the poker machines to the latest versions, which is why you're losing business – everyone wants to play the latest and greatest. Plus, they've put in drinks and bar snacks service direct to the machines, so punters don't need to leave their machine for any reason. Add that to the improved restaurant menu and there you have the reasons why your business has dropped off. Plus, the sporting clubs have already been told that there won't be any ongoing sponsorship support from the hotel next year.'

I couldn't help the gasp that escaped my lips.

'I know,' she said, 'it sounds horrific. And I think

we can assume that's what they have in mind for the Royal.'

'Yes, that's a safe assumption.'

WHEN ANGUS CALLED in that evening, I told him what Jenny had told me. 'Have you heard from the broker since you sent the email?' he asked, a concerned look on his face.

'No, we haven't, but I suspect we will. I did some quick research on what other hotels Emano Holdings owns, and they have another three in New South Wales. I'd hazard a guess that all of them have been acquired in the past couple of years and in similar circumstances – not that I can know that for sure. In a previous job, I worked as a business analyst on a credit portfolio that included a few hotels, so while I've probably forgotten more than I remember, what I do know is that the value of a pub is based on three things – the value of the poker machine permits, the value of the land and buildings – both as they stand and for alternate use – and the turnover from bar and dining.'

'So,' he mused, 'in the case of the Royal, what you're saying is that now that the dining, bar and poker machine turnover is down and there's limited options for reuse of the land and buildings, they could pick up the Royal for not a lot more than the value of the licenses.'

'Yes, especially if Mum and Dad are under pressure from the bank to sell.'

'And to increase the value, you'd need to increase the turnover?'

'Uh-huh. The pokies licences are worth what they're worth, and the building will only increase if there's a demand in that town, but the turnover you can influence – and relatively quickly. They were able to do that easily at the Commercial by updating the pokies, updating the dining, attracting patrons from Mannus Ridge, and giving them fewer reasons to leave the machines once they had them there. If that hotel was revalued now, I suspect it would have increased.'

'But doesn't that lead to an increased gambling problem? And that's the last thing communities like ours need.'

I sipped at my wine as I considered his question. 'From the sounds of it, the community isn't getting a say, and the Neilsons were told what they wanted to hear by the broker.'

'Do you think they're buying up the pubs to flip them? Sell them off quickly?'

I mused over his question for a second or two.

'Maybe, but I think it's more likely that they want to increase the value of the assets so they can borrow more against them. If they want to break into the Sydney pub market – and if they're building a portfolio like this, I'd say that's their aim – that will take a lot of money and a lot of security to back it.'

'In other words, they're capitalising on publicans who've struggled during the lean years, buying up pubs for the value of their licences and not much more as the owners are pressured into making a quick sale, increasing the turnover by either bringing in patrons from another town or making the pokies more attractive and then using it as leverage for the next purchase or selling it off.'

'Yes. Our challenge now, though, is twofold.' I stood and paced the verandah as I spoke, my bare feet soft against the worn timber floor. 'If Mum and Dad decide to sell, we need to maximise the value of the hotel to potential purchasers while ensuring they can meet their payments in the meantime, and to do those things, we need to increase turnover. Somehow, we need those dining, gaming and therefore drinking in Millers Creek to do that in Mannus Ridge. Plus, we need to fill the accommodation that Mum and Dad spent so much to renovate.' Pausing, I leant back against the railing and faced him, smiling wryly. 'Simple, really.'

'Too easy.' He chuckled. 'Have you got any ideas?'

I nodded and returned to my chair, warmth spreading through me at the way his eyes were drawn to my legs as I stretched them out. 'A few, but only the start of an idea – and I need to run it by my parents first.'

'I understand,' he said. 'Well, I have a big day tomorrow, so I'll be off.'

He placed his glass on the table and stood, stretching so his t-shirt separated from his shorts, exposing a patch of tanned, flat belly I couldn't look away from. When I did manage to drag my eyes back to his, there was a knowing smile on his lips and an intensity in his gaze that made my heart flip-flop and my breath come faster.

'I'll see you around,' he said as he did every evening. Almost as an afterthought, he turned back and said, 'Seeing how your sister is away, I'll be working in the cellar door tomorrow afternoon, so if you get a chance, why don't you come down? I'll show you around and give you a tasting.'

'Umm, sure,' I managed, my breath catching. 'I'd like that.'

'Great, I'll see you then.'

As always, I stayed in my seat until he'd gone inside and the lights in that part of the house had been switched off. Tonight, though, I sat there for longer, wondering if he was undressing for bed and whether he was wondering the same about me.

SEVENTEEN

The anticipated call from the broker came the following morning.

I'd dropped into the Royal after dropping the kids off – just as I did most mornings. This morning, though, I was having difficulty concentrating on Mum's conversation; my mind was full of the invitation Angus had issued last night. It had sounded so casual, the sort a friend would make to another friend, but his eyes and smile had said it was a date – but of course it couldn't be a date ... could it?

'You seem to be off with the fairies this morning, Lee.' Mum chuckled as if she knew where my mind was.

'Sorry, Mum, what were you saying?' I dragged my

attention from the dishwasher I'd finished unstacking towards whatever my mother had just said.

'I was just asking what you were planning to do today,' she said.

'Actually, Angus thought I'd like to have a good look around the cellar door, so I might pop over there this afternoon,' I said, hoping the heat on my cheeks would be attributed to the steam from the recently completed dishwasher.

'That sounds nice,' she said, the gleam in her eye at odds with her benign smile. 'Why don't I pick the kids up from school to give you a bit of a break and you can all have dinner here? Maybe—'

Before she could say more, Dad was there, holding his phone out to me. 'It's Evan Johnson, the broker we've been dealing with. I suggested he might like to speak with you.'

I nodded and took the phone from him. 'Ainsley St James speaking.'

'Ms. St James. My name is Evan Johnson, and your father and I have been discussing an offer from my client to purchase the Royal Hotel.'

'Yes,' I said, 'I'm aware of that. I'm also aware that they've declined your client's offer.'

He cleared his throat. 'I understand your parents have given permission for you to speak on their behalf, but I wanted you to understand the precarious position they're in should the bank choose to enforce the mortgage it has over the hotel, so I'd urge you to use any influence you have to change their minds. My client has made it clear that their offer remains on the table, but their patience is wearing thin.'

Bristling at his threatening tone, I kept mine businesslike. 'Thank you, Evan – may I call you Evan?' Without waiting for his response, I continued. 'I'm fully aware of my parent's financial situation – although I'm surprised at the extent of knowledge you seem to have ...' When no response was forthcoming, I added, 'Your information is, however, out of date. The arrears on the loan have been cleared, so there is no longer any immediate imperative to sell.'

I heard murmurings on the other end of the phone as if Evan had muffled the receiver to speak to someone else.

'I wasn't aware of that change in circumstances,' he finally said. 'The offer on the table is a good one – but if turnover continues to reduce, so will the hotel's value. And my understanding is you're losing patrons every week to Millers Creek.'

'Your information is excellent,' I said through clenched teeth. 'However, should my parents decide to sell the hotel, before they sign anything, we'd like to know a little about the purchaser and their intentions for the pub in relation to a continuation of community support, also—'

'I can assure you—' he began.

'Please don't interrupt me,' I said firmly, rolling my eyes at Dad, who was wearing the biggest grin I'd seen him wear since I arrived home. 'As I was saying, my understanding is that certain promises were made regarding the hotel at Millers Creek, which have since not been honoured, so your assurances, Evan, mean very little. Further, we'll be obtaining an independent valuation of the hotel as it stands, and I don't believe that your client's offer will be sufficient.'

'You're making a huge mistake, Ms. St James,' he said. 'If your turnover reduces any further, the only value your hotel will hold is in the gaming permits – yet my client's offer also takes into account the value of the land and building and the hotel income.' That threatening tone was back.

'That's where we disagree, Evan. As I see it, your client's offer makes very little allowance for the value of the land and building and none at all for the pub as a going concern.'

Evan remained silent for a beat. 'Our offer will remain on the table for another seven days. If I were you, I'd think very carefully about rejecting it.'

'Well, Evan, you're not me, and as I hope I've made clear, my parents will not be selling to your client as the offer stands. Should your client wish to reconsider their offer, along with formalising the assurances you're so quick to make on their behalf, my parents will, at that point, reconsider. And now, Evan, we have a pub to open. Goodbye.'

I pressed the button to end the call with a flourish of satisfaction, and while Mum and Dad certainly seemed happy with the conversation, the implicit threats that had been made left me hoping we were doing the right thing.

The pressure was certainly on to come up with a way to bring back the patrons we'd lost to Millers Creek and fill the rooms upstairs. If we couldn't ... It didn't bear thinking about.

DRESSED in one of my new printed sundresses from Tysons, the tan sandals I'd bought in Millers Creek and a straw hat I'd found in the cottage, I set off with Bella down the lane towards the winery. I was tempted to take Hayley's bike but figured the walk might help calm my nerves. Besides, it gave me long enough to repeat to myself, 'this is not a date; this is not a date.' By the time I reached the bottom of the lane, I might even be ready to believe it.

The Talbots had created a cellar door that fitted perfectly with the rural landscape. Barn-like in structure, the exterior was clad in vertically striped corrugated iron, rustic timber barn doors and window frames providing a warm accent. To the side of the structure was a long, covered deck strung with fairy lights and home to communal wooden tables, which were obviously intended for large tastings or private functions.

Inside was warm and inviting with polished concrete floors, timber-panelled walls, a fireplace, high tables and stools, and a timber bar area. A Christmas tree stood in one corner, and tinsel had been hung here and there in deference to the season.

It was behind the bar that I found Angus. Dressed in a navy polo emblazoned with the winery label, he was holding a bottle aloft and chatting easily to an older couple there for a tasting. When he saw me hovering in the doorway, his eyes lit up, a broad smile spreading across his face. It was enough to make my heart stop beating, and the nervous butterflies were replaced by a whole different chaos.

Beckoning for me to approach the bar and take a seat, he said, 'I was just telling these two customers –

Lauren and David?' When Lauren nodded enthusiastically, I almost rolled my eyes at his ability to turn on the charm when he wanted to. 'I was just telling Lauren and David how we have high hopes for last year's vintage. Dom here'—he bobbed his head towards the man who had just — 'is our winemaker, and he reckons it was a perfect year for pinot. Isn't that right?'

If Angus didn't already have my heart, Dom could very quickly have captured it. With curly tawny hair, a tawny beard and a set of cheeky dimples that matched the laugh lines around his eyes, Dom, who I would place at a similar age to Angus, was built like a rugby player and filled out his heavy cotton work shirt very nicely.

'That's right, Angus.' Directing his laughing hazel eyes to me, he added, 'It's good when the boss pays attention.' Angus chuckled and raised his eyes to the ceiling. 'Now, can I be helping anyone with a tasting?' Again, his focus was on me, and I couldn't help but respond to his flirty manner with a flick of my hair.

'Lauren and David were asking about water management of the vines,' said Angus, 'so why don't we swap positions and I'll help Lee with a tasting?' To the other couple, he said, 'It's very rare Dom ventures into the tasting room, so take advantage of him while you can.'

Dom had raised his eyebrows at Angus at the mention of my name but said with a grin, 'Absolutely ... so, what can I tell you about our growing process? You know, of course, that we model ourselves on Central Otago?'

'You came,' Angus said, leaning his elbow on the counter and resting his cheek against the back of his fist.

'Well,' I said, trying very hard to tear my eyes from his – and failing dismally. 'I was promised a tasting and a look around, so how could I resist?'

'And I thought it was me you were here to see.'

My breath caught in my throat at the gleam in his eyes and the wicked tilt to his mouth. This was the Angus of old, not the Angus who had done his best to ignore me for the first few days I was here. While we had been growing easier in each other's company, this was a massive leap forward and completely threw me – and had me wondering whether Jenny had been meddling in the background.

'That goes without saying,' I said lightly, trying to match his manner but feeling as though there was a subtext behind the words. 'But it really is the wine I'm here for.'

He punched at his chest as if wounded and said, 'Wine it shall be then. Once we've finished the tasting,

I'll show you around the operation. What time do you need to pick the kids up?'

'I don't today – Mum's doing it. She'll take them back with her, and then I'll meet them all in town for dinner.' I nearly added, 'so I'm all yours for the afternoon' but caught myself just in time.

'Excellent, I'll give you the spiel and we can go from there.'

'Sounds good.'

The wicked grin was replaced by a smile, but his eyes still held a sparkle that I was finding difficult to look away from. Concentrate, Lee.

'As you probably already know, we're a cool climate area here. While chardonnays and pinot noir are what we're mostly known for, we also produce pinot meunier, pinot gris, sauvignon blanc, riesling, shiraz, merlot, tempranillo and viognier in the region.'

'Do you grow all those here?' I hadn't realised there were quite so many varieties coming from Mannus Ridge.

'No, it's mostly chardonnay and pinot noir, but we also have a little pinot meunier, some pinot gris and a bit of tempranillo. We'll start with the sparkling and work our way through – how does that sound?'

'It sounds fabulous.'

As we worked through the tasting, I relaxed more,

as did he, and allowed him to tell me about each wine, what to notice in the aroma and taste and what their process was. As he spoke, the idea I'd had last night grew into something more fully formed.

When Lauren and David left, Dom joined us, the flirtatious manner from before gone as both men got into the swing of their business.

'I didn't know you knew so much about this,' I said, surprised at the breadth of Angus's knowledge. He'd been brought up on the farm, but growing grapes was very different from growing cattle.

'I didn't at first, but I did some courses at Charles Sturt University when I began to think about diversifying our land. Dad, as you know, had no time for grapes – thought it was a mug's game – but it fascinated me. So, when Talbots wanted to sell, it was a no-brainer to join it with McGuire land and keep the ownership local. I'd met Dom in Albury when I was studying and he agreed to come on as a winemaker.'

I shook my head in disbelief. 'I had no idea.'

The phone on the wall rang, and Dom left us to answer it.

'Why would you?'

I searched his face for a hidden meaning, another reminder that I'd left and hadn't made contact for so many years, but there was none.

Dom was back. 'It's for you,' he said. 'Georgia ... and before you ask me to tell her you're not here, she heard your voice in the background.'

Angus squeezed his eyes shut briefly. 'Fine. I'll take it.'

'So, you're the Lee I've been hearing so much about,' Dom said when Angus was out of earshot. 'Now it makes sense.'

'Yes, my name is Lee, but I don't know if I'm the one you've been hearing about,' I said, knowing full well that I had been the subject of much discussion over the past week. Had it only been a week ago that I arrived?

'Jazz's sister and the one who is going to single-handedly save our local pub from the corporate marauders – or so I heard.'

'I don't know about that. I am Jazz's sister and helping Mum and Dad with the hotel, but that's all.'

'Hmmm, that's not what I hear, but I'll take your word for it. Here's Angus back. Trouble in paradise, mate?'

Angus glared at him, but it was the type of good-natured glare men do when they're stirring each other up. 'Hardly paradise, but trouble, maybe.' He shot me a glance and Dom grinned again.

'How about you show Lee around, and I'll man the

fort here in case anyone comes in for a tasting?' Dom suggested.

'Sounds good.' I slid off the bar stool and grabbed my hat.

'Shall we?' Angus placed his hand on my back and led me through the office and out the back of the barn towards the modern-looking structure a short walk away. While he dropped his hand when we got outside, I could still feel the heat of where it had been through the thin cotton of my dress.

'What did you think of Dom?' he asked as we walked, his voice casual.

'He seems really nice,' I said, just as casually. 'He obviously knows his business. How come he wasn't at the wedding?'

'He'd already made arrangements to duck back over the ditch – go home to Queenstown – for a week and, as Jazz hadn't told anyone that she was getting married ...'

I nodded my understanding.

'Did you find him ... umm ... do you think he's ... umm ...?' Angus fell over his words.

'Are you trying to ask if I find him attractive? Yes, I do.' I couldn't help laughing at his discomfort.

'Right,' he said. 'Would you go out with him if he

asked?' He was looking straight ahead as he asked the question.

'Seriously, Angus? What are we, thirteen? Next you'll be passing me a note saying: Dom wants to go with you; do you want to go with him?' I parodied a teenage voice as I followed him through the open door into the winery.

His chuckle was self-conscious. 'No, I wasn't asking for him; I was just wondering ...'

He'd paused next to one of the steel vats, just a step between us, and looked down at me. My eyes flicked to his, the navy in his shirt making them appear as dark as the deepest of lakes.

'It would depend,' I finally said. 'But if he were to ask me right now, this very minute, my answer would probably be no.'

He held my gaze for a few beats longer and swallowed hard. 'That's good,' he said, his voice almost a whisper. Reaching out, he brushed his thumb lightly across my lower lip. I closed my eyes, a tiny moan escaping my parted lips.

'What is it about you, Lee?' he whispered. 'I thought I was over you, completely immune. I told myself that you'd changed and you were now some hard-hearted city bitch with posh hair and posh clothes and a posh car, but here you are – and as much as I wanted to hate you, if you take away the posh car and the designer clothes it doesn't take long to see you're still the same Lee.'

'You don't like my car?' I asked, trying to bring some lightness into a moment that had become super-charged.

'A ridiculous thing,' he said.

'And you want me to lose the designer clothes?'

'Oh yes,' he said with the same wicked grin that had always brought me undone. 'More than anything, I want you to lose those.' He sighed heavily. 'I was such an arrogant shit back then,' he said. 'So sure you'd stay just because I asked you to – no, told you to. I should never have given you an ultimatum; maybe if I'd given you the space you needed ...'

'Ssssh.' I lifted a finger to his lips. 'Let's not ... not yet.'

'Then when? You know we need to talk ...' He captured my hand and kissed the palm, his eyes boring into mine, dark, intense and for a second I forgot to breathe.

I lifted my other hand and stroked his cheek. 'We will, I promise.'

His gaze flicked from my eyes to my lips, my breasts under the strappy dress, and back to my lips. As he lowered his head to mine, Bella and Red came tearing into the shed, Bella winding between my legs, ecstatic at having found us.

With a rueful grin, he stepped away, the mood broken.

'You promised me a tour of the winery,' I said, not knowing if I was disappointed, relieved or confused, but deciding that all three emotions applied.

'Then a tour of the winery is what you'll get.'

AFTERWARDS, he offered to drive Bella and me back up the lane, but I refused. My head was full of ideas that the visit had firmed up, and I was keen to get stuck into some research for what was left of the afternoon. Besides, after that moment in the winery, I didn't trust myself alone with Angus.

Sitting at the kitchen table with my laptop open in front of me, I closed my eyes and took a deep breath, feeling again the soft brush of his thumb against my lips, the roughness of his stubbled cheek under my hand, the promise in his eyes when he kissed my palm. No, I didn't trust myself alone with him.

EIGHTEEN

'How did you go this afternoon?' Mum asked. 'With the winery tour?'

We'd finished our meals and Cody chose that moment to ask whether he and Jackson could leave the table to play with some friends sitting with their parents at one of the only other occupied tables in the restaurant. The interruption gave me time to compose my face and my voice. 'Really well. Dom, the wine-maker, was there too, so between him and Angus, I learnt a lot about what they're doing.'

Mum sighed heavily and looked like she wanted to ask a follow-up, but Dad stepped in. 'It's a good operation they've built up, and they're getting some favourable reviews. Between them and Mannus Ridge

Wines and a couple of smaller producers, they're putting us on the map as a wine region worth watching.'

'Why don't we sell local wines here?' It was a question that had been burning inside me since this afternoon – and was another piece in my strategy for the Royal.

'We sell some – the pinot and the chardonnay – but you're right, we don't market them.' A grin formed on his face. 'You have an idea, don't you?'

'I do. I think I know how we can move forward.' I flicked a glance over to where the boys were playing to check they were okay before I proceeded. 'While the Imperial has live music, it's always had a different crowd to those who come here – it's the only reason Mannus Ridge can support two pubs; you both have always known your place. The Imperial is where you go for live music and a flutter on the pokies—'

'And a punch-up on a Friday and Saturday night,' Mum cut in.

'That too.' I chuckled. 'As for here, the Royal used to be where you'd come for a nice meal. If you wanted Chinese, you'd go to the golf club, and for a schnitzel and fish and chips, it would be the RSL. Here, though, you could bring the family, and it was always special enough for date night. Sure, we always had our regulars that would come in for a drink and stay to play the gaming machines, and diners might come for a meal and stay for a drink and the pokies, but it's always been more about the food and the bar than gaming.' I waited for them both to nod their agreement before continuing. 'The problem isn't so much that we lost business during covid, but that turnover has continued to fall since the Commercial changed hands, and you lost your chef to them. That's meant we effectively haven't had a full dining option here – a daily roast of the day, sausages and mash, and a couple of burgers isn't going to cut it.

'For a start, it's competing with the RSL, and secondly, people know they only need to travel thirty kilometres down the road to get food like they used to get here. So instead of coming here, they're going to Millers Creek. The longer this goes on, the more your turnover will decrease. The regulars will begin to drink at the Imperial where there's more of a vibe or go to one of the clubs for a drink, a meal and a flutter. I don't need to tell you what that does to your cashflow or what that does to the value of the hotel. It's the main reason country pubs go out of business.

'The second part of the issue is that without a good

dining option, you're not going to be able to fill the guest rooms upstairs. Why pay for boutique accommodation if you can't get a good meal there?'

'So, what you're saying is that the restaurant is the key to our strategy moving forward?' Dad had leant forward as I spoke and now sat back in his chair, a thoughtful look on his face.

'Yes, but not just a restaurant; we need a point of difference – a reason for people to eat here and a reason for people to stay here. Tourism is concentrating on wine and the cycle paths, which means people with reasonable disposable incomes – which also means it will never really take off until the infrastructure is here to support it.'

'By infrastructure, you're talking about quality accommodation and food options?' Mum said.

'Exactly. The rooms upstairs are fabulous and suit that demographic perfectly, but we need to amp up our dining. I had a look at what some of the country hotels in Victoria are doing – the destination-style pubs. They all have good food and an interior that's a mix of contemporary with traditional touches. The first thing we need to do is fancy it up here -- replace these tables with new black or timber ones, open the fireplace, paint the walls in a dark red or deep blue, and string some mood lights about.' I showed them the photos I'd found.

Hayley, who had also been listening intently, leant in for a look. 'These places look really cool,' she said. 'I can help you paint, Aunty Lee.'

'I'll hold you to that.'

'And we could give the restaurant a proper name too,' she added.

'Great idea Hayles – that's your job,' I said. 'How about you come up with five or six options for us?'

She beamed enthusiastically, overjoyed to be included.

'We were going to replace the carpet in the dining room,' said Mum, examining the images. 'But we didn't get around to it. Maybe we can pull it up instead.'

'Last time I looked, the floorboards were in good nick,' added Dad. 'We can probably do that ourselves, too.'

'The way I figure it, we can do everything but the electrical work ourselves – or with help from friends. I've done some research this afternoon on the amount we'd need to spend on furniture and to update crockery, and I think we could get away with it for this amount.' I pulled up the spreadsheet I'd put together on my phone. Noticing the worried look Mum sent Dad at the cost, I added, 'Put the cost to one side for now because it's not just about improving the decor. Each of these examples I've shown you have a point of difference to whatever else is on offer in their towns. In every case, that point of difference is a focus on local produce. We've got access to fabulous beef and lamb and some good wineries within twenty kilometres – and that's what we should be showcasing. It would also tie in with what the council is doing from a tourism point of view. It's not just about regaining our share of the Mannus Ridge market; we also want to increase the number of people visiting here to discover the wine, produce and landscape of the region. We want them to stay and eat here.'

Dad slowly nodded as I finished speaking. It was as if he could finally see his way out of the problems they'd been dealing with – a bigger picture with more possibilities.

'A couple of these towns have annual food and wine festivals, and there's no reason we can't instigate something like that here.' Once I'd begun to put the plan together this afternoon, the ideas had come thick and fast.

'That would be great,' said Hayley. 'Make a really big deal of it.'

'I can see what you're saying, and it makes complete sense. It could be the boost we need. I have two questions. What do we do next, and how do we pay for it?' Mum counted them off on her fingers. While I knew I'd sold Dad on the idea, Mum had always been the more practical of the two.

'Firstly, we need to hire a chef – but rather than placing an ad, I think we should try and get Tilly back,' I said. 'She knows the market, and after googling her, I know she had a successful career in the Yarra Valley and came here for family reasons. It must be a drag for her to commute to Millers Creek every day, so I think if we gave her a brief that allowed her the freedom to develop a menu based on local produce that could be matched with local wines, she'd jump at it. Sure, she'd need a good basic blackboard menu with weekly specials and the types of dishes the regulars have come to expect, but this would lift her profile at the same time as it lifts ours. Plus, I don't think you'd need to pay her any more than what she's already on – although we could offer annual bonuses based on increased turnover … something else to think about.

'We'd close the restaurant completely for two weeks, get the work done, develop our menu and market extensively on social media, but hold a big pre-Christmas opening night – at a set price for three cours-es. Call it, I don't know … Christmas at Mannus Ridge. The timing would coincide with the weekend the Christmas street market is held, and we could offer bed and dinner packages for the event.'

Mum's brow was furrowed, and she tapped against her forehead with her knuckle. 'It seems you've thought of everything,' said Mum, 'but we still need to discuss the cost. Where's the money going to come from?'

This was the part I knew would get the most resistance. 'I'll use the rest of my payout and invest in it,' I said. 'And before you push back, hear me out.' I took a deep breath. 'Coming back here has made me realise what I've been missing in my life and what I've missed most about Mannus Ridge. It feels like home, and I truly wish I hadn't waited so long to come back.' A tear snuck out and slid down my face. 'Spending time with these three'—I grabbed Hayley's hand and gave her a watery smile— 'and helping at the hotel, doing the things I've been doing, has meant more to me than anything I've done in years. I hadn't realised how much of myself I'd lost on the path to what I thought I wanted.' I wiped at my eyes and noticed Mum dab at hers too. 'Mind you, if I hadn't done all that, I wouldn't be able to afford to do what I'm about to do, so it hasn't all been a waste. The thing is, I want to invest in this town, in us, in our pub. If it works and you decide to sell and retire, so be it – you'll have increased the value, but it will be your choice to make, and from the bottom of my heart, I want to be part of that.'

'Are you saying what I think you're saying? That you're here to stay?' Mum didn't seem able to speak, so Dad did the talking for her.

'Yeah, I think that's exactly what I'm saying. And while I'll help in the hotel, that's not what I intend to do going forward. I'm thinking of setting up a one-stop business shop for tradies or small businesses that need someone to do their human resources or compliance type of admin work – but I haven't thought it through properly. But yes, I'll be staying.'

'If that's the case,' said Dad, 'then thank you, we accept – on the condition that you take a share in the hotel.'

I waved his words away. 'We can deal with the fine print later,' I said. For now, we have some serious planning to do.'

WHEN WE EMERGED from the restaurant into the bar, Angus was there with Dom, Spider and a couple of other men I didn't know.

'I'll drop you home, but I just have to check on something first, so you guys wait here, and I'll be right with you,' said Dad, leaving the kids and me just inside the bar area.

Dom lifted his hand in greeting, Spider nodded his head, but Angus strode over to our little group, the other men looking on curiously. 'Hey Lee, kids,' he said, ruffling his nephew's heads and kissing Hayley on the top of her head. 'Good dinner?'

'The best,' said Hayley, unable to keep the smile off her face. 'We're going to paint the restaurant and Aunty Lee is staying forever.'

'That *is* good news,' he said, his look turning my insides to mush. 'That's the *best* news.' To me, he said, 'How were you guys getting home?'

'Dad's going to take us,' I said.

'No need to worry about that – I'm ready to go so can drop you guys off if you like.'

'Are you sure you have room?'

'Absolutely. The kids will fit across the back seat. You stay here and I'll let the others know. Hayley – can you run and tell your grandpa?'

She nodded enthusiastically and took off to update Dad on the change of plans while I watched Angus farewell his mates. While there was some good-natured backslapping from Dom, Spider eyed me with a narrowed, speculative stare. I'd put good money on the fact that he'd be straight on the phone to Georgia with the news.

During the short drive home, Hayley chattered about our plans and how she had the job of coming up with a name for the restaurant. 'Aunty Lee can tell you all about it when you're on the verandah having a wine tonight,' she said.

I turned around and almost laughed out loud at the sly look on her face. The little minx had known all about his evening visits.

Angus's eyes flicked to mine, his body shaking with suppressed laughter. 'There's not much anyone can keep from you, Hayles,' he said.

'Don't worry,' she said, 'your secret is safe with me, but I can't promise to keep quiet under questioning from Grandma, Mum or Aunty Jenny, so you've been warned.'

She sounded so grown-up; this time I couldn't suppress the giggles.

'What's so funny?' asked Jackson petulantly. 'What secret are we talking about?'

'It's okay, mate,' said Angus, with another side gaze at me. 'You're not missing anything, just boring grown-up stuff.'

When we pulled up at the cottage, I thanked Angus for the lift as the kids piled out of the car and the two youngest raced into the house, Hayley dawdling behind in case she missed anything.

'Thanks for the lift,' I said.

'You're welcome.' Then after a pause, 'Is it too late to come over after I drop the car at home?'

I made no attempt to hide my smile. 'Not at all.'

NINETEEN

Despite it being later than their usual bedtime, the kids settled remarkably well. By the time I took my shoes off and retrieved the open bottle of wine from the fridge and a couple of glasses, Angus was walking up the verandah steps. He'd changed into his usual footy shorts and a t-shirt, and although we'd been meeting like this for most of the week, tonight, the warm air around us felt alive with sparks.

I poured the wine and told him about my idea for the restaurant and a proposed partnership with local growers.

'That's a great idea, Lee,' he said. 'I reckon the other wineries would get behind you – and pairing wines grown here with local produce, well, it's not rocket science, so why no one's thought to do it here is beyond me.'

'I'm glad you think so – I think it's exciting. Mum was a bit hesitant at first, but they're both fully behind it. We don't have much of a window to get things done. I'll put some orders in on Monday for the furniture we need, but delivery from Canberra might be an issue. Once Jazz is back, I'll go to Melbourne for a couple of days and pick up the crockery we need – there's a great warehouse down in South Melbourne that supplies to the trade, so I should be able to get it all from there. My first task, though, is to convince Tilly Stone to come back, so that will be my job on Monday.'

I hadn't missed how his face had fallen when I mentioned heading back to Melbourne – but he'd recovered so quickly I could've imagined it.

'What do you need from me?' he asked.

'Wine, of course'—he laughed at that— 'but also some help promoting the reopening. We're planning on a Christmas at Mannus Ridge theme, and while I have a friend in Melbourne who knows people who can help us get the word out, we also need to promote it in town – and I know that could be more difficult. I need to sort out some more details and then we can talk, okay?'

'Sounds good.' He picked up his glass and sipped from it. 'Speaking of talking,' he said slowly, 'you and I need to talk.'

'Isn't that what we've been doing?' My heart had risen into my throat at the possibility that the wrong words or words taken the wrong way could destroy the tentative friendship we'd established.

'You know what I mean,' he said.

I nodded, my finger tracing the condensation on the edge of my glass.

'I meant what I said this afternoon – I was an arrogant shit and blamed you for far too long when I was just as much at fault. I should never have given you the ultimatum.' He put his glass back on the table and stood, walking over to the verandah railing, his back towards me, gazing out into the darkness towards the homestead. Turning to face me, he said, 'You're the biggest regret of my life, Lee, and I didn't know it until you came back.' He grimaced and added, 'What's worse is the awful things I said to you that night – how I'd never speak to you again and how you'd never be welcome here. I had no idea that you'd take it literally ... My only excuse is that I was very young and way too proud. I'm sorry, Lee. So sorry.'

I took a deep mouthful of my wine before setting it

down next to his. 'We were both so young,' I said. 'And both so proud.'

Standing, I walked across to where he stood and wound my hands around his waist, pressing my cheek against his chest, allowing hope to fill my heart. With a groan, he wrapped his arms around me and held me tighter than he'd ever held me before, my head tucked under his chin.

'God, I've missed you,' he said throatily.

'I've missed you too,' I murmured, loving the hardness of his chest against my cheek, the faint tinge of his spicy cologne filling my senses and mixing with the aromas of the wine, the feeling that now I truly was home.

Pulling back enough to look up into his face, I stood on my toes and kissed his lips softly like the way his thumb had brushed against mine this afternoon. 'I've missed you so much,' I whispered against his lips.

My words were his signal to lower his mouth and kiss me properly, the way I'd wanted him to kiss me for days, the way I'd been missing for years. When his tongue met mine, I didn't know whether the sigh I heard came from him or me, but I didn't care. As I gave in to his kiss, everything in the world came down to this man, the softness of his hair below my fingers, the way our bodies seemed to instinctively remember how to fit together, the stubble of his jaw against mine. Angus. It had always been Angus.

When he finally lifted his head, we were both breathing heavily. 'The kids ...' he said, groaning as I moved against his hips. 'Christ, Lee ...'

'I know.' I closed my eyes in frustration.

'I don't want to let go of you yet,' he said.

'Then don't.' I burrowed back into him, back where I belonged.

'Is it true what Hayley said? That you're staying?' The question was asked tentatively as if he didn't couldn't bear to hear the answer but knew he needed to.

'Yes. It's true.'

'And not just for Christmas?'

'Not just for Christmas.'

If it was at all possible, his arms tightened even more.

'You know,' he said, 'I'd already decided that if you needed to go back to your city life, then we'd make it work somehow. One thing I've learnt over the years is that for this to work, compromises will need to be made ...'

'On both sides.' I lifted my head again to look into his eyes. 'You know, Angus, I've never really gotten over you.'

'Nor me, you.'

'But Georgia?'

'I called it off with her yesterday – it's why she came to see me last night, to try and change my mind by reminding me what a bitch you were, what you'd already done to me and how you were only going to hurt me when you left again.'

Even though he wouldn't ask me outright, his eyes were pleading to tell him she was wrong.

'I can't do anything about what Georgia thinks about me, but I know how much it hurt to leave you last time, so I'm not going anywhere ... for long, that is.' I added the last with a smile, but it was enough for him. For now, anyway.

It was after midnight when we finally stopped talking and kissing for long enough to say goodnight and go to our respective beds. I'd promised the kids that if the day was as hot as it had been forecast to be, I'd take them for a picnic and a swim at the river, so before he left, I asked Angus if he wanted to join us.

'The swimming hole where we used to go?' I nodded. 'Sounds great. I'll pick you up, though – you won't get that posh car of yours down there.'

The dig about my beloved car earned him a playful thump. 'Should I ask Jenny and Dave and their kids too? It will be just like old times then.'

'Except we'll be there with kids and there'll be no sneaking off to make love,' he said, the memory almost leading to more kissing, 'but yes, I'll call her in the morning.' He grinned and kissed me one last time. 'Sleep well, Lee ...'

Back in my room, I sat on the bed, tired after the events of the day, but at the same time feeling more awake and alive and energised and hopeful than I had in years. This time last week I'd just arrived in town and had no hope of getting past the weekend, but now? Now everything was so different. It was, in fact, quite the opposite.

Before I slid into bed, I checked my phone – one missed call. From Otis. Unable to help myself, I listened to his message. 'Hey babe, just thinking about you and wondering where you are. Give me a call when you get this.' Then a pause. 'I miss you, Ainsley. Call me?'

I deleted the message, made sure my phone was on silent and pulled the sheets up. Not even Otis could dampen my mood tonight.

THE FOLLOWING DAY WAS FINE, so to the river we all went.

While I was shy about making our relationship public so soon after we'd reconciled, Angus had no such qualms, holding my hand or putting his arm around me whenever he had the opportunity. Hayley couldn't take the smile off her face, Jackson screwed his nose up and Cody didn't care. Dave was, at first, a little stand-offish, as he had been at Jazz and Mark's wedding, but once he saw that Jenny had relaxed her stance with me and that Angus and I were again together, he also unbent with me, and it wasn't long before we were bantering among ourselves the same way we had all those years ago.

Seeing Angus bare-chested in swimming shorts, the water dripping down his torso, his eyes laughing, the drops flying off his hair and flashing in the sun when he shook it, had all my hormones on alert, but watching him splashing about in the cold water with the kids, also made my ovaries take notice. I'd never considered being the maternal type, but the sudden yearning to have a family with him took me by surprise. I supposed that it wasn't so much that I hadn't wanted to have children rather than I didn't want to have children with anyone but Angus. And when he held me in the water, kissed me, and murmured, 'That bikini needs to come with a warning,' I wanted to take him by the hand and start the baby-making immediately.

'When did this happen?' Jenny asked as we lay back on our towels on the sandy bank, our legs stretched out in the sun.

'Yesterday, or rather, last night,' I said, not even bothering to hide the warmth that came to my cheeks.

'You both seem happy,' she added. 'I'm glad, really glad. You two have always belonged together.'

'Yes, it's early days, but so am I.' As if he knew we were talking about him, Angus paused, quirked an eyebrow in my direction and flashed me a wide grin. Jackson took his momentary distraction to splash him, the surprised look on his face causing Jenny and me to burst into laughter.

'And you're really staying this time?' Her voice held the same hope in it that Angus's had last night when he asked me that exact question.

'I am,' I said simply. 'I'm here to stay.'

THE REST of the weekend sped past. In many ways, it seemed as though we were living a hazy summer holiday like the ones we'd had when we were young – filled with sun, water, fun and love. Neither of us had said the actual words to each other yet, but I was sure he felt the same way I did; it was there in every touch, glance and kiss.

It was also as though I'd given myself permission to take two days off to relax before the work started on the restaurant, as planning in earnest kicked off on Monday morning. Orders were placed for new tables and chairs with delivery scheduled for the day before we reopened – nothing like cutting it fine – and I managed to convince Tilly to come back to us, although that hadn't been as difficult as I thought it would be.

Not only had the daily commute been getting her down, but the early assurances of a free hand in the kitchen had not come to pass and she'd found the new licensee of the Commercial difficult to deal with and penny-pinching.

'I've been asked to cut corners on everything,' she said, 'yet as your parents know, I've never been one to waste ingredients and am always cost-conscious. I would never have gone there if your parents had been able to guarantee me a job.'

As much as she was happy to come back to work for Mum and Dad, it was, however, my promise that we were adopting a local-first strategy that made her clap her hands with glee. 'That's exactly the right path to take,' she said. 'We have great beef and lamb and fabulous wines here, so if you trust me with it, I can guarantee the Royal will be known as *the* destination foodie pub in this region. We'll have people from Melbourne and Sydney fighting to get a room and a table here ... trust me.'

I explained what we were doing with the restaurant and the plans for our reopening dinner. 'We're thinking a set three-course menu – with vegetarian options, of course – designed to match with local wines, although patrons don't need to go with the wine matching if they don't want. The theme is Christmas at Mannus Ridge.'

Tilly, not much taller than me, with a riot of short black corkscrew curls and pinchable appley cheeks, the brightest Irish blue eyes I'd ever seen, had the kind of face that showed every thought that went through her mind. Right now, her thoughts were coming fast and furious. 'Perfect, it's a great opportunity to tweak the Christmas dinner by including local native ingredients.' She paused and grinned widely. 'This is exciting; thank you for the opportunity. I know you're closing the restaurant, but can I use the kitchen in the meantime as a test kitchen for menu planning?'

'Absolutely,' I said. 'Just let me know what you need. I'm talking to each of the winemakers we'll be featuring over the next few days, so we'll line up a tasting for you too.'

We agreed on the salary she'd previously been on and added an annual bonus tied to restaurant profits, and Tilly left for Millers Creek to give notice – effective immediately.

TWENTY

Jazz and Mark arrived home on Wednesday, tanned and relaxed and full of gratitude for me looking after the kids; we celebrated their homecoming with barbe-cued sausage sandwiches that evening at the homestead.

Although Hayley hadn't been able to wait to tell her mother about Angus and me being back together, Jazz still reacted with surprise when Angus put his arms around me to kiss me hello as if he hadn't only seen me a few hours before.

'Just how together is together?' she asked, a wicked grin on her face.

'Not *that* together,' I said. 'We've been very well behaved around the kids ... more's the pity.' I rolled my eyes to express my frustration, earning a giggle from Jazz.

'I'm pleased to hear it! But now that you won't be under the same roof as my children, what are you going to do, sneak Angus into your bedroom like you used to?' She waggled her eyebrows, and I couldn't help but laugh.

'Puh-leeese. We're so much more adult these days. Besides, it all has to wait until I get back from Melbourne.'

'Does it? Mum and Dad aren't expecting you to move back in tonight; you're off to the city tomorrow; no one will notice if you do a sleepover tonight.' She looked across at the barbecue where Angus was turning the sausages. 'You can't tell me the thought hasn't occurred to him too.' I shrugged a shoulder. 'Besides, you can thank me when the pair of you finally make it down the aisle.'

I choked on the wine I'd just sipped. 'Seriously? We've only been back together for two minutes.' She waved the detail away. 'Why should I thank you?'

'Because if I hadn't organised a wedding because I thought Dad was going to die and if I hadn't guilted you into coming back and if I then hadn't asked you to look after the kids so you two would be forced into close proximity, you wouldn't be together now.' She performed a little flourish with her hand and took a bow. 'Now, repeat after me: thank you very much, Jazz.'

'Okay, maybe you did have a small role in it. Regardless of the guilt, I probably wouldn't have come home if I hadn't been sacked, so the thanks are all down to my ex-boss for seeing me as the bitch that I am.'

'Was,' she corrected. 'That was Ainsley in the city; now you're back to being the same Lee we've all missed and who my Hayley has a massive dose of hero worship for. The bitch has left the building.'

I chuckled. 'I love her too – Hayles, that is, not who I used to be – and I'm glad you're back, but now I'm off to mingle.'

'Which means you're off to see your boyfriend because the two of you can't keep your hands off each other,' she teased. 'The sooner you shag, the better; so much unresolved sexual tension in the air is making us old marrieds uncomfortable.'

I pushed at her arm playfully and walked over to where Angus was talking to Mark and Jenny, a beer in one hand, the barbecue tongs in the other. At my approach, he put his beer down, wrapped his arm around my waist, pulled me into his side and dropped a kiss on the top of my head.

'Who's that?' Mark said, peering down the drive.

'Christ,' said Angus as the small blue hatchback came into view. 'It's Georgia.'

She jammed the brakes on as she pulled up, missing the front fence by the smallest of margins and leaving a cloud of dust behind her. Slamming the door, she stormed across to where we all stood.

'Well, isn't this all bloody happy families?' she sneered, glaring at Angus and me.

Angus stepped from my side to placate her, but Jenny placed a calming hand on his arm. 'I'll deal with this.'

'Georgia,' Jenny said in a soothing voice. 'I know you're hurting, but you don't want to be here right now.'

'You McGuires and St Jameses – you all stick together,' Georgia screamed. 'And as for you'—she leaned past Jenny, her finger pointed at me— 'why couldn't you have stayed away like I told you to? No one wants you here. No one, do you hear?'

'Georgia ...' Jenny tried again, placing a hand on her arm.

'Don't fucking touch me!'

The kids stopped playing cricket and stood like statues, staring at the commotion.

'Hey,' said Dave firmly, 'enough of the language; there are kids around.'

Ignoring him, she shook off Jenny's hand and stalked to the barbecue, planting herself in my personal space, eye to eye. 'Why couldn't you have believed me and stayed away? He was finally seeing me. Why did you have to come back?' And with that, she picked up the glass of red I'd placed beside the barbecue and threw it all over me. 'Why didn't you stay away?' she said again before turning to head back to her car.

'What did you mean? What should she have believed?' Angus went to follow her.

I reached for his arm and said bleakly, 'Don't. She's hurting ... let her go. It's only wine; there's no harm done.'

I stood there in the Mannus Ridge twilight, red wine dripping down the front of my once-white t-shirt, yet somehow unable to move.

'Lee,' said Angus. 'What did she mean?'

I looked across at him, my thoughts coming wildly and scrambling in my head. 'Ummm, I need to clean up ... the sausages are ready, so don't wait for me.' I forced a smile. 'I'll just go back to my room and ...'

'Lee.' Angus caught my hand as I turned back to the cottage. 'Come inside. You can clean up and borrow one of my t-shirts.' When I continued to look blankly at him, reaction beginning to set in, he led me to the house. 'Come inside, babe,' he said soothingly.

As we walked up the stairs and onto the verandah, Jazz said with an overly loud, overly cheery voice, 'Okay, kids, who wants a sausage sandwich?'

I hadn't been in the homestead since I left, yet it felt as though nothing had changed. The walls had been painted, perhaps, but otherwise, as I ambled down the hallway, I could swear that I heard the spirit of Mrs McGuire shouting, 'Girls! No running in the house!' and how we'd then take our shoes off to see how far we could slide in our socks along the polished floorboards. Yet Angus's mother had been gone for nearly twenty years.

He led me down to what had used to be his parent's bedroom and what appeared to be the only part of the house that had been renovated. The heavy floral wallpaper I remembered had been stripped off, and the plasterboard replaced by timber cladding painted royal blue. Hints of the same blue were picked up in the plaid bedspread that covered the oak king-size bed. It should've made the room feel dark, but the white skirtings and sills around the double doors, framed by heavy cream drapes that led to the verandah on the eastern side of the house and the painted white surrounds of the fireplace would add brightness to the room during the day, but at night with the fire going, it would feel cosy and warm. An oil painting of a pastoral scene sat on the mantel, completing the chic-country-style look.

'Hey,' Angus said softly, turning to face me and resting a hand on my shoulder. 'Are you okay?'

I nodded solemnly. 'I feel sorry for her, you know. She's always wanted you, and just when she thought she'd won, I ruined it for her again.'

'What did she mean, Lee?' His words were quiet and patient, but the look in his eyes was despairing.

I took a step back, not ready to answer the question, not ready for the hurtful truth to come out, but knowing I couldn't delay that for much longer. 'I don't want to get your rug dirty,' I said as an out. 'And it's such a lovely rug ... I'll clean up, and then I'll tell you ... okay?'

He raised his eyebrows, then nodded. 'Fine, but I'm not going anywhere.' He handed me a t-shirt that had been folded neatly on the end of the bed. 'It'll be too big, but at least it's clean. The ensuite is through there, and you'll find a clean towel on the rack.'

Smiling my thanks, I went into the ensuite – almost an extension of the bedroom with the same blue panelling and white accents. Carefully, I took off my t-shirt and washed it in the sink. It would never be white again. My bra was also soaked through, so I washed it and ran the shower to remove the sticky wine that was even now smelling stale on my skin.

Picking up the bar of soap, I held it to my nose, closed my eyes and inhaled – leather, spices and a faint back hint of chocolatey tobacco – the scent of Angus filled my senses. It would be so easy right now to walk out there, push him onto the bed and make love to him in the way I desperately needed to, but the family was outside, and inside we had things to say first. I turned the shower to cold and quickly finished.

I could tell by the way his eyes lingered on my bare breasts under his t-shirt, my nipples standing to attention against the cotton, that he'd been having the same thoughts as I had. His next words confirmed it. 'God you look sexy in that,' he said throatily.

He was sitting in the worn leather stockman's-style chair beside the bed, his eyes stormy grey as they ran down my body, which now felt like liquid fire. I bit my lower lip, his eyes following the movement.

'This was such a mistake,' he said, standing to walk across to me, his eyes holding mine.

'It was,' I said, meeting him in the middle. And then I was in his arms, and he was kissing me as if he wanted to devour me whole.

'Oh Angus, I want you so much,' I moaned, moving my hips against his when his hand cupped my breast.

With a wrench, he pulled away, breathing as heavily as I was. 'We can't, not with everyone out there ... but later? Tonight?'

I nodded. 'Tonight.'

'Now though, you need to tell me what Georgia told you – and we can't have that discussion here ... not with you looking like that and with the bed way too handy ...'

He grabbed my hand and led me into the kitchen where we found Jenny and Jazz packing the food leftovers into Tupperware dishes.

'We wondered what had happened to you two,' said Jazz, a teasing smile on her face.

'Nice t-shirt,' said Jenny.

'Is it hot in here or is Lee blushing?' Jazz asked Jenny.

Angus stayed on the other side of the kitchen counter, looking as if we hadn't just nearly had sex a few rooms from where our sisters were standing.

'Lee was just about to tell me what Georgia meant when she said she told her to stay away,' Angus said. 'It's okay, you might as well say it in front of these two – they'll find out anyway, and then they can all leave.'

My face flamed again, but Jenny simply laughed.

'Okay, big brother, we get the hint. Lee, I'd start talking if I were you – the sooner you do, the sooner we take our kids home.'

'Okay,' I said slowly. 'It was the day after I'd told Angus about the university offer and how I wanted to go. I told him I still wanted to marry him but asked if we could delay the wedding just a few years – we were both young, so I didn't think a few years would matter. He wasn't happy, but he said he'd think about it and I thought maybe it could work.'

'But I was an arrogant prick and the next night issued her an ultimatum – stay or go, there was no in between. I was so sure she'd choose me, but what Lee didn't know is that Spider had been in my ear and told me that he'd heard you boasting about how you couldn't wait to get out of this hick town and get yourself a boyfriend with brains who was going somewhere,' Angus said, his expression bleak with remembered pain.

'I didn't say that,' I said, pleading with him to believe me.

'I know that now, but at twenty-two, I was full of pride and had a chip on my shoulder a mile high. I believed it because it was what I feared most – and Spider knew that.'

'Anyway,' I continued, 'the next day, Georgia

called by and told me how you and she had still been seeing each other and how she'd missed a period. She didn't come right out and say it, but the implication was that she was pregnant and that it would be your baby.'

'Oh Lee ...' He reached for my hand and held it. 'Why didn't you say?'

His touch nearly brought me undone but I swallowed hard and continued. 'She said that you told her I'd given you the out you'd been looking for – that you'd been trying to find the words to tell me you wanted to end it and your ultimatum was a way of blaming me. Then she said she'd make sure everyone knew how much I wanted to leave town and how much better than Mannus Ridge I thought I was. She told me never to return because my family would be embarrassed if I did and the whole town would hate me for jilting one of their favourite sons.'

'And later that day, I said much the same to you,' Jenny whispered. 'I said some horrible things to you that day ... It's no wonder you stayed away as long as you did. I'm so sorry, but I had no idea what Georgia had said.' She turned to Angus and said, 'Please tell me none of that is true.'

'Do you even have to ask?' He sounded offended. 'Of course it's not. I kissed her once – or rather, she kissed me – that time we broke up for a few weeks, but it didn't go any further. Not then. I should never have encouraged her to think we could be more than we would ever be. That was cruel of me, and if I'd known what she'd said to Lee ...' He rubbed his forehead and shook his head slowly. 'Fifteen years we've wasted because of Spider and Georgia.'

'Not just Spider and Georgia,' I said. 'I was too proud and too hurt. I could've told you what she said, but I was scared it was the truth and didn't trust you enough. So, I left and vowed I wouldn't return until I'd really made it and could show everyone that the sacrifice I made when I left you had been worth it.'

Reaching for my other hand and tugging me to stand in front of him, our eyes locking, he said, 'And I was too proud to come to you with what Spider had said because I was scared it was the truth.' A smile tugged at the corner of his lips, his eyes bright. 'I vowed that the next time I saw you, I would've made something of myself to show you what you missed out on.'

'Instead, I was broken down, wet through, muddy, my credit card was over the limit and the payment to my roadside assistance had bounced.'

'And I was rude and arrogant, made you drag your suitcases through the mud and refused to speak to you.'

As we smiled into each other's eyes, I vaguely

heard Jazz say to Jenny, 'I think that's our cue to get out of here.'

'Yep, before I throw up,' added Jenny, a laugh in her voice.

When the screen door shut behind them, I said, 'I love you, Angus. I always have.'

'I love you too,' he said. 'And I always will.'

'Then please, will you take me to bed?'

That wicked grin that had spent the last fifteen years in my dreams reappeared. 'With pleasure.'

TWENTY-ONE

If it wasn't for the fact that I had to drive to Melbourne and Angus had cattle to move and drench, I don't think either of us would have gotten out of bed the next day. Even now, as I approached Wangaratta, about two hours down the highway, I still had a little shiver of remembered delight.

We'd made love, talked some more, made love again and managed a few hours' sleep before waking to make love again. I should be exhausted – *he* certainly should be – but I'd never felt more alive, more energised and more convinced that, finally, I was on the right path.

He held me tight and kissed me slowly before I climbed into the car to leave – almost as if he wanted to remember every miraculous second of the kiss while we were apart. 'I'm going to miss you tonight,' he murmured.

'I'll be back tomorrow.' I nuzzled into his neck, savouring the woodsy smell of his skin.

'Yes, but then you'll be moving back into town, and I'll miss seeing you every morning and every night.'

'I'm only a few kays away.'

'That's a few kays too far.'

He pulled back, a forlorn look on his face which earned him another kiss.

'Why don't you just move in here with me?' he said. I laughed, thinking he was joking until he said, 'I'm serious, Lee. Move in with me. It might be early days, but on the other hand, it's long overdue.'

Even though my head was telling me to take my time, my heart wasn't listening, and I found myself nodding, slowly at first, thoughtfully and then ecstatically.

I stopped at Mrs Wilson's bakery for a coffee and a sausage roll (who is Lee St James and what have you done with Ainsley?) and was rejoining the highway when my phone rang. Thinking it was Angus, I answered automatically, a smile in my voice. 'Hello, darling? What's up? Do you miss me already?'

'Well, hello darling yourself,' drawled Otis. 'And yes, I do miss you, but I was beginning to think you'd forgotten me by the way you've been dodging my calls.'

'What do you want, Otis?' I asked through clenched teeth.

'I'm just calling to see how you are. I've been worried about you.'

'Not so worried that you couldn't wait to evict me when I was already at rock bottom. I was sick, yet you only gave me two weeks to find somewhere else to live.'

'That was a misunderstanding, darling. Maria got the wrong end of the stick – I was surprised when I discovered what had happened and phoned you immediately.'

It was typical of Otis to get someone else to do his dirty work – in this case, it was his executive assistant – and then blame them for the fallout, leaving his hands squeaky clean.

When I didn't respond, he said, 'So where are you?'

'Do you even care?'

'Of course, I do,' he said, and if I didn't know him better, I would've believed the sincerity in his voice. 'So where are you living?'

I hesitated only briefly before saying, 'Mannus Ridge.' This time it was his turn to be silent. 'Where I grew up – remember, I told you about it.'

'So you did, but I would've thought it was a bit too ... Hicksville and rural for you – unless they have a Ted Baker store in the main street.' He chuckled at his joke.

'If that's all ...' I said disparagingly, gripping the steering wheel tightly.

He sighed down the line. 'Actually, there was another reason for my call. I wasn't as supportive as I could've been when JC booted you out—'

'You think?'

'My only excuse is that Melanie had found out about us and it had thrown me. That's all sorted itself out now, so there's no reason we can't pick up where we left off.' He paused and then said, 'I miss you, Ainsley.'

Whether it was shock or amazement at the sheer effrontery of the man, I was speechless.

Taking my silence as permission to continue he added, 'And there's also a job offer I'd like to discuss with you. In fact'—he let out a rueful laugh— 'JC might have done you a favour. A senior management role has come up at one of the big four banks that you'd be perfect for. The title is right, and the package is even more generous than what we were paying you at CP; plus, I know the hiring executive, so you'd be a shoo-in. What do you say?'

'Thank you, but no,' I said, my knuckles turning white.

'To what? The job offer or'—he laughed again as if the thought of rejection was impossible to consider—'my offer?'

'Both. The answer is no to both of your kind offers.'

Another silence. I pictured him pacing his office, his phone to his ear, his brain turning over the plausible reasons for my answer.

'Who did you think I was when you picked up the call?' he finally asked. 'The one *you* called darling. Have you moved on from me already or did you have a Plan B waiting in the wings?'

I almost told him it was none of his business who I was involved with, but instead I said, 'Maybe you really did teach me well.'

And then I hung up.

IT WAS after six that evening when I pulled into Benji's drive. I'd been to the cook's warehouse and sourced the crockery, flatware and other bits and pieces Tilly had chosen from the catalogue and had boxes piled high in the back of the car. I'd also made another stop on the way.

'Darling, let me look at you,' Benji cried when he came out to meet me, holding me at arm's length. 'Whatever you've been doing out there in the sticks, it suits you, sweetie,' he said. 'You look fabulous.' He held up one of my hands and tutted. 'Short nails on Ainsley St James? I never thought I'd see the day where you were without your acrylics.'

'Let's just say there are some very good reasons I can't go to the local beautician.' I laughed, kissing his tanned cheek. 'It's good to see you too; thanks for letting me stay tonight.'

'You're very welcome. Come inside; Brendan has opened some bubbles, and we both want to hear about it all – especially the new man in your life.'

'How did you know?'

'You look too good for there not to be,' he said. 'Wait ... what is *that* in the driveway? Where's your Beemer?'

'I sold it.' My gaze followed his to the second-hand SUV sitting where he expected to see my BMW.

'Why? You loved that car. It was, you said, the sign that you'd finally made it.'

'I know.' I cringed inwardly at the shallowness of the statement. 'But it's impractical for Mannus Ridge, and I needed the money, so I traded it for this.'

He shook his head in disbelief and took my arm to

lead me inside. 'We certainly do have some catching up to do.'

———

'WELL, DARLING,' Benji said a couple of hours later. 'You've certainly got a better appetite than you used to have. I'd told Brendan not to worry too much about the food, that you'd only push it around the plate to be polite, but the country air must be agreeing with you. Or,' he added with a suggestive wink, 'you're more … energetic … than usual.'

While I'd begun to catch Benji up on the events of the last couple of weeks, Brendan had barbequed some steaks, which he'd served with a potato salad and a green salad, outside in their courtyard garden. I hadn't realised how hungry I was until I began eating. Now the three of us were nursing freshly filled wine glasses and enjoying the warm summer night.

Fanning the heat on my cheeks, I giggled like a schoolgirl. 'Perhaps it's both.'

'So, who is he, this new man?' As he asked me the question, his hand reached out to hold Brendan's.

'He's actually an old man. Not in terms of age,' I said hastily when Benji's brows disappeared under his hair. 'Old, as in, I was engaged to him many years ago.'

Benji's gasp was audible. 'He's the reason I left Mannus Ridge.' I took a sip of wine and added, 'And he's most of the reason I haven't been back in nearly fifteen years. I called off our wedding, you see, and … well …'

'But you … you never said!' For once, Benji seemed lost for words, so I told him our story – mine and Angus's – how we'd fallen in love, broken up, and how we'd planned to marry but hadn't quite made it.

'Looking back, we were both too young and too proud, and it probably wouldn't have worked,' I finished.

'And now?' Benji asked softly.

My smile felt as though it came right from my heart. 'And now I think we will make it. I'm not running away from him or giving up on us this time.'

'Does that mean you're planning to stay in Mannus Ridge?' asked Brendan.

My nod was exaggerated with excitement and anticipation. 'Yes, it does.'

'But …' Again, Benji couldn't seem to get the words out.

'I think what he's trying to say is'—Brendan sent a fond glance in his husband's direction— 'what on earth are you going to do with yourself?'

'That's exactly what I was going to ask,' said Benji.

'What are you going to do with yourself?'

'Well,' I mused, 'first, I'm going to save my parent's pub ...'

Benji choked on the mouthful of wine he'd just taken. 'You're what?'

'Haven't I told you that part?' I asked innocently.

'So, let's get this straight,' Benji said once I'd finished telling them about our plans to save the Royal. 'You're refurbishing the restaurant and having a grand reopening before Christmas to place Mannus Ridge on the foodie destination map.'

'That pretty well sums it up,' I said.

'Okay,' Benji dragged the word out. 'I have one question for you then: why haven't Brendan and I received our invites yet? After all, how are we to make sure we get the details right for when we're spreading the word?'

I placed my wineglass on the table and rushed out of my chair to hug them both.

Once I'd settled back down in my chair, Benji asked quietly, 'I don't want to upset you, but have you heard anything from Otis?'

I grimaced and ran my finger around the bowl of my glass. 'Yes, but not until last week, and then just messages telling me he missed me.'

Benji rolled his eyes. 'Of course he does. You

haven't spoken to him, though, have you?'

'I accidentally picked up a call from him this morning. I thought it was Angus.' The heat rushed to my face again as I remembered how I answered his call. 'He said there'd been a misunderstanding and Maria should've given me more time to get myself organised.' I grinned at Benji's scoff of disbelief. 'I know. It was a typical Otis thing to say. Then he suggested that as the dust has died down, we can recommence our affair as if nothing had happened.' I paused for a few seconds. 'And then he offered me a job – more senior, more money.'

'Whoa ... Really? Who with?' Benji leant forward, frowning.

'One of the big four – he didn't say who.' As Benji continued to frown, I said, 'Don't worry, I haven't fallen for it, and I said no to both of his offers. I'm not interested in going back to him or to corporate – it's not who I am anymore.'

'No darling,' Benji said softly, 'I don't believe it is.' He raised his glass in my direction. 'Here's to you, Ainsley, and your new life ... or is it your new old life? Whatever it is, I couldn't be prouder of you or happier for you.'

Dabbing a finger at the corner of my eye, I said, 'Thank you for everything.'

'You're very welcome, darling. But I do have one more question – what's happening with all those beautiful clothes? I can't see them being suitable for riding horses or tractors or pulling beers at the local pub.'

I grinned. 'I'm selling them.'

Benji looked horrified. 'What? All of them?'

'Most of them. After all, I've sunk all my savings into the pub; I need the money! Seriously though,' I said when their laughter had died down, 'I have no use for them and am embarrassed when I think about how much money I wasted on clothes and shoes ...'

'And manicures and injectables,' Benji added with a completely straight face.

'Yes, all of that. I truly thought I needed it.'

'Perhaps you did,' said Brendan. 'And now you don't.'

'No, I don't. Although I might keep a few favourite pieces ...' Benji shook his head at the cheeky look on my face. 'Anyway, I'm exhausted and have to drive tomorrow so I'm off to bed.' I stood and kissed each of them on top of the head. 'Thanks again, guys; I really do appreciate this.'

'Any time, Ainsley,' said Benji.

'Sleep well,' said Brendan.

I paused at the door. 'Could I ask one more favour?'

'Name it,' said Benji.

'Call me Lee.'

He grinned and nodded. 'Night, Lee.'

Once undressed and in bed, I phoned Angus. He must've been waiting for my call and picked up immediately.

'Hey, you,' he said, the deep timbre of his voice wrapping around me. 'I've missed you today.'

'I've missed you too.' An image of what we'd been doing this time last night floated through my brain and I was suddenly lost for words.

'Are you there?'

'Yes, sorry, I was just thinking ...'

'About last night? Yeah'—his voice lowered even though I knew there'd be no one there to hear him—'me too. I've been thinking about it all day – and how I can't wait to have you in my arms again.'

I couldn't help the spark of joy that ran through me. 'Part of me still doesn't believe this is true,' I said. 'That we have another chance.'

'I know what you mean, but it is true and we do have another chance. And this time, I don't intend to let anything or anyone get between us.'

When he finally hung up, I lay there for a while longer, my phone clutched to my heart, wishing he was beside me.

TWENTY-TWO

Just as it had been on that Friday afternoon two weeks ago, it was raining as I drove through the stands of poplars into Mannus Ridge the following afternoon. The weather was the same, but everything else was so very different.

That time I'd been dreading my arrival – so sure my presence wouldn't be welcome and so sure my stay would be short. The posh car was gone – and had been replaced by a much more practical and substantially cheaper second-hand SUV. The money that had been sitting in my bank account was gone, my acrylic nails were gone and the ice-queen tight bun was gone.

Even the posh clothes were gone. That had been my last stop in Melbourne earlier today – to take the clothes, shoes and bags that I'd left at Benji and Brendan's to a consignment store in Armadale that dealt in rehoming second-hand designer clothes and accessories. As I was handing them over to the appreciative store owner, I couldn't help but do another quick calculation as to how much money I'd originally spent on these garments. I mightn't be able to do anything about that now, but the money I'd receive from the sale would help my otherwise rapidly depleting bank balance. I'd go through what I had hanging in the wardrobes at home and do the same with them.

Mostly, though, the tummy-churning anxiety I'd lived with for so long that I couldn't remember not having it was gone; the tears were gone, and the fears were gone. It had been just over a month since that dreadful day when my life had fallen apart, and I hadn't felt happier. I wasn't quite at the stage where, if I saw JC in the street, I'd shake his hand, but I was close.

I was still smiling as I drove into the car park at the Royal.

'You came back then,' said Macca when I strolled into the bar.

'How could I possibly stay away?' I quipped, playfully patting his cheek.

'Oh, away with you, girl,' he said gruffly, trying and

failing to hide a smile. 'And while you're about it, a man could go thirsty sitting here.'

'I don't think you'll be dying of dehydration any time soon,' Mum said, sliding a fresh beer in front of him. 'Good trip, Lee?'

'Yes, it was.' Impulsively I hugged my mother, even though it had only been a couple of days since I last saw her. 'But it's good to be home again.' I ducked into the office and kissed Dad's cheek. 'Any chance of helping me unload these boxes?'

When I opened the back of the SUV, Mum didn't attempt to hide her confusion. 'Where's your beautiful red convertible?'

'I sold it,' I said, no hint of regret in my voice. 'It was beautiful but let's face it, it wasn't practical. It's a city car and didn't like the dirt roads and lanes that I've been taking it down.'

Mum seemed to accept this explanation, but Dad's eyes narrowed as he searched my face for another meaning. 'You didn't sell it on account of us, did you love?'

'Absolutely not. Now, where's Tilly? I want her to see what I've brought home.'

I WAS STILL SMILING when I drove into the entrance of Balloch Estate and Angus walked out onto the verandah to meet me. 'I thought you'd never get here,' he said, holding his arms out for me to run into. 'Welcome home, Lee.'

'It's so good to be home,' I said, raising my lips to his.

'You know there's a dinner at the pub tonight?' Angus said when finally, leading me into the house. 'Tilly wants to try out some of her menu items on us, and Hayley has a presentation about the new name of the restaurant.' He grinned down at me. 'I think you've created a monster there.'

I chuckled and slid my hands up under his t-shirt. 'How long do we have?'

'Well,' he drawled, his eyes darkening. 'That all depends on what you have in mind.'

'I don't suppose it will matter if we're a little late for dinner,' I said suggestively, loving how his skin tasted slightly salty on my tongue, his scent filling my nose. I stepped away and pulled my sundress over my head, allowing it to fall on the floor in a multicoloured pool of cotton.

As I reached behind to unclip my bra, he stopped me. 'No, you don't,' he said, scooping me up in his arms. 'I've been thinking about doing that all day.' And with that, he carried me through to the bedroom.

'DIDN'T Granny tell you the right time, Aunty Lee?' Hayley asked when we finally made it back to the pub that evening.

Angus chuckled softly at the colour in my cheeks, his arm around my waist tightening.

'Yes, Aunty Lee,' teased Jazz. 'You are later than we thought you'd be ...'

'Well, we're here now,' I said briskly. 'And before we eat, I understand you've got some names for us to decide between, Hayles.'

As Dad organised drinks for us, Hayley readied her presentation. She'd borrowed a flip chart from school and had set it up in the half-done restaurant space.

'Okay,' she began. 'Is everyone ready?'

'Yes,' we all chorused.

'Mum,' she said sternly, 'no talking while I have the floor.'

I suppressed my giggles, but Jazz, suitably chastened, made a locking motion on her lips.

'Right, our mission was to decide on a new name

for the restaurant, and we've put a lot of thought into it.'

'Pick mine!' yelled Jackson, earning him a glare from his sister.

She turned the first page to display a graphic drawing of a blue cow. 'Our first choice is Blue Bull,' she announced. 'Closely followed by'—she flipped over to the next sheet, which was the same cow but drawn in red— 'Red Cow.'

'I'm seeing a theme here,' whispered Angus.

'But our favourite is ...' As Hayley paused dramatically, Jackson and Cody banged the table with their spoons to simulate a drumroll. 'Lizzie's.' Hayley flipped the chart to show the word Lizzie's written in basic cursive print, in hot pink. 'After Gran,' she added.

As the confident smile on her face slipped and her shoulders slumped, I stood and clapped. 'I don't know about you lot, but I love it. It's simple, it's graphic and I can see it against the feature wall in hot pink lights just as Hayley's drawn it here. But'—I looked around the table at my family, my mother dabbing at a tear, Hayley now standing proud and tall, Dad suspiciously bright eyed— 'maybe we should put it to a vote. Does anyone want Blue Bull?' Jackson's hand shot up. 'Red Cow?' Cody's hand shot up. 'What about Lizzie's?' Every hand was in the air – including Jackson and Cody's.

'Lizzie's it is.' I held my glass in the air. 'So, I'd like to propose a toast to Lizzie's at the Royal!'

'To Lizzie's at the Royal!'

'Now, while I've got your attention, I need some volunteers to help me get some paint on these walls over the weekend.' Hayley's was the first hand to shoot up.

Later that evening, the kids having gone upstairs to watch telly, Jazz and Mark joined Angus and me in the bar.

'What's this I hear about you selling your car?' Jazz asked.

Angus reached for my hand. We'd had a similar discussion this afternoon, one that had begun with him telling me he could lend me what money I needed to tide me over and continued with me telling him it was my decision to make and ended with us making love again – hence why we were late.

'It was impractical for here,' I said simply. 'As beautiful as it was, it was a city car, expensive to maintain, with a temperament to match. It's not me anymore. Besides,' I said with a laugh, 'it really hates the lane to your cottage.'

'Fair call,' she said, but the frown on her face told me she suspected there was more to the story.

I hesitated and then said, 'And while I was in

Melbourne, I put most of my clothes and shoes in a consignment store.'

'Not all of them, surely?' Jazz looked and sounded horrified.

'Not all, but most. I kept a few favourite pieces.' I shrugged. 'Seriously though, can you imagine if I pranced down the main street of Mannus Ridge in a pair of Jimmy Choo platforms?'

Mark and Angus exchanged cheeky grins. 'Well,' said Angus, 'that would depend on what else you were wearing.'

Once the laughter had died down, Jazz said, 'So you really are staying.'

With a smile that hurt my cheeks, I said, 'I really am.'

She exchanged glances with her husband and then said hesitantly, 'In that case, I have something I want to talk to you about.'

'Go on ...'

'You know how Dad was always hoping that one or both of us would take over the pub when they retired – to keep it in the family?' I nodded. 'But you were away, and I didn't want to take it on ...'

'Are you telling me you've changed your mind?'

Jazz caught Mark's eye again. 'Yes, I think so. It

wasn't so much that I didn't want to take it on, but more that I didn't want to take it on without you.'

'Jazz ...'

'I know you don't want to be a publican; I've always known that, but you do know how to run a business and I've never known that. I just think that if this works and we save the pub, when the time comes for Mum and Dad to step back, Mark and I are thinking we might step up, but only if you're there to support us from the business viewpoint.'

A wave of warmth rushed through me, and I blinked back tears. Beside me, Angus rubbed his hand on my jean-clad thigh.

'What do you think? I know, it's probably a stupid idea ...'

Slowly, I shook my head. 'I think it's exactly what our parents would be hoping for – to keep the pub in the family for at least another generation.' I flashed her a quick grin. 'As long as I'm not expected to be in here pouring beers every night!'

'Isn't this a cosy little family scene?' The sardonic tones of Spider Webb cut into our mirth. Angus stiffened beside me, his hand gripping my thigh.

'What do you want, Spider?' Angus growled.

Spider shrugged and placed his beer on our table. 'I was just wondering how long it will be before Lee shoots through again. After all, none of us are good enough for her and she does have form.'

Before I could stop him, Angus was off his stool, grabbing a handful of Spider's t-shirt and pushing him backwards until he came up hard against the wall.

'Angus!' I shouted, rushing to his side, and reaching for the arm he'd raised, his fist clenched. 'He's not worth it.' A crowd was gathering around us; all other chatter ceased in the bar. 'Angus,' I pleaded with him to look at me rather than Spider. 'Please, he's not worth it.'

Without loosening his grip on Spider, he said, 'But what he and Georgia did broke us up and stopped you from coming home for all those years. How can I just leave it?'

'Don't you see? We won.' I stroked his back, feeling his muscles relax under my hand. 'We're together again, and this time nothing he says can change that.'

He turned to face me, his eyes meeting mine. 'You're right. We have won.'

As Angus released Spider, Mum came charging in. 'I won't be having any of that in this pub,' she said, hands on hips, glaring at both men. 'If you want to carry on like that, take it out into the street or up to the Imperial. Angus, I expected better of you.'

Angus hung his head, chastened, and I had to stop

myself from giggling at the ridiculousness of it. 'Sorry, Lizzie,' he said.

'But Mum,' began Jazz.

'I'm sure Angus was provoked, Jacinta,' Mum said, her eyes not shifting from Spider, who was making a production of brushing down his shirt and acting very much as the injured innocent party, 'but that's still no excuse. As for you, Spider, I know the part you played in what happened all those years ago and why my daughter didn't feel she could set foot in her hometown before now, so cause any more trouble and you'll be barred.' She stared hard at him until he, too, dropped his head. 'As for the rest of you,' she raised her voice to include the entire bar. 'The show's over, so as you were.'

Spider slunk away in the direction of the group he'd been drinking with before he'd approached us. As he passed, Macca shook his head and turned away from him.

I suppressed a yawn, but not before Angus saw it. 'You okay?' he asked.

I reached up and kissed his lips briefly. 'I am, but it's been a big few days, and I think I'd just like to go home.'

He slid his arm around my waist and tilted his head to rest against mine. 'Sounds good to me.'

TWENTY-THREE

As the reopening date for Lizzie's at the Royal drew closer, the days also flew by.

Thanks to Benji and Brendan, social media awareness was growing, and all the guest rooms were booked for the opening weekend. Restaurant bookings were also strong as the local community got behind the initiative. In what little spare time I could muster, I'd pitched the idea of the food and wine festival for the following spring to the local council and the regional tourism authority and had been asked if I'd take on the part-time role of festival director – something I jumped at and was looking forward to getting stuck into.

Tilly's menu had been finalised and comprised almost entirely of produce sourced within a fifty-kilometre radius of Mannus Ridge. She'd given it a practice run on Mum and Dad, Jazz and Mark, and Angus and I, and we all declared it to be a winner.

Jazz, Hayley, Angus and Mark and I painted the space, exposed the original brick surrounds of the fireplace and pulled back the old carpet. The result was even better than what we'd envisaged. We'd carried the same theme through the hall leading in from the car park and splurged on a custom neon sign for the hall wall that read 'Lizzie's' in script and another for the main feature wall inside. As a nod to the season, we'd also thrown around tinsel with gay abandon.

Even without the restaurant being open, the drain of custom to Millers Creek had halted, and without a decent restaurant over there, patrons were drifting back to the Royal. The tide was changing, and my parents were beginning to believe they might just be able to hold onto the Royal for the next generation to take over when the time was right. Knowing that Jazz and Mark were keen to do so had given them even more motivation to not only save the pub but also grow the business.

Although it was still early days, Angus and I quickly settled into a comfortable routine. We were both busy – him with the farm and the winery and me with the restaurant – but we made it a point to have breakfast together each morning after my run, and although I was enjoying having someone to cook for in the evenings, we shared that responsibility too. While our lovemaking was joyous and we couldn't keep our hands off each other, these days, we talked more than we ever did in the past and had truly become friends as well as lovers.

The only flies in the ointment were Georgia and Spider. Since that night when Angus had confronted Spider about his part in our separation and my lengthy absence from town, amongst our crowd, at least, they were on the outer. Word began to filter about Angus and me being back together and what had really driven us apart all those years ago – completing my redemption. I felt sorry for Georgia. At the same time, the lies she and Spider told had been designed to keep Angus and me apart. The motivation for Georgia was simple – she wanted Angus – but for Spider, it was more complex; he'd wanted me and, when I rejected him, had decided that not only should no one else have me, but that I had no right to be in town as a reminder of what he saw as a humiliation. It made no sense to me, but there it was.

It did, however, look as though their misfortune might finally drive them together, and while Angus grumbled that they deserved each other, I figured I could afford to be magnanimous in my happiness and hoped they'd find some contentment with their lot.

<hr>

ON THE AFTERNOON before our official reopening, I was up a ladder adjusting the hang of the lights when Jazz said, 'Umm Lee, there's someone here to see you.' There was something in the tone of her voice that made my stomach churn and my whole body stiffen.

'Who is it?' I asked.

'Do you have to ask that question, darling? You had to know I'd come and find you.'

I briefly squeezed my eyes shut before carefully backing down, hating the sudden weakness in my limbs.

'Jazz, this is my ex-boyfriend, Otis. Otis, my sister Jacinta.' I made the introductions stiffly, my mind busy searching for why he'd be here. Dressed in cream moleskin trousers, polished RM Williams riding boots and a crisp chambray shirt, he was obviously attempting to channel the wealthy grazier look but succeeded in looking like he'd just driven in from the city. 'And I'm not your darling.'

'The married ex-boyfriend?' Jazz asked, glaring at

him. 'The one who stood by while you got sacked and then kicked you out of your apartment? That ex-boyfriend?' Hands on her hips, her pointed chin jutting out, Jazz stared down his attempts at a smile.

'Yes,' I said, 'that one.' I brushed my hands against the back of my denim shorts.

'What's he doing here?' she asked as if he weren't in the room.

'I have absolutely no idea,' I said. 'What *are* you doing here?'

'I'm here to see you, of course,' he said easily, smoothing his hair back. 'And, as I've already told you, the apartment was a misunderstanding.' He flashed his million-dollar smile at Jazz who remained unmoved.

'Well, now you've seen me, you can go; I'm busy here,' I said dismissively, shrugging a shoulder, as if he meant nothing.

'So I see. A restaurant opening, I understand.' He gazed around the room, somehow looking down his nose at our efforts. 'But I've come to rescue you from all that,' he said. 'That job I spoke to you about – have you thought any more about it?' Jazz's eyebrows shot up, and her quick glance at me brought a satisfied smile to his mouth. 'Didn't you tell your sister about it?'

Ignoring his last comment, I replied evenly. 'I told

you I wasn't interested, Otis. There was nothing more to think about – or tell.'

With a meaningful look at Jazz, he said, 'Is there somewhere quiet we can discuss this?'

'There's nothing to discuss,' I said. 'I'm not interested in returning to the city or another corporate role. I'm happy here.'

'Babe, did you want me to leave these cases here or take them through to the bar?' Angus came striding into the restaurant, a case of wine in his arms. His grin faded when he noticed Otis. 'Who's this?'

Otis stepped forward and held out his hand. 'Otis Wilde, Ainsley and I were … close …'

When Angus made no move to adjust the box of wine to shake Otis's hand, Otis let his drop, but if he felt any awkwardness, it didn't show on his face.

'He's the *ex*-boyfriend,' Jazz put in.

Angus nodded slowly as if everything was suddenly clear.

'And you must be the Plan B,' Otis said, narrowing his eyes.

My heart was in my mouth as I waited for Angus to respond to the challenge. Rather than bristle, he sent me a slow, sexy smile and said, 'I don't know about being a Plan B. The way I figure it, I'm the long-term strategy.'

Looking at the pair of them sizing each other up, I wondered what I'd ever found attractive in Otis and was filled with a fresh wave of love for Angus.

'What brings you here, Otis?' Angus asked pleasantly, still holding the case of wine as if it weighed nothing but which made his biceps bulge very satisfactorily. As a show of strength, it was an effective one.

'I thought I'd make the trip to talk through the job I offered Ainsley the last time we spoke.' He said it breezily as if it were already a done deal and as if we were in regular contact.

Angus frowned. 'My understanding is that she already turned you down. I wouldn't have thought there was anything else to discuss.'

A flicker of surprise crossed Otis's face as if he hadn't expected me to have told Angus about the offer he'd made. I, however, had learnt my lesson from the past and had vowed never to keep anything from him again.

'I got the feeling that Ainsley was still harbouring some ... resentment ... from the misunderstanding we had before she left,' he said, still smiling that smarmy smile that had the ability to charm so many people.

Angus placed the case on the floor. 'Misunderstanding, you say? That's a new word for it, but then maybe betrayal is done differently in the city.' He shrugged. 'But then what would I know? I'm just a simple country boy.'

Jazz and I exchanged glances; it was all I could do to keep a straight face.

'Do you have any idea how much Ainsley is turning down to stay here and attempt to resurrect a pub that's well past saving?' Otis dropped the act and glared at Angus. Otis had always been so used to getting what he wanted that I'd never seen this side of him before.

'In terms of dollars? Yes, she's told me. But then'—he sent me that same loving smile— 'what she has here is priceless.'

I couldn't return his smile, though; there was something Otis had said that started a bell ringing in my head.

'Will she still say that when all her money has been eaten up trying to save this place?' He spread his arms wide to indicate the pub.

Jazz gasped, and that's when I knew she'd picked up on it too.

'As if fixing up the restaurant can save it.' Otis laughed bitterly.

'Otis,' I said slowly, 'how did you know where to find me?'

'You told me – the other day on the phone.'

'No, I told you I was in town; I didn't say I was here, so how did you know where to find me?'

'It's a small town. I'm sure you mentioned at some point that your parents were publicans here.' He waved my questions away as if he were swatting a fly.

'You never listened when I spoke about my family,' I said. 'You never wanted to hear about them, and you certainly were happy I never wanted to visit. In fact, you actively encouraged me not to.'

'I gathered you were happy staying away,' he said. 'I recall you telling me there was nothing for you here.' With that, he raised his eyebrows in Angus's direction, an 'I bet you didn't know that' look of triumph on his face.

What had been the name on that Heads of Agreement? Emano Holdings. Em an O ... M and O. 'You! You and Melanie are Emano Holdings, aren't you? That's how you knew about the pub. When did you find out I was here?'

Angus audibly inhaled as he worked out what Jazz and I had already surmised.

'When Evan Johnson phoned here after receiving your parent's refusal to sell and told me he'd spoken to an Ainsley St James, I couldn't believe it.' Otis must've given up all hope of pretence. 'And when Melanie found out it was you standing in the way of the sale ...'

'That's why you called and left that first message. It was the same day I spoke to that broker. It must've been a disappointment when you realised we'd cleared the arrears so there was no longer any leverage there. Speaking of which, how did you know about the arrears on the hotel's loan? Unless ... of course ... it would've turned up on the credit reports you receive. Is that how you acquired the other pubs too?' Otis's eyes skittered away from my stare. 'Wow, CP is going to be interested to hear about this. And your wife is part of it? That will go down well with the Law Society, I imagine – especially if it turns out that any of these hotels you two have been buying up have been mentioned in divorce settlements your wife has been dealing with.'

Otis swallowed hard, his usually suave expression making way for a hunted look. 'You wouldn't dare,' he managed.

'You don't think? Is that what the job offer was? A way of getting me out of here so we couldn't make the changes we'd planned? What was wrong, Otis? Were you worried they'd work and the pub would be profitable again? You must've been thrilled that we managed to halt the growth at Millers Creek. I hear turnover is already on the way down since your chef left.' I stepped closer to him and looked up at his smooth-shaven face. 'You underestimated me, Otis, and you have no idea how much I'm going to enjoy this.'

'You wouldn't dare,' he said again. 'Besides, do you think anyone will listen to you? You signed a deed stating you wouldn't take action against anyone in the company – you're going to sound like a woman scorned.' His face had taken on a strange redness.

I smiled dangerously. 'True, I did sign that document. But the thing is, *I* have no intention of taking action against you – I'll be giving JC enough ammunition to commence an investigation into you, and you and I both know how that will end. Privacy breaches are taken very seriously. How does it go? Zero media tolerance? I can't wait for the headlines.'

'You have nothing!' Otis took a step towards me, his hand raised as if to strike.

Angus rushed in and grabbed his wrist, twisting his arm behind his back. 'If I were you,' he said between clenched teeth, 'I'd get out of here now before I throw you out and before the townsfolk who rely on this pub chase you out of town.'

'Ainsley ...' Otis began, one last attempt to mollify me.

'Just leave.' I turned my back on him.

'Think of everything we were to each other.' It was his final desperate effort to bring me back onside.

I swung around, a red mist descending over me. 'What we were to each other?' I ground out. 'I was nothing to you. Nothing except a pawn you could manipulate to do your dirty work for you. I hate the person I became when I was with you. I hate the things I did and the people I hurt so you could keep your hands clean. You used me, Otis – and you almost broke me, but you didn't. Coming back here has shown me that the person I used to be was still inside. I mightn't have the fancy title and the six-figure salary and the designer clothes, but I've got so much more. I'm doing work that means something with people who mean something to me. So yes, you almost broke me, but now I'm going to break you – not because of what you did to me, but because despite your best attempts, I still have integrity and there is no way I'm going to let you do to anyone else what you've tried to do to my parents.' I looked him up and down, unable to believe that there had ever been a time I'd been in this man's thrall. 'Get out of my sight.'

I folded my arms, relishing the sound of his footsteps down the hall. Once I was sure he'd gone, I began to shake. Angus wrapped his arms around me until I'd calmed down. 'It's okay, love,' he crooned. 'He can't hurt you anymore.'

'You said he was a dick,' said Jazz, 'but I didn't realise how much of a dick.'

'Let's not tell Dad about this just yet,' I said, stepping out of Angus's embrace. 'I don't want anything overshadowing tomorrow night.'

She nodded. 'Yep, good idea. We can tell him when we're back up and running.'

'Will you report him?' asked Angus.

'Absolutely,' I said seriously. 'He's breached privacy – and he's exposed CP to some potentially massive financial penalties as well as adverse publicity. What they choose to do with him is their business, but I imagine their investigation will also raise uncomfortable questions for his wife.' I forced a tremulous smile. 'As long as they can't do that to anyone else.'

'They would've succeeded if it wasn't for you, Lee,' said Jazz. 'I can't believe Mum and Dad had kept it from me for so long.'

'Well, we're on the way back now,' I said. 'And we have a restaurant to launch.'

TWENTY-FOUR

Benji and Brendan arrived early the following morning and were in raptures about what we'd created. Brendan disappeared into the kitchen to talk to Tilly about her inspiration and the ingredients and, in the process, managed to shoot several images we'd be able to use on our social media posts going forward.

It was, however, Benji's opinion I was most interested in – and not just regarding Lizzie's.

'Nice choice, darling,' he said midway through the afternoon. He'd been helping me set up the restaurant (although he called it 'styling'), and we'd both finally called it done and had sat down with coffees.

'The wall colour?' I asked ingenuously.

'That's good, but no, the man. Very nice choice. He looks straight out of an episode of *Farmer Wants A*

Wife, but more importantly,' he added, all banter gone, 'he adores you, and it's about time you were adored. Yes, my darling Lee, being back in Mannus Ridge with your family suits you.'

'It does, doesn't it?' I tried to sound flippant, but a ball of gratitude had lodged in my throat and the words squeaked past.

He glanced at his watch. 'But now you need to get that delectable arse home and get your glad rags on to welcome your guests.'

BENJI AND BRENDAN were a hit with Angus and my family and friends – especially Hayley, who declared she wanted to be a stylist or designer when she grew up. Before they left to return to Melbourne, Angus made them promise to come back in the new year, but this time they'd be staying with us.

The launch was an outstanding success, and the restaurant was booked solidly through to Christmas. While I knew that this could change in the new year once the newness wore off, I was quietly confident we'd turned around the decrease in trade and had built a base we could grow from.

Among the early visitors were some restaurant critics organised by Brendan and whose positive reviews for the dining and accommodation options offered at the Royal ensured we had excellent forward bookings for our room packages. Chatter about the Royal at Mannus Ridge had filtered through to Sydney and Melbourne, and I'd taken requests from two travel magazines to feature us in the new year. We weren't quite on the map yet but were undoubtedly heading in the right direction.

ALTHOUGH ANGUS HAD SAID he never bothered with a Christmas tree, I insisted on getting their tree out of the storage box where it had been languishing for years. The lights needed to be replaced, but with the help of Jazz and Jenny and all the kids, we soon had a Christmas tree in the corner of the living room.

I brought out a bottle of champagne and some parmesan shortbread, and we popped the cork and toasted the tree.

'What would you call that style?' asked Jenny. 'Homemade?'

'Eclectic,' I offered.

'Is it my imagination or is it leaning to the left?' asked Jazz, her head tilted to the side.

'There's a definite lean,' I said.

'You know,' said Jenny, 'I don't think there's been a Christmas tree up in this room since Mum passed away.' There was a catch in her voice.

'I think this is the most beautiful tree ever,' announced Ivy.

Jenny reached out to wrap her arms around her daughter. 'I agree. It's the most beautiful tree ever because Christmas has returned to Balloch Estate.'

'I haven't had a Christmas tree since I left Mannus Ridge, so I think it's the most beautiful tree in the world because we all put it up together,' I said, trying to push away the memories of those lonely Christmases spent apart from people I loved.

'And I think it's the most beautiful tree in the world because you're here,' Jazz said to me. 'And that's our Christmas miracle.'

'I think Angus would say exactly the same thing,' Jenny said softly.

WAKING up with Angus on Christmas morning was like a dream I hadn't even dared to dream had come true. A similar thought must've occurred to him because when I woke, it was to see him lying on his side, a broad smile on his face as he gazed at me. As my eyes flickered open, he said, 'Waking up with you every day is the best Christmas present ever.'

'Yeah,' I murmured. 'Me too.'

'Did you ever dream that we could be together again? Like this?' He reached out a finger and lazily ran it down my arm, leaving lovely sparkly shivers in its wake.

'No.' I closed my eyes briefly, and my breath hitched as his finger strayed to my hip. 'I dreamt of you, wild and lovely dreams, but never thought they'd come true.'

He grinned, a twinkle in his grey eyes. 'What were we doing in these wild and lovely dreams of yours?'

He hooked a strong leg over mine to pull me closer, his fingers now trailing lightly over my back, my bum, my hips. 'Almost exactly what we're doing now,' I moaned as his mouth sought mine. 'But this is so much better.'

ANGUS and I hosted Christmas lunch for our families at the homestead, erecting long tables on the front lawn and filling those long tables with food-laden platters and bowls. I'd baked a ginger and bourbon glazed ham, Mum had done her special brined turkey with pigs in blankets, and Jenny brought along roast pork with crackling. We shared making the side dishes, and for dessert, we had Christmas pudding, a mango pavlova and Mrs McGuire's trifle which caused much reminiscing between her and her brothers. By popular demand, Jazz was given the job of chips and dips to start and sweets and lollies for the table.

'Are you trying to tell me something?' Jazz had asked.

Mark had put his arm around his wife and said soothingly, 'Everyone has their strengths, babe, and we love you for more than your cooking ability.'

After the food had been demolished, Angus stood and tapped his glass with his knife.

'Well,' he said, 'there's plenty to celebrate this Christmas. Lee came back to Mannus Ridge where she belongs, and the family – our families – are finally able to spend Christmas together. The Royal has a new restaurant and, fingers crossed, we'll have a new wine and food festival next spring. Mark and Jazz officially joined our families together—'

'Finally,' said Dave, rolling his eyes.

'—with their surprise wedding – congratulations,

guys.' He raised his glass in their direction, and the rest of us did the same. 'And I hope we'll have another reason to celebrate soon ...' As he reached inside the pocket of his shorts, all eyes flew to me, and when he pulled out what looked suspiciously like a ring box, there were gasps around the table, although I couldn't be sure one of those gasps hadn't come from me.

'Lee,' he began, casting a bone-melting look down at me, 'I know you've only been back for a few short weeks, but ...' He hesitated and then said with a wry laugh, 'Who am I kidding? You're the love of my life, and I knew from the minute I saw you standing there on the road in those tight white capris with those ridiculous sandals, soaked to the skin, that that had never changed and never will change. You've always been the only one for me.' He smiled again, hope flaring in his eyes. 'So, as I was saying, I know you've only been back a few short weeks, but we've waited nearly fifteen years. I don't want to wait another second.' He opened the box, and this time, the gasp came from me. Inside wasn't the ring I'd given back to him all those years ago, but something different. This ring was vintage in style, with a single diamond in a Celtic-inspired gold band. 'Will you marry me?'

Tears had begun to pool in my eyes as he spoke, but now they ran freely down my cheeks. In the background, I vaguely heard Mark say to Jenny, 'Is that Mum's ring?'

'Yes,' I said, accepting his hand and rising to my feet. 'A million times, yes.'

His smile was wide, his eyes watery as he slid the ring onto my finger. 'God, I love you, Lee,' he murmured before dropping his head to kiss me deeply.

When he raised his head, he asked quietly, probably not entirely joking, 'No running away this time?'

'No running away this time,' I assured him before we were inundated with hugs and kisses and congratulations.

'Why is Aunty Lee crying?' asked Ivy.

'Why is Uncle Angus crying?' asked Ethan.

'Why are Mummy and Grandma and Aunty Jenny crying?' asked Jackson.

'Because they're happy, idiot,' said Hayley, playfully punching his arm. 'Don't you know anything?'

'I'm so happy things have worked out,' said Mum, hugging me tightly. 'And glad you'll finally get to wear that beautiful dress, although'—she looked me up and down— 'it might still need taking in a little bit.'

After everyone had left, all the plates had been cleaned away, the leftovers packaged up and the trestle tables returned to their place in the shed, Angus and I settled down on the wicker chairs on the verandah, each nursing a glass of Talbot's pinot.

'Well,' I said, lifting my hand to marvel again at the ring on my third finger. 'Today certainly turned out very differently to what I imagined.'

He reached out his hand to hold mine. 'Happy?'

I smiled through watery eyes. 'Unbelievably so.'

Dropping my hand, he placed his wineglass down on the table between us and jumped to his feet. 'Come on,' he urged, holding his hand out for mine and leading me down the steps and onto the lawn.

Taking me in his arms, we swayed to imaginary music. I tipped my head back and laughed with joy at the romance of it all. Angus and I, the sun setting on a perfect Christmas Day, dancing to music only we could hear. It was too corny for words, but at the same time, it was absolutely right.

'We need to talk about what song we want for our bridal waltz,' he said, a mischievous gleam in his eyes.

'We do,' I replied with mock solemnity. 'But you know how that ended last time.'

'No,' he replied, the same affected seriousness in his voice. 'Tell me, how did that end last time?'

'With us arguing and making love instead,' I replied, winding my arms around his waist and resting my head against his chest.

His chuckle rumbled through his body. 'How about we skip the argument and head straight to the making love part?'

'Now *that's* the perfect ending to a perfect Christmas Day,' I said, leading him back up the stairs.

EPILOGUE

And so it was that fifteen years to the day of our originally scheduled wedding, Angus and I said our 'I dos' on a sunny autumn afternoon in the little white church on the hill, the sun streaming through the stained-glass windows just as I'd pictured. I wore the dress I'd bought all those years ago, although rather than hanging off me as Mum had feared, it was now quite snug thanks to the presence of Spud McGuire – although that was still a secret from all but our nearest and dearest.

Just as we'd done last time, we argued over the song for our first dance but finally agreed on Shania Twain's 'Still The One'. We really had taken the long way, but we'd made it.

BEFORE YOU GO ...

If you enjoyed *Christmas at Mannus Ridge* I'd love it if you left a review in the usual places. If you'd like to stay up to date with what Philly gets up to next, you can sign up for my newsletter here: http://eepurl.com/hWhlcD or via my website.

You can also drop by and see me – virtually speaking, of course – here:

My website: https://joannetracey.com

My blog: https://andanyways.com

Facebook: https://facebook.com/joannetraceywriter

Instagram: https://instagram/jotracey

ACKNOWLEDGMENTS

The most common question people ask me upon hearing I'm an author is: where do your ideas come from? In this case, the answer is simple – from a song. To be more specific, from Dire Straits's 'Telegraph Road'.

The song tells the story of how a long time ago, a man walking a track set his pack down in a place that looked as if it would be nice – and decided to stay. He built a shelter and made a life, and around him, a town sprang up. And that's exactly how the two main families in this novel came to be in Mannus Ridge – their respective ancestors, a long time ago, put down their packs where they thought it was best.

As for Mannus Ridge itself, it doesn't exist, but it could be any country town in southern New South Wales or northern Victoria. Many of the memories I've given Ainsley about Mannus Ridge are those I have of the country town in the foothills of the Snowy Mountains of New South Wales, where my ancestors decided it would be a great place to make a life. I have, however, used that only as a broad outline; Mannus Ridge and the people within it have come from my imagination with one exception – the sausage rolls at the bakery really are the best.

Having said this, this was not a novel I intended to write until:

- a scene sprang into my head almost fully written (in case you're wondering, it was the one where Ainsley is stranded on the side of the road in the rain) and
- after being portrayed as such an unlikeable secondary character in previous novels, (*Wish You Were Here, Careful What You Wish For* and *It's In The Stars*), Ainsley herself needed to set the record straight. Hopefully, I've managed to do that on her behalf.

Indie publishing is a team effort, and I'm eternally grateful for the people on my team. Firstly, to my editors Nicola O'Shea and Jo Speirs for helping me wrangle my ideas and words into a story and for helping me become a little better at my craft with each outing. Thanks also to Louisa West for the super cover and for formatting this one.

Thanks also to my team of first readers – Pieta, Donna, Debbie and Sue. Your continued support makes my heart swell – in the best possible way

The usual thanks to my family – Grant, Sarah and Kali (aka Adventure Spaniel) – for being there.

Mostly though, my thanks go to you, my readers. You have so many books to choose from, yet you still picked up this one. Thank you for helping make my authorial dream come true.

ABOUT THE AUTHOR

Joanne Tracey lives on the Sunshine Coast in Queensland Australia with her husband and a cocker spaniel who takes her role as resident flop-dog and guardian of Jo's office very seriously. An unapologetic daydreamer, eternal optimist, and confirmed morning person, Jo writes contemporary romance, romantic comedy, women's fiction and cosy crime. When she isn't writing or day jobbing, Jo loves baking, reading, long walks along the beach, posting way too many photos of sunrises on Instagram and dreaming of the next destination and the next story.

Jo's life goals (apart from being a world-famous author) are to be an extra on *Midsomer Murders* and to cook her way through Nigella's books.

facebook.com/joannetraceywriter

instagram.com/jotracey

amazon.com/author/joannetracey

ALSO BY JOANNE TRACEY

The Philly Barker Series (Cosy Crime)

Philly Barker Investigates

Philly Barker Is On The Case (coming soon)

The Melbourne series (contemporary romance)

Baby, It's You

Big Girls Don't Cry

I Want You Back

Careful What You Wish For

It's In The Stars

Christmas At Mannus Ridge

Escape To The Country series

Wish You Were Here

Happy Ever After

The Little Café By The Lake

Escape To Curlew Cottage

www.ingramcontent.com/pod-product-compliance
Lightning Source LLC
Chambersburg PA
CBHW020253120726
47904CB00001B/182